WITHDRAWN

COLLARED

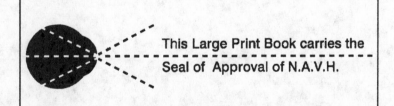

This Large Print Book carries the
Seal of Approval of N.A.V.H.

AN ANDY CARPENTER MYSTERY

COLLARED

DAVID ROSENFELT

THORNDIKE PRESS

A part of Gale, a Cengage Company

Farmington Hills, Mich • San Francisco • New York • Waterville, Maine
Meriden, Conn • Mason, Ohio • Chicago

LIBRARY OF CONGRESS CATALOGING-IN-PUBLICATION DATA

Names: Rosenfelt, David, author.
Title: Collared / by David Rosenfelt.
Description: Large print edition. | Waterville, Maine : Thorndike Press, a part of Gale, a Cengage Company, 2017. | Series: An Andy Carpenter mystery | Series: Thorndike Press large print core
Identifiers: LCCN 2017028689| ISBN 9781432841454 (hardcover) | ISBN 1432841459 (hardcover)
Subjects: LCSH: Carpenter, Andy (Fictitious character)—Fiction. | Missing persons—Investigation—Fiction. | Animal shelters—Fiction. | Dog rescue—Fiction. | Large type books. | BISAC: FICTION / Mystery & Detective / General. | FICTION / Suspense. | GSAFD: Suspense fiction. | Mystery fiction.
Classification: LCC PS3618.O838 C65 2017b | DDC 813/.6—dc23
LC record available at https://lccn.loc.gov/2017028689

Published in 2017 by arrangement with Macmillan Publishing Group, LLC/St. Martin's Press

Printed in Mexico
1 2 3 4 5 6 7 21 20 19 18 17

COLLARED

This would not let her come to terms with what she had done. Though that had long ago ceased to be a goal. This act today could never erase her actions; nothing could. But this was the right thing to do, and she had been planning it for a long time, since that day three years ago. She was thirty-six years old, but it felt like those three years had consumed half of her life.

No, getting rid of the guilt was not going to happen. This might ease the pain some, but it would never entirely go away. Not even close. So the best she could hope for was not to feel good, but rather less bad.

She had known she would do it for a long time, far too long. But even in her self-loathing, she was self-protective. So she waited until she was sure she was safe and that they could never find her.

She had tried once, and it had been a disaster and only made things worse. Much worse . . . a man had died. She couldn't be sure it was as a result of what she did, but she believed that it was.

She knew even then that there would be a time she would try again, and that time had come.

She had her reasons for what she did back then, but looking back, they seemed so insufficient. They convinced her it was the right thing, and they gave her all that money. She needed that money, and somehow they knew it.

She pulled up to the building and waited to make sure the people weren't there. She knew they wouldn't be; she had patiently observed their arrival every day for a week. They would pull up in twenty minutes sharp; they were very punctual that way. That was why she chose this time to arrive; this way he would be outside and unprotected for only a short time.

She turned off the car and got out and then opened the rear passenger door. The border collie perked up; he just figured he was going for a walk.

Which he was, in a way. But that walk was only about twenty feet, to the front of the building. Once there, she had to work quickly. With gloved hands, she tied his leash to the door handle and taped the envelope with the note to the door.

She gave the dog a small pat on the head and turned to go back to the car. It was then that she realized she was crying. It did not surprise her.

The woman made the mistake of looking to her left, toward the gas station / convenience store. She saw a man watching her through the window, and then she quickly turned away. She doubted he could recognize her or identify her from that brief moment, but either way, there was nothing she could do about it.

She got in the car and pulled away, not looking back at the dog. By now she was sobbing, so much so that it was hard for her to drive.

But it was over now, out of her hands. They would do what they would do, and she would be alone with her pain.

I place the paper on the table and say, "It's time for a Carpenter family meeting." I'm pretty sure that Laurie and Ricky are surprised by this, since they're in the middle of breakfast, and we've never had a breakfast family meeting before.

Actually, this will be the first family meeting we've ever had, regardless of the meal, which is why I'm not opening with the reading of the minutes from the last meeting. Of course, we haven't even been a family very long; it's just been eighteen months since Laurie and I got married and adopted Ricky.

"What about?" Laurie asks. She points to the paper. "What's that?"

"It's a renewal form for my law license. If I want to remain certified to practice law, I need to sign it and send it in." I've been a reluctant lawyer for some time now; while I have no financial need to work, I seem to get drawn into taking cases even when I don't want to. If I'm not certified, then that can't happen, so not signing would be a form of self-discipline. I continue, "I think this should be a family decision."

"So you want our opinion on whether you should send it in or not?" Laurie asks.

"Yes."

"Send it in," she says.

"Just like that?"

She nods. "Just like that." Then, "Are we done with the family meeting?"

"Wait a minute. Why are you saying this?"

"Because you're a lawyer, Andy, and a wonderful one. That's what you do."

"Not if I don't send in this form; that's the whole point." I turn to Ricky. "What do you think?"

"If I send it in, can I be a lawyer?" he asks.

"Not without going to law school."

"That's not fair," he says.

I'm not making much progress here.

"I already went to law school, before you were born. Now, do you think I should send it in or not? Think about it carefully before you answer."

"Yup. Send it in," he says. If he took the time to think, then he's a really quick thinker.

"Why?"

"Because that's what Mom said."

11

"Thanks, Ricky, that's really helpful." Then, "This is one of the worst family meetings we've ever had."

"What will you do with yourself if you don't practice law?" Laurie asks.

"Well, for one thing, I'll spend more time here at home."

"Definitely send it in," she says, a hint of desperation creeping into her voice.

"You don't like having me around during the day?"

"It's a treat having you here, but it's a treat that's best enjoyed in moderation. Sometimes you get a little cranky when you're bored. And sometimes you get a little cranky when you're not bored."

"Okay, then I'll spend more time at the foundation helping out." My friend and former client Willie Miller and I are partners in the Tara Foundation, a dog rescue operation. Willie and his wife, Sondra, run it day to day, but I help out whenever I can.

It's named after Tara, our beyond wonderful golden retriever. Right now, she and our basset hound, Sebastian, are lying on the floor next to me; they are technically a part of the family meeting but have so far shown no desire to contribute.

"I think I can speak for Willie and Sondra when I say, 'Send the form in,' " Laurie says.

"They don't like having me around either?"

She smiles. "I refer you to my previous comments about 'crankiness' and 'moderation.' "

Getting nowhere with her, I turn back to Ricky. It's a desperate move, and one likely to backfire. "Wouldn't you want me around more?"

"Would I still get to play with my friends?"

"Of course."

"Would we have to let you play with us?" he asks.

"No."

"Then I don't care."

"Well, this has been very enlightening," I say. "I don't think I'll be calling any more family meetings anytime soon."

"Andy," Laurie says, draping her arm around me. "We love you deeply. As far as Ricky and I are concerned, the sun rises and sets on you. And it is from that place of love and that place of the rising and setting sun that we say this to you: 'Sign the damn form and send it in.' "

The phone rings. I hate to break up this heartwarming family moment, but I drag myself away to answer it. "Hello," I say, which is a breezy bit of repartee that I have found often opens the door to further conversation.

"It's me," says Willie, confident enough in his own skin to feel sure that he's on an "It's me" basis. I, on the other hand, have only started using "It's me" on Laurie, and I still am afraid she'll think it's a crank call.

"Would you and Sondra want me to spend more time at the foundation?" I ask.

"Definitely not. But I do want you to come down here now."

"Why?"

"I'll show you when you get here."

14

The Tara Foundation is only about ten minutes from my house. I bring Tara with me, since she always likes to play with the dogs that are there. I don't bring Sebastian, since playing really isn't his thing. Sleeping and eating are his two main interests, though he puts up with occasional walking.

Willie and Sondra are both waiting outside for me when I get there, which seems a bit unusual. Willie is holding a border collie on a leash; it's not a dog I have seen before.

We say our hellos, and Sondra takes Tara into the play area. Before she does, she asks, "Willie says your plan is to spend more time here?"

I nod. "What do you think?"

"I love you, Andy, you know that. But . . . ."

"But what?"

"I think you should come up with a new plan," she says.

"You too? Why are you saying that?"

15

"Well, don't take this the wrong way, but there are times when you can get a little —"

I interrupt. "Cranky?"

"I was going to say *annoying,* but *cranky* works," she says and then heads inside, leaving me with Willie and the border collie.

"This one just come in?" I ask.

He nods. "This morning. Somebody tied him up before we opened. They left a note."

He hands me a piece of paper that I hadn't noticed he was holding. The message on it is short and more than a little weird, since it's made up of pasted-in letters that look like they were cut out of a magazine, much like one of those old movie ransom notes.

It says, "You'll know what to do with him."

"They didn't leave any identification? We don't know who left him?"

Willie shrugs. "That's all."

"Okay; idiots like that don't deserve a dog," I say. "Let's find him a good home."

"The thing is, I scanned him," Willie says, "even though it was an owner turn-in . . . because of the weird note and because the person who left him could have found him as a stray."

He's referring to a device we have that scans for imbedded chips in the dogs that come in; it's a way of identifying who their

16

owners are, provided the owners have registered the chip. We don't usually bother doing so with dogs that owners turn in to us, since we obviously don't have to find those owners to reunite them with the dog. But in this case, Willie couldn't be sure that the person who left him was the owner.

"What did you come up with?" I ask.

This time he reaches into his pocket and comes out with another piece of paper. I recognize it as a scanner report. He hands it to me.

"Can't you just tell me?" I ask.

"You probably should read it."

So I do, and I'm three lines in when I say, "Holy shit."

Willie nods. "That's what I thought you'd say."

If the chip scanner is correct, and I've never known it to be wrong, then the owner of this dog, whose name is Cody, is Jill Hickman. And that is going to send shock waves through North Jersey and beyond.

"Do you think it's real?" Willie asks.

I nod. "Seems like it. That is definitely her address, and I remember she had a border collie named Cody. If it's a scam, it's a beauty."

"There was a whole DNA thing, right?"

"Right."

17

Jill Hickman was a very successful businesswoman who suddenly decided three years ago, at the age of thirty-five, that she wanted to have a child. What she didn't have available was a husband; she and her fiancé, Keith Wachtel, had broken up about six months earlier. So she adopted a one-month-old boy that had been anonymously abandoned at a local hospital. She named the child Dylan.

Not wanting to give up her career, Jill hired a full-time nanny, Teresa Mullins, to care for Dylan while she was at work. One day, two months after the adoption, Teresa took Dylan in a stroller, along with the family border collie, Cody, for a walk in Eastside Park.

Once they were deep inside the park, a car pulled up and a man jumped out. He had some kind of covering over his face and was holding a gun. He pistol-whipped Teresa, who was the only witness to the crime, and then took off with the child and dog.

The brazenness of the midafternoon crime stunned and panicked the community. Mullins pointed to Keith Wachtel, Jill's former fiancé and also a former top employee at her company, as the kidnapper. Mullins had met him on a few occasions and claimed to recognize his eyes and voice. She also got a partial license plate number, which matched Wachtel's car.

The police searched Wachtel's house, and while there was no sign of Dylan or Cody, they did find dog hair in the house, on Wachtel's clothes, and in his car. They also found some trace hairs in the car that they matched to the blanket surrounding Dylan when he was taken.

The police matched the DNA of dog hair to that found on the brush that Laurie used to groom Cody. It was the first known use of DNA in this manner, and Cody became known as the "DNA dog."

Wachtel had no explanation for the presence of the hair or blanket fibers, or at least none that the authorities found credible. He was arrested for the kidnapping, though, to my recollection, murder charges were never filed, simply because Dylan's body was never found. It didn't matter anyway; he received a sentence that will likely keep him in jail for the rest of his life.

I was not involved legally in the case, but my connection to it was that Jill Hickman was a high school friend of Laurie's and lives just a few minutes from us on Derrom Avenue. I wouldn't describe them as close, but since Laurie is an ex–police officer, Jill accepted her offer of advice and support during the months after the abduction.

Dylan would be three years old now, though a more hopeful way of saying it is that he *is* three years old now. But the truth is that none of us know whether Dylan is alive or dead, which is why back then Laurie had nothing to say that could ease Jill's pain. Only the return of her son could do that.

Laurie had offered my help to Jill in dealing with the legal side of the issue, and I met with her a few times, always with Laurie present. I also brought nothing substantive to the party and wound up having no role, since no leads ever turned up as to Dylan's fate and Wachtel was continuing to deny his involvement in the crime.

I'm not really sure what the apparent return of Cody means; it could be nothing. Perhaps Wachtel took them both and just let the dog run stray later. Or maybe the dog ran off during the abduction, and Mullins, having just been pistol-whipped, didn't realize it.

It could be of little significance, but when the word gets out, the media will jump all over it.

I tell Willie to keep this to himself for the time being and to take care of Cody. Then I head home to discuss it with Laurie. I pretty much discuss everything with Laurie, but in this case, it's a no-brainer.

But I'm just going to walk in and talk to her; there's no reason to call a family meeting about it.

"Are you sure it's the same dog?" Laurie asks.

"I can't be 100 percent positive, but everything fits. And he seems to answer to the name Cody. But I'd never been around Jill's dog."

"I need to call her," she says.

Laurie does just that and tells her that we'd like to come over and talk to her. She says it in as casual a way as she can, but I can tell from the rest of the conversation that Jill's guard is up.

Finally, Laurie says, "Jill, it's nothing to worry about, and we can clear it up for you as soon as we get there." When she gets off the phone, she turns to me and says, "She knows it's about Dylan."

"How does she know that?"

"Intuition. And the fact that you're coming also. Let's go."

"Should we bring Cody?"

She shakes her head. "One step at a time."

We drive over to Jill's. On the way, I ask Laurie what Jill has been doing with her life and whether she is still working. I remember that she started and owned an Internet venture that had progressed from struggling start-up to very successful, and the nature of that company contributed to the public interest in the case. Jill's company, called Finding Home, was one of the pioneers in retail DNA. People could send in a sample and find out their heritage. By all accounts, Jill has made a fortune.

Keith Wachtel worked for Finding Home as the company's chief chemist. He continued in that role for quite a few months after their personal relationship broke up, and I don't know why he subsequently left the company.

Laurie tells me that when Dylan was taken, Jill initially pulled back from work entirely. At the time, she had just spent months raising enough money to save the company and ensure its ability to compete at a high level. It was an intense time in Jill's life; the money was crucial to the company's survival and, therefore, crucial to preserving her life's work.

Laurie had been out of touch with her during that period of time; she said that

Jill's fund-raising efforts had been all-consuming and required a lot of travel.

Jill eventually returned to the company, but in a less active role. Laurie is not sure but thinks Jill might be more of a figurehead at this point than a hands-on executive. Dylan's disappearance has apparently left her with a different perspective on her career than she had before.

Jill's house can best be described as *stately,* though *enormous and stately* probably fits better. It is probably the most impressive house in Paterson, and while some might consider that faint praise, it really is an imposing place. I know through Laurie that Jill has often talked about moving, since the house reminds her of Dylan.

Of course, on the flip side, the reason she hasn't moved is that the house reminds her of Dylan. Laurie has told me that it's well known that Dylan's room is exactly as it was when he "left"; nothing in it has changed. Leaving the house would feel to Jill like cutting off the last tie to him, providing a closure that she doesn't seek.

Jill is waiting for us on the porch when we get there. She skips the "Hello" part of the conversation and starts with "What is it?" She's literally cringing when she asks the question, and I realize that she fears we are

24

going to tell her that Dylan's body has been found.

"Let's go inside," Laurie says, and we do.

As soon as we're in the den, Laurie says, "We think we've found Cody."

The statement jolts Jill, apparently literally, as she takes a step back. "Alive? Where? How do you know it's him?"

Laurie answers those three questions, and many others, in a calm, unruffled way. It just takes a few minutes, and I don't say a word. When she's finished, she walks over and hugs Jill.

"Can I see him now?" Jill asks.

"Of course."

We go in my car to the foundation, and I call on the way to alert Willie. He's standing there with Cody on a leash when we arrive, and Jill starts to cry when she sees him. As for Cody, he goes into major tail-wagging mode; this is someone he seems to recognize and like.

She finally composes herself and walks over to him, taking the leash from Willie. "Roll over," she says, and Cody immediately assumes the sitting position.

While I don't know what to make of the fact that he obeyed the wrong command, Jill seems to understand it quite well. She goes to her knees, hugging the surprised

Cody so hard that I'm afraid she's going to strangle him.

Jill explains. "Keith thought it was funny to train him to the wrong commands. If you tell him to shake hands, he plays dead. If you tell him to play dead, he twirls around."

She demonstrates these commands, leaving no doubt that this is her Cody. We all go into the back room, which we use to talk to potential adopters of the dogs. Sondra comes in with coffee, but then she and Willie leave, and we talk a bit about the implications of what has happened.

Jill asks, "What does this mean?" about ten times in ten different ways, but neither Laurie nor I can effectively answer any of them.

"But we need to bring this to the attention of the police," I say, and everybody agrees with that.

"Can I bring him home?" Jill asks while petting Cody.

"He's your dog," I say. "I'll bring him by later."

"I can't keep him now?"

"I need to introduce him to the authorities. I'll get him to you as soon as I can."

"I'll wait at the house with Jill," Laurie says.

"You'll bring him back today?" Jill asks. I nod. "Today. I promise."

I nod. "Today I promise."

I call Captain Pete Stanton and tell him I'm on my way to see him.

"What for?" he asks.

"You'll know when I get there. But it's police business."

"You going to turn yourself in?"

"For what? I haven't done anything."

"Damn," he says. "I guess I'll have to put them away."

"Put what away?" I ask.

"I've got handcuffs with your name on them."

When we're not insulting each other, Pete and I are actually best friends. He's an outstanding homicide cop, and I'm a pretty good attorney, but he and I would never compliment each other under penalty of death.

When I get to the precinct, I tell the desk sergeant that I'm here to see Captain Stanton. He points to Cody, sitting calmly and respectfully next to me at the end of a leash. "He can't go back there."

"Yes, he can," I say. "He's evidence."

As a defense attorney, I am rather widely hated by the members of Paterson's finest. If you're trying to talk yourself out of a speeding ticket, it's probably best not to mention that you know Andy Carpenter.

This particular sergeant is not an exception to that rule, and he's about to argue with me when we see Pete coming toward us.

Pete points to Cody and asks, "What the hell is it with you and dogs?"

"I find they're smarter and more reliable than people, present company included." I point to the desk sergeant. "Eliot Ness here says I can't bring the dog back to your office."

"You can't."

"Okay, then you can read about him in the paper."

I turn to walk away, and Pete says, "That dog is the reason you're here?"

"He is."

He sighs. "All right. Bring him back. But if he shits on the floor, you're cleaning it up."

We walk back to Pete's office, and that's when I notice that Cody has a slight limp in

29

his rear back leg. It doesn't appear serious, but I make a mental note to check it out with our vet.

When we're finally in Pete's office, I ask Pete, "I assume you remember the Dylan Hickman abduction?"

My question hits him right between the eyes, and the realization comes a split second later. "That's the dog?"

"One and the same."

"Where's he been for the last three years?"

"Beats me."

"How do you know it's him?"

I tell him the entire story, including the chip identification and Jill's certainty that this is, in fact, Cody.

"It could be a hoax," he says.

"That's not possible, but I knew you'd say it, which is why I brought him down. You can run his DNA; you've certainly got a sample to compare it to."

He nods and picks up the phone to request a forensics team. They are here within three minutes, and in another three minutes, they leave with a hair and saliva sample. Cody is completely cooperative throughout; he clearly has nothing to hide.

When they leave, Pete says, "This doesn't change anything." He was the lead investigator on the case and certainly believes that the right man is behind bars.

"It changes one thing for sure," I say.

"What's that?"

"The missing dog isn't missing anymore."

"But the right guy is in jail. There could be a million explanations for this, even if it's the same dog. None of them exclude Wachtel's guilt."

I don't really disagree with anything he is saying, but I don't tell him that, since I wouldn't want to give him the satisfaction. Our friendship is a really mature one.

"Well, this has been a real treat," I say, standing up. "It's always comforting to spend time with the protectors of our community, no matter how incompetent they may be."

"Where are you taking him?" he asks, pointing to Cody.

"Home. If you need to question him further, I'll bring him back. I'm his attorney."

"Don't you already have enough dogs?" he asks.

"I didn't mean my home. I meant his."

31

Laurie and Jill are in Jill's kitchen when Cody and I get back. Coffee cups sit in front of them; if they've been actually drinking coffee this long, they're going to be awake until August.

Cody runs right over to Jill, and as he runs, his limp is a little more pronounced. But he has no trouble hopping up into her lap and licking her face. If ever there was a case in which a DNA test was not necessary to determine identity, Cody is it.

"What did Pete say?" Laurie asks.

"That it doesn't change anything." I can see Jill react, and I realize that she somehow is holding out a faint hope that Cody being alive means that Dylan might be alive as well. "He's running a DNA test on Cody."

"So that's it?" Jill asks.

I nod. "As far as the police are concerned. To them this is a curiosity but doesn't change the facts. They've got their man, and

32

in their eyes, the dog was never a real factor."

She pets Cody's head. "He always was to me."

At the time of the investigation and trial, the fact that the abductor took Cody was always puzzling. The prosecution portrayed it as possibly a way to keep Dylan calm and not scream, but that was only one of the theories they advanced. The other was that Keith Wachtel knew that Jill loved Cody, so killing him was an extra act of revenge.

"So where has Cody been all this time?" Jill asks.

"I have no idea. He could have been found as a stray back then and maybe ran away. Or maybe the people that had him just didn't want him anymore."

"God, I wish I knew what this means," Jill said.

I see a look in Laurie's eyes that makes me very nervous. I get even more nervous when her mouth starts to move, since I assume it's connected internally to the look in her eyes. I don't even have enough time to cringe before she starts talking.

"Jill, Andy and I will look into this. If there's anything to find out, we'll find it out for you."

"I can't ask you to do that," Jill says.

"You didn't ask," says Laurie. "We offered."

Clearly, her use of the pronoun *we* in that sentence was somewhat inaccurate, but I don't have the guts to point it out. The other thing I don't have the guts to point out is that there is no upside to injecting ourselves into this situation. We'll get nowhere, and it might give Jill false hope.

I'm trying to summon up the courage to verbalize a form of that when Laurie jumps back in.

"I'm not saying we'll get anywhere," Laurie says, "but it won't be for lack of trying."

"I've hired private investigators in the past," Jill said. "I've tried everything I could."

"I know that," Laurie says. "We know that. But I've got plenty of time on my hands, and Andy has decided to renew his law license. We're happy to do it." I think she's noticed that I haven't said a word, so she adds, "Right, Andy?"

"Absolutely," I lie. "What is it we're happy to do?"

"To find out whether Cody's turning up has any significance to the overall case," Laurie says.

"Are you going to tell Keith?" Jill asks.

I hadn't thought about it, mainly because I hadn't thought about getting involved. "Sooner or later," I say. "He has a right to know, and maybe it could get him talking."

Jill nods. "Okay."

"I think we can hold off on that for now," Laurie says. As an ex-cop, she is somewhat less concerned with the rights of the convicted than I am. She continues, "At least until we know whether this is of any real significance."

I don't say anything because I'm too busy mentally kicking myself for the casual way in which I handled the note left with Cody at the shelter. I should have protected it and brought it with me to the precinct so that it could be tested for fingerprints.

We promise Jill we will keep in touch and inform her about any progress, and we leave. The first thing I do is call Willie and tell him to put the note in plastic to protect it. He says he'll do so and offers to drop it off at our house later.

"That's okay. We'll stop by and pick it up," I say, and Laurie and I drive over there.

Instead of pulling into the foundation parking lot, I stop next door at the gas station / convenience store. I've become friends with the owner, Bert Manning, who seems to work a twenty-four-hour day. I don't think I've ever been in there without Bert being on the premises.

Laurie comes in with me, and after we exchange greetings, I ask Bert if he happened to see anyone leave a dog in our parking lot that morning.

"You mean the border collie?" he asks, which, as questions go, is a fairly promising one.

"Exactly."

"Sure did. I saw her tie the poor thing up. I was going to wait a little while and then go bring it inside here, but then Willie showed up. How does someone just dump a dog like that?"

"It was a woman?" Laurie asks.

"Definitely."

"You know what she looked like?"

"Not really. Youngish, and seemed on the tall side. But I didn't get a good look at her face. I called out to her, but she quickly got in the car and took off. Like she was embarrassed that someone saw her."

"What kind of car?"

"Nothing unusual, just a sedan. Dark green, I think."

"Any chance she stopped in here for gas or anything before she left the dog?"

"You mean, would our cameras have caught her? No, I'm pretty sure she didn't.

But I can check; I know what time it was."

"Please do that," Laurie says.

"The dog okay?" Bert asks.

"Fine. Reunited with his rightful owner."

When we park at the foundation, I'm surprised to see Pete walking out. He's with two guys that I don't recognize, one of whom is holding an evidence bag.

"You here to get a dog?" I ask. "Because we usually adopt to a higher class of people."

"I'll come back tomorrow looking for code violations."

I point to the evidence bag. "Is that the note that came with Cody?"

"It is. I understand from Willie that you did everything but run it through the washing machine."

"Guilty as charged," I say. "Will you let me know if you get any prints?"

"So you're conducting another one of your independent investigations?" he asks. "Let me guess . . . there's a paying client involved."

"I believe that it's my money that keeps

you in beer and hamburgers." I think the last time Pete paid for his food or drinks at our favorite sports bar was during the Reagan administration.

"Good point," he says.

"But no money this time; I'm doing it for a friend. I'll wait to hear from you on the prints."

"Don't hold your breath."

Laurie has been pulling off the remarkable feat of watching all this and rolling her eyes at the same time. She obviously feels it's time to intervene, because she says, "Pete, we'd appreciate any information you can give us. Jill's pretty upset and anxious, and we can be your conduit to her."

Pete respects and likes Laurie as a former police officer and all-around decent human being, so he says, "Sure, Laurie. As long as I can deal with you, I'll help in any way I can."

Pete and his evidence buddies leave.

"I guess we told him," I say.

Bottom line is that I'm pleased that Pete showed up to get the note without my having to bring it down to him; it shows he's taking it seriously. He has far more resources to get to the bottom of this and find the person that left Cody than I do.

Laurie and I head home, since Ricky is

due home from school pretty soon. After he gets there, I take Tara and Sebastian on an early walk in Eastside Park. These walks are the time when I do my best thinking, and right now, I have to figure out the next steps in the "Cody investigation."

I'm loath to get into the nuts and bolts of the original investigation. To do so, I would have to read the trial transcript, go through the discovery, and completely familiarize myself with all aspects of the case. Since I have none of that material and it would take considerable effort to get it, to say nothing of reading it, I rule that out.

When it comes to effort, I am a minimalist.

The only new event here is Cody's appearance on the scene, so it would make sense to put my focus on where he's been all this time. It would be nice if he would tell me that, but he doesn't seem to be talking.

On the other hand, there might be a way to get him to talk.

When I get home, I call Jill and ask her if she and Cody can meet me at Dr. Dan Dowling's office in an hour. He's my veterinarian, and I'm hoping he can get information out of the close-mouthed Cody.

She agrees, so I call and set up the appointment. It's one of the few times I don't dread going there. Usually I'm bringing Tara or Sebastian in for some ailment or general checkup, and I start panicking the night before in fear of what he might find.

Jill, Cody, and I are ushered right in to an examining room, and Dr. Dowling is surprised to see that I've brought a border collie. I explain that it's Jill's dog and that we want him fully examined.

"Do you have his medical history?" he asks.

"Well, that's sort of why we're here," I say. "We're hoping you can tell us."

"I don't understand."

"Cody has been missing for a while . . . almost three years. We're trying to figure out where he's been."

"That isn't clearing it up much," Dowling says. "What do you mean, 'where he's been'?"

"We're hoping that you can find something medically, maybe a surgical procedure, which is only performed in certain parts of the country, maybe something else, which we can use. Any little bit helps."

"Let me make sure I understand. You want to know if there is anything physically unique about this dog that will tell you where he's been living?"

"Right."

41

"Okay, I'll give it a shot, but don't expect much. It will take a couple of days to get a full blood panel back. The x-rays we can shoot now, but the blood is more likely to reveal whatever there is to reveal."

"Fine. I appreciate it." Then, "Also, you haven't seen him walk yet, but he has a slight limp. I think it's in his rear hind leg."

"I'll check it out," he says. "Give me a couple of days on the other thing."

"You think you can come up with something?"

He shrugs. "It's a long shot, but you never know. This is a first for me; there isn't usually much call for forensic veterinary medicine."

I smile. "Glad we could expand your horizons."

Jill and I wait for almost an hour as they put Cody through his medical paces. That gives her a chance to ask me many more times if Cody reappearing will have significance for the case.

Cody comes out looking none the worse for wear, and Jill leaves with him. I have no idea where this is going to go, if anywhere, but I do know what I have to do next:

Mail in the renewal for my law license.

Just in case.

Tara starts barking at six thirty the next morning, and Sebastian joins in. This is highly unusual; Tara almost never barks in the morning. She's always happy to sleep in, but if nature calls and she needs me to take her out, she accomplishes that by coming to my side of the bed and rubbing her nose against my arm. Sebastian is very different in that regard. If I were to put a diaper on him, he'd be content to sleep the entire day.

I get up to determine the cause of the outburst. Tara makes that rather easy, since she is standing at the window looking out. When I do the same, I see three local news media trucks and a group of maybe eight reporter types and cameramen. I can tell they're cameramen because I am a born investigator, and because they are carrying cameras.

Just then, the phone rings, and that serves

to do what the barking did not, which is wake Laurie up. She answers, listens for a few seconds, and then says to me, "There are media people outside Jill's house."

"I think I detect a pattern," I say.

"What's going on?" Laurie asks.

"I suspect if we turn on the news we'll find out all we need to know, but in the meantime, I'm going to take my media fans on a walk through the park."

Laurie turns on the television as I get dressed, and sure enough, Cody's reappearance is the lead story on the local news. I'm sure it will get at least some national play as well, because Dylan's abduction was a pretty big story back then. Many kids are unfortunately victimized each year, but the national media only latches onto a few. Think JonBenét Ramsey, Elizabeth Smart, and Caylee Anthony. Dylan Hickman made it to that list.

Once I'm dressed, I grab two leashes and say to Tara and Sebastian, "Come on, gang. It's showtime."

We go outside and head for the park. The assembled reporters and cameramen follow me, both on foot and in their vans. We're quite a procession as we trudge along; Tara seems to be enjoying it, and Sebastian is basically oblivious to them.

The reporters bombard me with questions and pay no attention to the dogs, except for one close call when Sebastian almost pisses on one of their legs.

They are asking where Cody is, how we know it's the same dog, and what it means to the case. They already know the details anyway, including the fact that Cody was dropped off at our foundation. It's why they came to me in the first place.

My responses are basically that I am not positive it's the same dog, that we have no idea what, if anything, it means to the case, and that it's none of their business where he is.

"But I can tell you one thing," I say. "He's damn cute."

It's a fairly quick walk at a brisk pace, except for once on the way back when Sebastian stops to squat. "Any of you guys good with a plastic bag?" I ask, and this seems to disperse them quite a bit. They head back, no doubt to breathlessly report all the information that I haven't provided.

I don't know how the information about Cody got out. I'm sure it wasn't Willie or Sondra; they know better. It's possible that it was a police department leak, but more likely, Jill told one of her friends, who blabbed about it.

There's no great harm in it happening, and probably some benefit. Now the public can help in trying to figure out where Cody's been; somebody out there has to know.

The other result, whether beneficial or not, is that now Keith Wachtel will be aware of the development. I've been thinking about going to the prison and meeting with him, but I wasn't sure I wanted to pull the trigger and inform him. Now that doesn't matter; if he doesn't know already, he will by the end of the morning.

Of course, Keith either will have no information to add to this puzzle, or if he does, he won't reveal it. If he did, and it was helpful to his situation, he would have come forward long ago. If he kept it secret because it represented a negative to him, that would likely still be the case. In either event, I don't see him being helpful in that regard.

Having said that, there is one area in which he could be very helpful. Since I was not a participant in the original case, my knowledge of it barely extends past media reports. Much as I would dread it, if I'm going to jump fully into this investigation, that has to change.

That brings me back to the trial transcript

46

and the discovery information. Even though I don't want to immerse myself in it right now, I should put myself into position to do so if I change my mind, or if Laurie changes it for me.

I can get the transcript on my own; it's part of the public record. But the discovery I can only get by either being Keith's attorney of record or having him authorize his prior attorney to provide it.

Each of those possibilities presents a problem. First of all, I don't want to be Keith's attorney, which precludes avenue one. Avenue two, getting it from Keith's attorney, presents one major difficulty.

He's dead.

Stanley Butler was a credit to the legal profession, which is still my profession now that I've sent in my license renewal. He graduated from Columbia Law near the top of his class, which means he could have punched his ticket to pretty much any top law firm in the country.

Instead, he went to work for Passaic County as an assistant prosecutor. One could say he became spoiled by success, as he won case after case. He came to the conclusion that most of the defendants that he put away did not have the resources to mount an effective defense against the

47

government. Unlike most of his colleagues, that bothered him.

It was not that he thought they were innocent; on the contrary, he knew in his heart that most were guilty. It's just that he believed for our system to work in a fair and just way, the playing field had to be more level.

So he went to the other side and joined the public defender's office. Eventually, he left and opened his own practice, but he continued to defend those that in many cases were too poor to pay him. His win-loss record turned around permanently toward the negative, but he felt he was doing the right thing.

Stanley represented Keith Wachtel in his murder trial. By all accounts, at least as I remember it, impartial observers thought he did a creditable job. He lost because there was a mountain of evidence stacked against his client, not because he provided inadequate representation.

I knew Stanley Butler pretty well; I shared a few meals with him, and he and his wife, Phyllis, came over to the house a couple of times. He was a major dog lover, so we obviously had that in common. In fact, they rescued a Lab mix from the Tara Foundation.

Life was not always easy for Stanley. He battled drugs and alcohol and founded an AA group in Paterson. He was proud of his sobriety, and we were going to have dinner one night to celebrate his hitting the five-year mark.

Two nights before that dinner, he was killed in a car crash when he drove his car off a road, down into a ditch, hitting a tree. He was killed instantly, and subsequent blood tests showed there were drugs in his system.

It was a double blow to those who cared about him. He had kept it from all of us, and we weren't aware enough to have realized it and offered help.

I had heard that Stanley's practice was turned over to the public defender's office after his death; I assume his clients were divvied up by the lawyers there. But his not being around certainly complicates my getting up to speed on the case, should that be what I decide to do.

Here's the problem: I know myself. If I go see Wachtel, it effectively means I'm diving in all the way. I'd much prefer to just dip my toes in a bit and find out if the water's cold.

When I get home, Laurie greets me with, "You just got a call from the prison. Keith

Wachtel wants to meet with you."

So much for toe-dipping. Andy Carpenter is about to do a full gainer with a high degree of difficulty.

East Jersey State Prison was originally called Rahway State Prison. This was a cause of some dismay among the citizens of Rahway, since the prison wasn't actually located there. They were understandably not thrilled being known for having hardened criminals in their midst, especially since the criminals were really housed in somebody else's midst.

In this case, the somebody else was Woodbridge Township, which is where the prison happens to stand. The Woodbridge citizens had been fine with the Rahway name but were less fine with having their own town attached to it. They must have known more people in high, prison-naming places than the poor Rahwayians, because suddenly East Jersey State Prison came to be.

Of course, calling it East Jersey State Prison comes with its own silliness. New Jersey is only seventy miles wide. You could start a drive across the state at the opening kickoff of an NFL game and get to the other side before halftime, even with no endless replay reviews.

In New Jersey, east and west are pretty much one and the same. It's one of the few states where "the twain shall meet."

One can see the prison from miles away because of its most distinctive feature, a large dome roof. The shape is reminiscent of a woman's breast, and the lore is that it was built that way to further taunt the all-male inmates. That, of course, makes no sense, since the only people on earth who have absolutely no chance of seeing the outside roof of the building are the people imprisoned inside.

Keith Wachtel is one of the fifteen hundred men who can't see the dome. I've met him once or twice in the past, through Jill and Laurie, but we never really got to know each other. That's unlikely to change today.

Getting to see someone in a maximum-security prison is not quick or easy. There's a lot of waiting, scanning, waiting, metal detecting, and waiting involved. I've been here quite a few times, which is common among criminal attorneys when they don't go undefeated.

The good news is that I know some of the

people who arrange for the visitations. They're aware that I'm a lawyer, so they make the natural assumption that my meeting with Keith is to be a private lawyer/client conference. Therefore, we wind up in a separate room, rather than one of those crowded rooms where you talk on phones through glass.

"How's it going?" I ask when I first see Keith, which is near the top of the list of stupid questions to ask inmates in a maximum-security prison. It ranks just below "Get out much?" and one rung above "Do you believe this weather?"

"Every day is the same," Keith says, which is not really on point but moves the conversation to the next stage.

"You wanted to see me," is my next salvo.

"Yeah. Thanks for coming. It's about Cody being found."

I know I take dog-loving to a somewhat absurd degree, but what he just said pleases me. Someone who doesn't care about dogs, or this one in particular, would have said, "It's about the dog being found." But he said *Cody* instead of *the dog,* which to me is a sign of respect and caring.

I may need to get out more.

"What about it?" I ask.

"Is it really him?"

53

"They're doing a DNA test, but in my mind, there's no doubt that it is."

"Jill would know for sure — better than any DNA test."

I nod. "We can stipulate that it's him."

"What about Dylan?"

Saying *Dylan* and not *the kid* chalks up another point for Keith on the Carpenter grading scale. "No news on that front at all."

"So bottom line, what does it mean?" he asks.

"To you?"

"Of course to me. I do have something of an interest in this."

"To tell you the truth, Keith, I don't have the slightest idea. But the fact that Cody is alive doesn't exactly give you a 'get out of jail free' card. There's just too many credible explanations."

"But there has to be more to it. Cody didn't just turn up; he turned up with you."

He's just hit on something that's been bugging me, but which I've not been paying attention to, or at least not verbalizing.

He continues, "You remember when we all had dinner at the Bonfire? You and Laurie, me and Jill?"

"I think so," I say, even though I don't.

"Well, I remember it. We were discussing

some murder trial in the news, not one you were involved in. And you were talking about it, and you said, 'In murder cases, there's no such thing as a coincidence.' "

I don't remember saying that at a dinner with Keith, but I have no doubt I did, since it's what I believe. To be completely clear, it's not that coincidences can't happen, it's just that as a lawyer it is always best to discount the possibility.

I offer a grudging nod. "You're talking about the fact that the dog came to me. A criminal attorney, and one who knows the players."

"Right. Somebody wanted to draw you in."

Another nod from me, less grudging this time. "It's certainly possible."

"That's why I wanted to talk to you. I need you in."

"I'm not your lawyer, Keith. If I do this, it's for Jill and for Dylan. Maybe even for Cody. I'm sorry, but my goal would not be to get you out. It would be to find out what has happened and why."

He nods. "Good enough for me."

"How's that?"

"I've got nothing here, Andy. When Stanley died, they gave me a public defender. Kid must have been out of law school for about an hour. We met, and you know what he told me? That I should stay on good behavior; it would serve me well with the parole board. You know when my first parole hearing is? In seventeen years."

What Keith is telling me is that any action, any movement, on his case can't be bad. It could either have no effect on his situation or be a positive. That in itself is something for him to grab on to.

I nod. "I understand. And even though I just said I'm not your lawyer, I'm going to need you to hire me, on a temporary basis."

"Okay. Why?"

"Because I'm going to have to request discovery from the prosecutor's office, and I can only do that if I'm representing you."

"Fine. Great. But you know I can't pay you, right?"

"Fee is one dollar."

He smiles. "That I can manage."

My next stop is the Passaic County prosecutor's office. I could have accomplished this by phone, but it's on the way home, and it gives me a chance to see Richard Wallace.

There's one thing you can say about Richard that you can't say about any other prosecutor on the entire planet: he likes me. The main reason for that is his connection to my father, who ran the prosecutor's office when Richard first arrived. Richard loved and respected my father, and he and I got to know each other back then as friends, not adversaries.

We've tangled on a couple of big cases over the years, and I've been lucky enough to come out on top in each trial. It hasn't affected our friendship, which is a good thing for me, since Richard now runs the office. It's good not to be hated at the top.

I called to confirm that Richard could see me, and he said he'd make time. After we

57

exchange pleasantries and a few stories of the old days, he says, "So is this about the Hickman abduction?"

"What makes you ask that?"

"Come on, Andy, you're all over the news."

"Were you involved in the case?" I ask.

"Only as a supervisor. Mitch Kelly tried it."

Mitch Kelly is an excellent prosecutor, if not exactly my favorite human. He's a sore winner, and if there's anything I hate more than winning prosecutors, it's smart, sore-winning ones. "So he's still on it?"

"At this point, no one's on it. The case has already been tried."

"So you don't think finding the dog means anything?"

"It's a human-interest story, Andy. Not a legal one. You don't agree?"

"You're probably right, but I promised Jill Hickman I'd look into it. So I'm going to need a copy of the discovery, as well as a trial transcript if you have one lying around."

"You have an official role?"

"I'm Keith Wachtel's attorney. He just hired me on a temporary basis, basically for this purpose. I can get you paperwork."

"No need; I believe you. Maybe later for

the file."

"Great. Thanks."

"Last time we had dinner, you said you were going to retire," he says. "I think your plan was to become a placekicker for the Giants."

I nod. "I gave up on that idea. Stadium is too windy, and I found out you have to wear a jacket and tie on road trips."

He smiles. "Damn, and you were so close."

Richard promises to send the discovery over as soon as possible, so I head home. On the way, I contemplate just how far to go with this. If it's going to be a full-fledged effort, it would mean involving the whole team.

I call Laurie and ask her opinion, and unfortunately, she gives it to me. "Bring them in," she says. "I really want to do this for Jill."

"Let's set the meeting for tomorrow afternoon at the house," I say. "We should have copies of the discovery tonight, which will give me a little while to skim through it."

"Okay if I include Marcus?"

She's talking about Marcus Clark. "Maybe wait on him," I say.

"Maybe not; he brings a lot to the party."

"He scares me. I'm always afraid he's going to do something I don't care for."

"Like what?"

"Like kill me."

"Come on, Andy, you're a big boy. And I'll protect you."

"If I say no, are you going to call him anyway?"

"Of course."

"Then you have my permission."

I spend the morning reading the trial transcript. It's all Richard could get on such short notice; he called and said I should have the rest of the stuff later today. He's still not assigning a prosecutor to it; he'll follow it for the time being himself and will bring someone in if it appears that there is reason for us to go into court.

God forbid.

The jury deliberated nine hours before finding Keith Wachtel guilty. It's a relatively short time for a case of this magnitude, but the question that comes to mind in a reading of the transcript is, what took them so long?

The key pieces of physical evidence were Cody's hair, which was found in Keith's house and car, and the blanket fibers, found only in the car. Stanley Butler, his now-deceased attorney, argued that he had previous contact with the dog and that explained the hair. He had no good explanation for the blanket fibers but still disputed its significance.

But it didn't fly with the jury. When Keith and Jill broke up, he moved out and got a new car and house, so Cody had never been in either. The amount of dog hair was just too great for simple transference, and the time since he had last been with Cody weighed heavily against that argument as well.

Also contributing greatly to Keith's conviction was the testimony of the nanny, Teresa Mullins. She had met Keith a couple of times, and though the abductor wore some kind of mask, she was able to successfully identify his voice and eyes. She also said that the car the abductor drove was identical to Keith's, and had even gotten a partial license plate identification, which matched.

Even though the prosecution doesn't have to demonstrate motive, in this case, there was plenty to go around. Keith and Jill had what could be called a double breakup, both somewhat contentious, though they were months apart. Not only did their personal relationship end somewhat acrimoniously, but Keith was also later fired from his job in Jill's company.

The firing was particularly ill-timed. It was while Jill was on the desperate, but ultimately successful, fund-raising mission. Using the money she brought in enabled the company to go from what had been a struggling start-up to a thriving enterprise. All this happened right after Keith left, making Jill a fortune and leaving Keith in no position to profit from it.

Altogether, it was more than enough for twelve citizens to decide that Keith should never see the light of day again.

I'm having the team meeting at our house since there's really no reason to do it at the office. I haven't been down there in a while; my assistant, Edna, has been going in every few days to get the mail. Edna sees occasionally having to get the mail as akin to working in a sweatshop; she's in no danger of locking up the Employee of the Year Award.

Laurie made the phone calls and tells me that Edna was not pleased that actual activity looms on the horizon. Edna discovered the world of crossword puzzle tournaments in her sixties and spends all her time preparing for and competing in those tournaments. She's had a few top-ten finishes, which means she's a hell of a lot better crossword puzzler than she is legal assistant.

The entire legal dream team is assembled by 2:00 P.M. Sam Willis is my accountant turned computer whiz kid, capable of hacking into anything. Hike is the only other lawyer in the firm, very capable but also always positive that the worst thing that could happen is about to happen.

Then there is Willie, who has no real function other than to provide general help, especially of the physical variety, when we need it. He is a karate expert and possesses absolutely no fear. He would be the toughest person I know, if I didn't know Marcus.

The advantage of having Marcus come to the house in broad daylight is the effect it has on my neighbors. Nobody is going to block my driveway, or have their dog shit on my lawn, or play loud music at night, for fear that I might have Marcus pay them a visit. And no one would dream of robbing our house.

"First of all, we don't really have a client in this case," is how I start the meeting. I pause to let Edna finish her sigh of relief, and then I continue. "Technically, Keith Wachtel has hired us, but only for the purpose of allowing us to effectively investigate."

I then proceed to start at the beginning, with Cody showing up at the foundation's door. Everyone has a recollection of the details of Dylan's abduction, just from the media reports. I give them more details based on the trial transcript.

When I'm finished, Laurie adds, "We're really doing this on behalf of Jill Hickman."

"So we're not doing anything other than investigating? No contact with the court system?" Hike asks.

"Not at this point."

"So there's nothing for me to do?"

"Not so far," I say.

"Am I still getting paid?"

"Yes."

"Great. My recommendation would be to make the investigation long and thorough."

"What have you got for me?" Sam asks. He's become increasingly frustrated at being computer-bound during our cases; he sees himself as a cross between Marshal Dillon and Bat Masterson. Sam has recently acquired a gun permit, and in an even worse development for the citizens of New Jersey, he's also gotten a gun. I caught him practicing his draw once in his office; based on what I saw, he should stay off the streets at high noon.

Marcus doesn't say a word during the entire meeting; he just sits there looking scary and unnerving me. Marcus almost never says a word, or at least not one that I can understand. Fortunately, he reports to Laurie on our chain of command; they like each other and work well together.

I don't really have any specific assignments for anyone yet and may never have any. I just wanted to bring them up to date and alert them to the fact that I may be calling on them.

It's not until they all leave that the only potentially significant event of the day happens. It's a call from my vet, Dan Dowling.

"Andy, I've got something for you."

"What?"

"I think I have some good news. You should come down here."

"I'll be right there."

"The blood tests and x-rays showed nothing. I even did ultrasounds. Nothing," Dowling says.

"Have we gotten to the good part yet?" I ask.

"Of course not. I'm just taking you through the process. So I was about to call you and report my lack of success, but I still wanted to figure out what was causing the limp. Diagnostically, I saw no reason for it."

He pauses as if waiting for me to jump in, but I'm not inclined to jump. I just want to wait to find out where this is going and, hopefully, where Cody has been.

"So I ran some additional blood tests, called titers, which screen for specific diseases. We had eleven negatives, and one positive — for anahlichtia."

I nod. "Just as I suspected." Then, "What the hell is anahlichtia?"

"It's a tick-borne disease . . . very rare. It can cause paralysis in dogs, and even when it is treated, there can be permanent physical effects. Like a limp."

"What does that tell you about where Cody has been living?"

"That's the good part. It was first discovered in southeastern Canada about twenty years ago and has very slowly been making its way south. I did some research, and 80 percent of the reported cases in the U.S. have been in Maine. The other 20 percent has been divided evenly between Vermont and New Hampshire."

This is good news, even if I don't yet know what to do with it. Hopefully, other things will come up that will make this information more valuable. Of course, as with anything else, there are caveats. Cody could have spent the last two years in Florida but acquired the disease while on a one-week family vacation in Maine.

So right now, what we know is that Cody may or may not have been in Maine, New Hampshire, Vermont, or Canada. It's not exactly a case-cracker.

Dr. Dowling prescribes some medication for Cody to take to make him feel better, which I will get to Jill. I thank him and leave to go home and read the remaining discovery material that Richard Wallace has sent over.

Going through discovery documents is never any fun. It's like reading a terribly sad novel of human suffering, except it's a true story. One moment Jill Hickman had a child that she loved more than anything, and the next moment she didn't.

All she was left with was pain.

And questions that were never answered.

If we're going to find out where Cody has been, it's going to be by someone coming forward. Pete called Laurie to tell her that there were no prints on the note, which leaves us with no other options. Pete has also set up a tip line, through which members of the public with knowledge about Cody can report it. He has promised to update Laurie if it bears fruit.

So if I have no way of finding out where Cody has been, I might as well try to figure out how he got there. Of course, the police have already conducted an extensive investigation, without bothering to focus on that question.

They deemed it at least semi-irrelevant. They concluded, and the jury agreed with their conclusion, that Keith Wachtel took Dylan and Cody. The presumption was that he murdered the little boy, though no evidence existed to demonstrate that. Their reasoning was based on that lack of evidence and the theory that if he placed Dylan somewhere, they would have been likely to uncover where that might be.

As far as Cody goes, to the extent that they thought about it at all, they just assumed that Keith either killed the dog as well or perhaps let him loose somewhere. If the latter were the case, then Cody's reappearance on the scene is consistent with their suppositions.

The only witness to the crime, if you don't include Dylan, Cody, and the perpetrator, was the nanny, Teresa Mullins. She was the one who got pistol-whipped in the process and who identified Keith's car and voice.

There is very little about her in the documents other than her testimony regarding the abduction and the fact that she was a trusted employee of Jill's. She was hospitalized briefly for her facial injuries and then released.

I'm going to need to find her, if only because I can't think of anyone else to find. It's possible that Jill has kept in touch, and I'll ask her, but for now I'll put Sam on the case to find out whatever he can about her, starting with where she lives now. If the information is in Internet-land, and everything is in Internet-land, then Sam can shake the cybertree until it falls out.

Sam answers the phone on the first ring, as he does every single time I've called him. He must take the phone into the shower and who knows where else.

"Talk to me," he says, a new opening he's picked up.

"I was already planning to," I say. "That's why I dialed your number."

"What's up, boss?"

"I need you to find Teresa Mullins. She was the nanny in the Dylan Hickman case."

"That's it?"

He's disappointed; the assignment provides little opportunity for shooting. "For now. Keep it holstered, Wyatt."

"I'm on it."

Leaving the dog at the rescue place eased her mind more than she expected. Not all the way; she never even had the slightest hope of that. But she had done something, no matter how little, and now there were other people who could run with the ball.

The last time she had tried, with the lawyer, it had gone horribly, and her guilt had only increased. This would end differently, or at least she hoped it would.

So now she was heading home, although she would never really consider it home. The only place that really felt like home was a thousand miles to the north, and she had lived in three places since then. At first, she had tried being close to home, but she gradually moved farther and farther away, just to be safe.

Moving all those times was probably not necessary, but she took no chances. She wanted to make sure that they could not find her.

She stopped at the grocery store when she got into the town, fifteen minutes from her house. The people who lived in the town called it a supermarket, but that's only because they did not know what real supermarkets were like. This was a grocery store, pure and simple, but it served her needs.

She didn't talk to anyone in the town; she rarely did. A few times she had ventured out, trying to be sociable, but had quickly pulled back.

She briefly entertained the thought that now that she had given the dog back, it might signal a turn in her life. Maybe she would move one more time, not home but to someplace more to her liking. And then she would make friends and live a normal life.

A life not full of fear.

Exhausted from her ordeal, she arrived home just after eight o'clock in the evening. She left the shopping bags in the car while she went inside to turn on some lights.

As always, she hated walking into a dark house, and as it turned out, this was the last time she ever would. She felt the hands grab her and instantly knew she could never escape them.

She also knew that the owner of those

hands was the man called Kyle. And Kyle simply said, in the voice she had hoped never to hear again, "We trusted you and let you live. Big mistake."

"Jill hasn't seen or spoken to Teresa Mullins since before the trial," Laurie says.

We're using Laurie to do most of the contact with Jill; Jill seems more comfortable with her.

"That makes sense," I say. "But does she know where she's living or how to reach her?"

"No. The old number she had for her is disconnected."

"How did she come to hire her in the first place?"

"It was through an agency; they're the ones who checked and provided her references. You have any reason to think she is part of this?"

"No, but at this point, I have no reason to think anything. A woman dropped Cody off at the foundation, and she's the only woman involved in the case right now except you." I look at Laurie suspiciously. "You didn't leave Cody at the foundation, did you?"

Laurie smiles. "No."

"Great," I say. "We're really narrowing it down now."

I ask Laurie to call Jill and get the name of the agency that she used to hire Teresa Mullins, and she does so. I call it and ask to speak to the manager, who I'm told is a woman named Kathe Iovene.

"Ms. Iovene, my name is Andy Carpenter. I'm an attorney, and —"

She interrupts me. "*The* Andy Carpenter?"

I like this woman already. "I think so. I'm the only Andy Carpenter I know, so at the very least I'm one of the Andy Carpenters."

"The big-time attorney, right?"

This is a conversation I never want to end. "I believe that's me, yes."

"Wow. I'm sort of a courtroom junkie, so I've followed a lot of your cases. This is so cool. How can I help you?"

"I'm calling about a nanny you placed a while back named Teresa Mullins. She was —"

"Oh, I remember Teresa," she says. "She was there for that terrible kidnapping."

"Yes. I've been trying to reach her."

"Join the club, Mr. Carpenter."

"What do you mean?"

"We have money for her. Not too much, just about $300. There was a mix-up in accounting, and we owe it to her. I've given up trying to find her."

"What's the last address you had?" I ask.

She asks me to hold while she goes to find it. It takes a few minutes, during which Laurie asks me what's going on. "She's trying to find the address," I say. "She's a big fan."

"She's an address fan?" Laurie asks.

"No, a Carpenter fan, of the Andy variety. She worships me."

Laurie shakes her head. "That is one strange cult."

Iovene finally comes back on the line and gives me the address: 432 Jefferson Road, in Nobleboro, Maine.

Maine, home of the anahlichtia tick.

Iovene also gives me a phone number that she had for Mullins but says it's been disconnected for years.

"When was the last time you talked to her?"

"I think it was just after the kidnapping. I wanted to make sure she was all right and see if there was anything we could do. She was pretty shaken up . . . I mean, who wouldn't be?"

I thank her and hang up and then call Sam

to see what he's learned.

"I was just going to call you," is how he answers the phone.

"Good. What did you find out?"

"Nothing. Teresa Mullins, at least the Teresa Mullins that you're looking for, no longer exists."

"She's dead?"

"Could be, but I doubt it. When I say she no longer exists, I mean under that identity. If she died while still using her name, there would be a record of it."

"So what are you saying?" I ask.

"I'm saying that going back for a few years, Teresa Mullins has left no imprint on the planet. She hasn't used a credit card, had a telephone or a bank account. She hasn't gotten sick, or maintained a driver's license, or even died. She has to have assumed a new identity and effectively disappeared."

"Could she have legally changed her name?"

"No," Sam says. "I would have found a record of that. She's gone, Andy."

"Maybe she changed her name because she wanted to get out of the spotlight," Laurie says. "She could have just wanted to put the entire terrible experience behind her."

I shake my head. "That makes sense, but according to Sam it's not possible. He claims he would have found a record of her changing her name, of records being transferred from one name to another."

"So what do you make of it?"

I shrug. "I'm not sure. Can you go down to the agency to press them further? Maybe they'll have more information in the file."

She nods. "Absolutely."

"Good. Right now, it's time for a session with Tara."

Laurie knows what I mean by that. When I need to think through something, I take Tara and Sebastian for a long walk. Sebastian doesn't often add much insight to the issue at hand; his main concern is where to

79

sniff and piss. But Tara is different; she often leads me to conclusions I wouldn't otherwise have reached.

"Try not to take too long," Laurie says. "I ordered a pizza."

"With what on it?"

"Same as always. Ricky and I have half, and you have the other half. Your half is plain cheese, the way you like it."

Laurie puts all kinds of healthy, vegetable-ish toppings on her pizza, and she's somehow co-opted Ricky into liking it the same way. It's as if they order a salad with cheese and crust under it. I never thought I'd see the day when a son of mine would eat broccoli on pizza. Or broccoli on anything. Or just broccoli.

"Here's the problem," I say. "You guys never finish your half, and then if I want more, I have to pick off all the vegetables. The cheese sticks to them and comes off as well . . . and I can never get all of them. It is no way to treat a pizza; it's a form of pizza abuse."

"That's a serious problem. You want to call another family meeting about it?" she asks.

That shuts me up, and I head out for the walk so that Tara and I can try to figure out what to make of the apparent disappearance of Teresa Mullins. One thing I don't have to wonder about is if she's really gone; if Sam can't find her in cyberspace, then she really doesn't exist, at least under that name.

In my mind, this sends our little investigation to a new level. It's not DEFCON 1, but it is definitely sending off warning alerts. There could be a benign explanation for Mullins's disappearance; maybe she was so psychologically damaged by the abduction and attack that she went to these drastic levels to leave society.

But I don't buy it. It's one thing to escape the press and curiosity seekers; it's another to completely disavow your identity and escape the world. I feel like if I'm going to find out anything, I first have to find out where the hell Teresa Mullins is.

While I may not know where she is, I certainly can't say the same about Pete Stanton. He's at Charlie's, the greatest sports bar / restaurant in the Western or Eastern Hemispheres, sitting at our regular table with Vince Sanders, editor of the local newspaper.

After I'd dropped off the dogs, I called ahead and told them I'd be a little late, but once they heard that I was coming, they would wait until four o'clock in the morning just to see me. It's heartwarming, but would be even more touching if their gesture wasn't totally a function of knowing I'd get stuck picking up the check.

As I walk in, I notice on one of the many TVs that the Knicks are up by fourteen in the second quarter. Based on their recent performance, that gives them maybe a 15 percent chance of winning. But it should be enough to put both Pete and Vince in a temporarily good mood.

Vince stands up as I approach, and for a fleeting instant, I think he is doing so to welcome me and shake hands. Instead, he walks behind me and appears to stare at my ass.

"What the hell are you doing?" I ask.

"Just making sure you brought your wallet."

"It's so nice to be around such caring friends."

Pete nods. "That's what it's all about."

I've been to Charlie's so often for so many years that I don't even have to order. They just bring me my hamburger, french fries so crisp that it's impossible to believe they were once living potatoes, and a light beer.

We settle in to watch the game, and between the third and fourth quarters, with the Knicks now down by eight, I ask Pete,

"Did you get the DNA results back?"

He nods. "Yeah. Same dog. Means nothing."

"And Laurie said there were no prints on the note?"

"Not true; yours and Willie's were all over it. Good job, Sherlock. You can play the lead in *CSI: Paterson.*"

I ignore that, mainly because he's right. "You might be interested to know that Teresa Mullins is missing."

"That the nanny?"

I nod. "That's the nanny. We can't find her."

"I'm surprised you can find your hamburger."

"So your prize witness disappears from the face of the earth after the trial, and that doesn't even strike you as odd?"

He shakes his head. "Nope."

"Amazing. You have the intellectual curiosity of a gerbil." I turn to Vince. "What do you think of a star witness who goes missing?"

"Here's what I think," Vince says. "I think the Knicks are about to make a comeback in the fourth quarter, and I want to watch the rest of it."

"I'm leaving," I say. "You guys can pay for your own food."

"On the other hand," Vince says, "it is quite intriguing. Compelling, really, on a conceptual level."

Pete nods. "Certainly worth pursuing; should be fascinating to see where this leads."

"You guys are pathetic," I say, getting up to leave.

"Where are you going?" Vince asks.

"To look for Teresa Mullins."

"Come on, stay for a while. In the spirit of friendship," Pete says.

"Don't worry, I'll tell them to put it on my tab."

"Good," Vince says. "That friendship-spirit shit can get old real fast."

I'm going to have to go to Maine. As much as I'd like to avoid it, I don't really see as if I have a choice. Laurie has called the agency and gotten the names of the people that Mullins used as a reference, as well as the name of her landlord there, since she was renting.

Laurie or I could probably conduct those interviews by phone, though in-person conversations are usually more productive. But I also want to talk to friends and neighbors of Mullins's, and there's no way to identify those people from here.

I'm going to go tomorrow, which means I have to find stuff to fill up the rest of today. I'm not exactly bursting with investigative leads to follow up on, so with nothing better to do, I decide to go visit with my one-dollar client.

As soon as Keith is brought into the attorney meeting room, I'm sorry I came.

That's because he brightens up with obvious hope and expectations when he sees me. Since I'm not bringing anything with me that is positive, he's about to be disappointed.

It's a weird situation for me; I've never had a client that I basically had no interest in helping before. Maybe that will change; maybe my investigation will reveal that he was wrongly accused and convicted. But the evidence is the evidence, and it was compelling. For now, I have no reason to disbelieve it.

Once I disabuse him of the notion that I am bringing good news, I ask him how well he knew Teresa Mullins. She had testified at trial that she recognized his voice and even his eyes.

"Not well at all," he says. "I met her a couple of times at the house."

"So she was the nanny while you were living there?"

He shakes his head. "No, she arrived probably eight months after Jill and I split up. But I came back to the house a couple of times to get my stuff. I had left a lot of it in the attic; Jill had been okay with me using it as a storage space. But as things with Jill deteriorated, I started getting the stuff out of there. Those are the times I met

Teresa. It wasn't much more than a hello and good-bye thing."

"So you and Jill weren't on decent terms at that point?"

"I didn't shoot her, which is a tribute to my self-control, considering the circumstances."

"You mean the fact that you broke up?"

"Much more than that. I . . ."

He stops, so I prod him to continue. "I need to know as much as possible," I say.

"The personal relationship ended months before I left the company," he says. "I'm not really sure what happened. It was a stressful time for her. The company was in trouble, hemorrhaging money, and she was spending all of her time trying to find investors. She was obsessed with it; that's all she talked about. But I didn't blame her; Finding Home was her baby." He realizes what he said and adds, "Her other baby."

"She found the investors?"

He nods. "Eventually. Some big equity firm. But she spent a huge amount of time on the road; later on, even a couple of months overseas. But by then, we were already done, and I think the business stress probably took a toll on our relationship. I also had a strong feeling she was seeing someone else, but she never confirmed that for me, and I still don't know if it was true."

"So it was all on her?" I ask, my skepticism probably evident.

"No, I did my part. She was busy, or away, and I wasn't a Boy Scout. I had some . . . is there a nicer way to put it than I cheated on her with a few people? In any event, it ended in what I guess is a typical fashion. Life goes on, you know?"

Having once been divorced, I sort of know, but I let him continue.

"The business relationship was something else," he says.

"What do you mean?" I ask.

"She thought I was stealing from the company; not money, but proprietary information. Somebody gave her a tip to that effect while she was overseas raising money."

"Were you?"

"Absolutely not. But they . . . we . . . were developing a new process at that point. So they shut me out of it; it should have been under my supervision, but I wasn't allowed anywhere near it. I confronted them, and they told me of their suspicions. So I left."

"Fired?"

"Absolutely. It was positioned in the press as a mutual decision to save face, but that's not what it was, and that's not what I wanted. I took steps to sue them and bring

88

it all out in public. They'd have to testify in court and show evidence that I stole those materials, which they wouldn't be able to do, because I didn't."

"What happened to the lawsuit?"

He makes a gesture as if to indicate the prison surroundings. "This."

"So you left the company before Jill adopted Dylan?"

He nods. "Yes, I left while she was still in Europe. She adopted Dylan maybe a month after she got back."

"Do you know why Mullins would have testified against you at trial?"

"I never thought she lied; I just figured she was wrong. I mean, she was attacked herself, and she must have been scared to death. The cops told her that I did it, and she must have bought into it."

It's a rather generous, understanding answer, and it impresses me.

"Who would have told Jill that you were being dishonest in your dealings with the company?" I ask.

"I don't know; that's the weird thing. If you had asked me at the time, I would have said I didn't have an enemy in the world. But I obviously did. The funny thing is, the way they froze me out, I couldn't have given out any information to anyone. I didn't have any."

"What was the process they froze you out of?"

"They developed a new DNA test. It's apparently faster, requires a smaller sample, and is more accurate. They've made a fortune off of it; or at least the stock went through the roof."

"Can you give me a list of people I can talk to that might have been involved or might have an insight into what happened?"

"Sure, but the players have moved on. Once I left, they cleaned house, anybody who had worked with me became toxic. They brought in a whole new staff; it was very unfair to my people. Although I was told they gave them very rich severance packages." He writes out a list of people for me to talk to and gives it to me.

"Okay," I say. "I'll keep you updated as best I can."

"I really appreciate this. I haven't had any real hope since Stanley died."

The timing of that surprises me. "He died well after you were convicted," I say. "Weren't you in here by then?"

He nods. "Absolutely. But he told me he was working on something that could help me."

"Did he say what made him hopeful?" I ask.

"No. He was probably just trying to keep my spirits up, but if that was it, it worked. Until he died."

Billy Cameron is a dedicated, incredibly hardworking lawyer, passionate about the law and helping those in need. He is exactly like I would be, if I were a completely different person.

Nicknamed "Bulldog" because he was a star college football player for Georgia, the name fits his legal approach as well. His tenacity is legendary; he'll leave no stone unturned on behalf of his clients.

He's certainly not doing it for the cash. Billy runs the public defender's office, so his clients are almost exclusively those who can't afford to pay an attorney. It's a completely admirable thing to do, especially since he and his staff are terribly overworked.

On occasion, he would call and ask me to take on a client when they simply couldn't handle the load. I did so on a couple of occasions; that was before I learned to screen his phone calls.

"You come in to offer your services?" he asks after we get the greetings and a little small talk behind us.

I turn around and look behind me, as if he were talking to someone else. Then, "I'd love to, but I have all the clients I can handle."

"How many?" he asks.

"All together? One."

"I'm awed by your dedication."

I shrug. "I do what I can."

The actual reason I'm here is because of Keith's comment to me that Stanley Butler, his lawyer, had told him he was working on something that could help Keith's position, that he was hopeful in the days before he died.

I knew Stanley very well, and if he had one defining characteristic, it was that he told the truth. He would not have said that to Keith unless there really was something that had come up that would provide some reason for hope. I want to find out what that was.

That real motivation is not something I want or need to share with Billy, so I simply say, "I'm representing Keith Wachtel."

He perks up at the mention of the name; it was a big case around here. "Really? You

93

filing an appeal?"

"Not sure yet," I say. "For now, I'm just looking into it."

"You must have a reason," he says, which is his way of prodding me to reveal more.

I nod. "Yes, I must."

"But you apparently don't want to share it with me."

"Apparently not," I say.

"Does it have to do with the dog being found?"

"You're getting either warmer or colder," I say.

He laughs. "Okay . . . . I give up. So what can I do for you?"

"Stanley Butler's files were turned over to you when he died, right? Wasn't that in his will?"

"They were, and it was. It gave us a whole bunch of new clients that we didn't need."

"Well, I'll take a potential one off your hands. I'd like his files on the Wachtel case."

"You have official representation?"

I nod. "I do."

"You want some other cases while you're here?"

"I don't."

He laughs again and calls his assistant and tells her to bring in the file on Wachtel. That gives him ten minutes to once again recount the story of the touchdown pass he caught to beat Auburn. "And then the next week we turn around and lose to Tennessee," is how he always finishes. "We win that game, we're in the Sugar Bowl. We win the Sugar Bowl, and I'm in the NFL. I get to the NFL, and I'm doing color on ESPN today."

"If it's any consolation," I say, "I bet Tennessee and made money off your pain." Of course, I have no recollection of the game, and as Billy is at least ten years older than I am, I would have been more likely watching cartoons than football that day.

"I feel much better now," he says.

His intercom rings, and he picks it up. "Yes?" After a pause, he says, "Are you sure? I'll be right there."

He hangs up and says, "Give me a second." Then he gets up and walks out of the room.

He doesn't return for about five minutes, carrying a folder much smaller than I would have expected. "We don't have any documents on the Wachtel case. There's a file there, but it's empty."

"But everything he had was supposed to be given to you, right?"

"Definitely."

"Have you noticed anything else missing?"

"Not that I'm aware of. It's strange."

95

I point to the folder in his hand. "What's that?"

"Photographs from the case. Stanley kept all his photographs in a separate area in his files. Makes no sense, but that was Stanley. I'm sure he knew what he was doing."

He hands me the folder, and I open it. The one on top is a photograph of Teresa Mullins and a small infant, taken fairly close up, so I assume it was a selfie. Having never taken a selfie myself, that's not in my area of expertise.

I also assume it's Dylan Hickman with her, since the stroller is the same type as the one in the crime pictures. This particular stroller is enormous, with all kinds of compartments and shelves for carrying things. In the 1800s, families traveled cross-country with less storage space than in this stroller.

If nothing else, the photograph of Teresa will give me something to show people in Maine as I wander around aimlessly, looking for a clue to strike us from out of the sky.

The rest of the photographs are standard-issue crime-scene stuff. Whoever took Stanley's files, if they had a sinister purpose, was not damaged by not noticing that the photographs were missing. There doesn't seem to be anything I can use, or anything that might have accounted for Stanley's apparent surge of optimism.

"If anything else turns up, let me know, okay?" I ask.

"Sure. The fact that we don't have that file is strange."

Yes, it is.

The trip to Maine is a momentous one, but not because of the investigation. Laurie has decided to come with me, which means we're leaving Ricky, Tara, and Sebastian for the first time. Willie and Sondra are going to stay at our house, along with their dog, Cash. We both trust them and know everything will be fine, but that didn't stop Laurie from tearing up when she said good-bye to Ricky.

We have been incredibly lucky in that Nancy Ohman, the sixteen-year-old girl who lives with her family next door to us, babysits for Ricky whenever we need her. I'm not surprised she does; at current babysitting rates, a few hours a week can put her through college and graduate school. But she's almost always available, and completely reliable.

But when we're out of town, we're more comfortable with Willie and Sondra being there. Tara and Sebastian seemed pretty sanguine about our departure; they like Willie and Sondra and love playing with Cash. It's only going to be for a day or two, the length depending on what we learn, but Laurie acts like we're heading off to war.

I've been to the Portland airport before, and it is so perfect that I wouldn't mind having an apartment there. It's never remotely crowded, the gates are all close to baggage claim, the restaurants serve fantastic lobster rolls, and the rental car places are literally attached to the terminal. It's like JFK, except completely opposite.

Once we get the car, we head straight to Camden, about an hour and a half from the airport. That's where the Fitzgeralds live, and they are the people who gave Teresa the reference that got her hired by Jill in the first place.

We had called ahead, and they said they were happy to talk to us. The town of Camden is picturesque and stylish, and a bit upscale, maybe Maine's version of the Hamptons. The Fitzgeralds live right in town, and Peter and his wife, Susan, greet us with smiles when we show up.

They've got both coffee and tea made and waiting for us, as well as an assortment of cakes and pastries. So we all sit down to eat, drink, and chitchat for a while until we get down to business. And business in this case is Teresa Mullins.

I ask what they know about her, and Susan says, "Teresa is wonderful, just wonderful."

We need a little more detail than that, so I prompt her a bit. "How did you come to know her?"

"We had a housekeeper back then who recommended her. I think they were friends. Our youngest was ten or eleven at the time, so we needed more of a babysitter than a nanny. But I would have recommended her for anything. She was very responsible and reliable, especially considering what she was going through."

"What was that?"

"She didn't talk much about it," Susan says, "but her husband had recently left her. Apparently just walked out. Then her mother had early onset Alzheimer's, so she had that on her plate as well."

"Is her mother still alive?" Laurie asks.

"I don't think so," Peter says. "I had heard she was in a facility, and a pretty expensive one at that. I'm not sure how they pulled that off; they had very little money. But then I heard that she passed on."

"How long since you've seen her?" Laurie asks.

"Probably three years," Susan says. "Not since she left here."

"Do you know how to reach her?"

Susan shakes her head. "I tried a few times, but her phone in Nobleboro was disconnected with no forwarding number."

"Didn't Fred say he saw her?" Peter asks, which is the most interesting thing I've heard since we walked in.

"Fred?" I prompt.

Susan nods. "Right, I remember that. Our friend Fred Patton said he saw her . . . I think it was in Bridgton . . . but she didn't recognize him, and she denied that Teresa Mullins was her name. It was strange, because Fred knew her pretty well, so I don't see how he could have been wrong."

At my urging, Susan calls Fred to ask if the woman he saw gave a different name, but he doesn't remember if she did or not.

Peter and Susan, much as they are trying to be helpful, have really nothing to add that's useful to us. They give us the address and phone number that they had for Teresa, but they're the same as the ones the agency had given Laurie.

We head for the address in Nobleboro, but it's dark by the time we get there. We take a room at an inn in nearby Damariscotta. Laurie immediately loves the place, because it has charm, character, and antique furniture, all things that are completely meaningless to me.

What it doesn't have, amazing as it may seem, are televisions in the rooms. No televisions! What kind of barbaric people are these? There is a football game on tonight, and there are no televisions! This is America? Who would stay in this place besides Communists?

Laurie calms me down some by taking me to a pub called King Eider's, where they have great lobster rolls, about four million kinds of local beers, and a television tuned to the game. The natural order of things has been restored.

In the morning, we head back to Nobleboro to talk to neighbors of the house that Teresa lived in, as well as her former landlord. No one has heard anything from her in years. It's a complete waste of time, and the same could be said for this entire trip, with the exception of the lobster rolls.

Our last stop before heading for the airport is Bridgton, the town where the guy named Fred said he saw Teresa, though she denied who she was.

We have even less to go on here; even if

Teresa did live in Bridgton, we don't know where and, therefore, have no idea who her neighbors might be. We brought the selfie photo of Teresa and Dylan that was in Stanley Butler's file, and we show it to a few passersby and shopkeepers, but none of them have a clue who she is.

We're leaving to go to the airport when Laurie asks me to pull over into a parking lot. When I look up and see the sign that tells us where we are, I understand why.

"Bridgton Animal Hospital."

It's a long shot, but no longer than our other shots. Laurie doesn't even have to tell me why we're here; we just get out of the car and head inside.

Laurie shows her private investigator's license to the woman at the front desk and says that we need to speak with the owner of the place. It works, and we're brought through the back area to an office within five minutes.

Her saying that she is a private investigator is a hell of a lot more effective than my saying I'm a lawyer. Had I done so, we'd probably be back in the parking lot by now.

The vet's name is Dr. Patricia Brenner, and she answers our first question by saying that she's owned this practice for twenty-seven years.

"So what can I do for you?" she asks.

"We're looking for a woman named Teresa Mullins; we have reason to believe she was a client of yours," I say, even though we have almost no reason to believe that.

Dr. Brenner thinks for a moment and then says, "I can't say I remember the name, but a lot of people and animals have come through these doors. When would she have been here?"

"Sometime within the last three years," Laurie says.

Another shake of the head from Dr. Brenner. "If it's that recent, then I'm sure I'd remember." She starts typing some keys on the computer on her desk, and after a few moments, she says, "No such name in our records."

I take out the picture of Teresa and show it to her. "Do you recognize her?"

"I'm not sure; she does look familiar," Dr. Brenner says. "What kind of animal would she have brought in?"

"A dog. A border collie, to be exact. The dog would have been suffering from a tick-borne disease called anahlichtia."

A longish pause from Dr. Brenner as she looks back at the picture and stares at it. "Of course. I remember this."

"Are you sure?" Laurie asks.

"Yes. Absolutely. This was the first case of anahlichtia that I had seen; I almost missed it. It's making its way slowly down from

Canada. We've only had five or six cases since."

"Can you remember the name the woman used?"

"No, but I can find it based on the medicine we prescribed. Like I say, we've only had a handful of cases, and the medicine is unique to that. It's all here in the computer."

She types some more, and this time the search takes longer. "Here it is. Her name was Linda Sanford. It was a four-year-old border collie named Joey."

"How can you be sure she's the one?"

"Because all the other dogs that received this medicine are long-term clients and have been back a number of times. We only saw Ms. Sanford and Joey that one time."

"Could the ailment have caused a permanent limp?" Laurie asks.

She nods. "Absolutely. Especially if the medication protocol was not followed as prescribed. But even if it was, a chronic limp is not unusual."

Dr. Brenner checks and tells us that "Ms. Sanford" paid her bill in cash. She gives us the address that was given to her. We thank her and leave, stopping off at the address to possibly talk to whoever lives there now.

That turns out to be tough, because there is no such address. It's a fake.

Heading for the airport, Laurie sums up the situation perfectly. "What we have here is a whole new ball game."

Heading for the airport. I sure sure up the situation perfectly. What we have here is a whole new ball game."

Ricky seems to have had a great time with "Uncle Willie and Aunt Sondra." I get the feeling that they didn't deprive him of much, as my secret M&M stash in the cupboard has been decimated. I had an aunt and uncle just like that who used to stay with me when my parents went away. It was so much fun that I was constantly slipping my mother travel brochures.

Tara and Sebastian seem considerably happier to see me than Ricky does, so I reward them by heading out for a walk, while Laurie updates Willie and Sondra on the progress we made in Maine.

As we walk, I tell Tara that it doesn't take deep thinking to understand the importance of what we learned. It appears certain that Teresa Mullins, using a fake name, had possession of Cody after the abduction.

The implications of this are huge. There is no way to reconcile her testimony that she was simply a victim of the crime with her possession of Cody. It just does not compute. The only way she could have gotten him would be if she were in some way conspiring with the abductors.

It's not exactly a leap from there to question her entire testimony. She could not have been truthful in her identifying Keith Wachtel as the abductor; it would make no sense for her to implicate and help convict the person she was conspiring with, not to mention the fact that Wachtel has not said anything about it.

Which leads me to a typical defense attorney conclusion: Keith Wachtel has been wrongly convicted.

And the next step in the progression is just as obvious and unavoidable: my temporary one-dollar client has just become a permanent one-dollar client.

Of course, I can't prove any of this. While I find the recollections of Dr. Brenner to be perfectly believable and reliable, it's fair to say that the police and prosecutor will have a different view.

I'm seeing this through the eyes of a defense attorney, since that's what I am. The law enforcement side would look at the anahlichtia tick, and a vet's vague recollections, and a supposed missing nanny, and they would say that, in legal terms, I am full of shit.

They would point to the other evidence, Cody's hair and DNA in Keith's apartment and car, and the blanket fiber in the car. If I accept the police expert's opinion that simple transference couldn't account for that much shed hair, then if Keith is actually innocent, the hair and fiber must have both been planted.

It's fair to say that Pete, and the prosecutors, would not think that highly of my dog-hair-and-blanket-fiber-planting theory.

Unfortunately, though we've learned a great deal about Teresa Mullins, we still don't know where she is. And that's a problem.

In addition to not having a promising way to proceed, I also have something of an ethical dilemma. Laurie and I undertook this investigation as a favor to Jill. She didn't ask us to but certainly didn't fight very hard when we offered. I think Laurie was right that Jill was feeling alone and needed us beside her.

Keith was only my client in the most technical of terms, and he understood the relationship. The sole reason for him to hire me was so that I could have legal access to the discovery information. I made him no promises and did not mislead him in any way.

So my loyalty was far more to Jill than to Keith. Now that has changed in a tangible way. Not that Jill is less worthy of my help than she was before, it's just that Keith has had a major status adjustment.

He has gone from someone I considered probably guilty, if I thought about it at all, to someone I now believe has been wrongly convicted. At the very least, the key government witness against him has been demonstrated to have a relationship with the abductor. It is certainly not a relationship she ever revealed in court.

One tangible difference is that I have to start treating Keith like a real client, and that includes confidentiality. I can no longer discuss our communications, or the progress of our case, with anyone who is not on our legal team. That means leaving Jill out of the loop.

Tara understands the subtlety of the legal process, while Sebastian does not. When we get back, Tara and I talk to Laurie about it, while Sebastian exerts just enough effort to climb up on the couch and go to sleep.

"I'll speak to Jill about it," Laurie says. "She'll understand."

I'm not so sure she will; I think she will

feel shut out. She's anxious for any information that in any way relates to Dylan, and that's understandable. But I'll let Laurie deal with her.

My next move is to call Sam and say, "I've got a new name for Teresa Mullins."

"Go," he says. Sam believes that if you use short, staccato words and speech, it sounds cooler and more detective-like.

"Linda Sanford."

"Got it," he says. When we're talking about a case, Sam can speak entire sentences without using a two-syllable word.

"Thanks, Sam."

"I'm on the case . . . . back to you soon," Sam says, proving my syllable point before hanging up.

It's time for another visit with my client. This time when Keith is brought in to meet with me, I'm not as distressed to see the hopeful look in his eyes, because this time it may be warranted.

"We've got a change in circumstances," I say.

"Uh-oh."

"Nothing negative," I say. "I've just learned some things, and it will affect our relationship one way or another."

"What have you learned?"

I tell him about Teresa Mullins being missing and how we have reason to believe that she was in possession of Cody well after the abduction.

"So she was a part of it?" he asks, not bothering to mask his amazement.

"It would seem that way. I can't think of another credible explanation, though one may exist."

113

"Can we get a new trial?" he asks.

"Don't get ahead of yourself, Keith. We are on another planet from a new trial at this point. What we have is reason to keep investigating. That's all."

He nods. "Okay . . . I understand. Great. How does this change our relationship?"

"Because my representation until now, as you know, has been a convenience to allow me to get discovery documents as your designated legal counsel. We're way past that now. If I continue on the case, I will be your attorney in every respect."

"Is there a problem with that?"

"No, not a problem. I just need you to understand that and accept it, or not."

"Are you kidding? I accept it."

"Fine," I say. "Next question. Last time I was here, you said Stanley gave you some reason to hope shortly before he died. You said he was working on something."

"Right. It was surprising, because before that, he always went out of his way to make sure I was being realistic about stuff."

"Did he say anything more about it?"

"Just that he had gotten some information worth checking out and that he would stay on it. I asked him what it was, but he wouldn't say. Said it could be a crank."

"Crank? Did you take that to mean he had

gotten a call or maybe a tip from someone?"

"That's what I figured, but he wouldn't tell me any more. Didn't want to get my hopes too high."

"Did he mention whether or not he was working with another lawyer on your case? Someone who might have been in possession of his files?"

"No. Never."

I promise Keith that I'll keep him updated but caution him that these things rarely move quickly. There's no reason to renegotiate the legal terms of our relationship or to change the fee structure, because he still has no money to pay me.

When I leave the prison, I drive for about twenty minutes before I see that there's a message on my phone. It's from Sam, and the message is a short one.

"I'm on the way to your house. I've got news."

Ten words, ten syllables.

I resist the urge to call home and find out if Sam is there yet, or if Laurie knows what's going on. It'll be easier to have the conversation in person, and I'll be there in a few minutes.

Sam is at the house when I arrive, and I of course immediately ask him what is going on.

115

"I found Linda Sanford."

"Where?"

"Outside of Greenville, South Carolina."

"She lives there?"

"She did until a few days ago, at which point she died there. Actually, she's that rare person who died twice."

"Sam, please don't make me drag this out of you. Tell me everything you know."

"Okay, okay. I found Linda Sanford through a credit card she used up in Maine. I was pretty sure it was her, but I became positive when I found a death certificate for the same Linda Sanford, who died nine years ago. Teresa Mullins took the identity of a dead woman; she got a driver's license and birth certificate. It's not that hard.

"She continued to use the card, not very often, but enough that I could trace her movements over time. She seems to have lived in three different states before South Carolina, maybe even four. I've got the stuff written down for you, but I have to flesh it out more. I did this fast, so I might have missed something."

"How did she die?"

"You mean the second time? She lived in a small cabin that burned down. She appeared to be asleep, but all I know is what the newspaper story showed. The only other

116

thing it said was that the fire department was investigating but had no comment at that point."

"We need to get somebody down there," Laurie says, and I agree.

Sam continues, "It also said that Ms. Sanford's next of kin was notified. I wonder what their reaction was when they heard she died again."

"Sam, you did great." Sam's ability to find out anything about anyone online is scary and a little disconcerting. I wonder if he knows about what Marcia Bergman and I did behind the gym in tenth grade. We swore we'd keep it a secret, but it's always possible that Marcia told someone. I know I never did, even though it still ranks as one of the highlights of my life.

"Thanks, boss," he says. "No coincidences, right?"

I nod. "No coincidences."

It's become clear that it was Teresa Mullins, a.k.a. Linda Sanford, who left Cody at the shelter. We don't know why yet; that is still to be determined. It may or may not have been her that contacted Stanley Butler and gave him a tip that made him hopeful he could secure Keith's release.

Teresa must have been fearful in the years since the abduction, since she changed her name and assumed an entirely new identity. And that fear was obviously justified.

The killers were either watching her, or more likely saw the publicity about Cody in the papers. Teresa may have thought they did not know where she was, living in that out-of-the-way cabin in South Carolina.

But they knew, and they killed her. And now she is not available to tell us what she knows, and what she did.

No coincidences.

All crimes happen for a reason. That may seem obvious. In fact, you could claim that everything, criminal or not, happens for a reason, but it remains a crucial fact in conducting an investigation.

In my world, the reason is the motive, and the common ones are money, sex, or power . . . sometimes all three. Even irrational crimes have a reason, though that reason may obviously be an irrational one.

The Son of Sam murdered people because he believed his dog told him to. Totally nutso, obviously, but the reason for the crimes was the imagined conversation between David Berkowitz and his dog, and the motive was to do the dog's perceived bidding.

Since I talk to Tara all the time, perhaps this isn't the best example for me to provide. But the most crucial step in uncovering a perpetrator is uncovering the reason for the crime.

What makes this case so difficult is that we don't even know who the target was, which makes it much, much harder to discover the motive. There are three target possibilities, and a case can be made for each of them.

Jill Hickman might well have been the intended victim; if you want to get revenge on, or simply hurt, a mother, there could be no more effective way than to take her child.

As a very successful businesswoman, and a person simply living on this planet, Jill might well have a lot of enemies, people who could hate her for reasons real or imagined. It's highly unlikely that money was the pure motive, since even with her considerable fortune, no ransom demand was ever made.

Another potential target is the child, Dylan Hickman. At this point it's impossible to know if there was something about his identity that specifically led to his being abducted. Further complicating the matter, and complicating it considerably, is the fact that he was initially abandoned and then adopted. Who are the natural parents, and could their identities have played a role?

Were the kidnappers after any baby or this

baby in particular? And if it was this one, was it because of who his adoptive mother is or maybe who his natural parents are?

Then there is Keith himself, in my eyes another victim of this crime. I believe he was set up to take the fall, but could that have been the purpose all along? Could the entire thing have been done simply to punish him? This seems the least likely of the three to me, but it's still possible, which means it's something we have to consider.

One thing is certain: this was not a random crime. Random criminals rarely, if ever, take the next step of framing someone to take the fall. And they don't track Teresa Mullins for years, despite all her efforts to disappear, and then kill her.

And there is another thing that is certain: Keith Wachtel did not kill Teresa Mullins in South Carolina this week. I can check, but it's very unlikely that the warden of East Jersey State Prison gave him a three-day pass.

I call Phyllis Butler, Stanley's widow, to ask her if she has any idea where his missing file on the Wachtel case could be. Laurie and I have taken Phyllis to dinner a few times since Stanley's death, and she is one of those people that you instantly like.

She's happy to hear that I'm taking over

one of Stanley's cases but cannot help me with this one. "Everything went to the public defender," she says. "I cleaned out the office myself."

I thank her and hang up. I'm afraid I've run into another dead end; there is simply no place else for me to look for the file. I don't know whether or not it was somehow stolen, but the way things are going, I sure wouldn't bet against it.

My next call is to Hike, who answers with a "Hello" that sounds like he's cowering in fear that I am going to give him an unpleasant assignment. The bad news for him is that I am.

"I need you to go to South Carolina," I say.

He repeats my words, but with an incredulous tone. "South Carolina?"

"South Carolina," I say. The conversation is not quite advancing at the rate I'd like it to.

"The actual South Carolina?"

"I wasn't aware that there is a virtual one," I say. "But just to be clear, if you look at a map and find North Carolina, I'm talking about the state that is slightly below it."

"What for?"

"A woman that we believe is Teresa Mullins died in a fire in her cabin in the woods.

We have no details, and I want all of them."

"You want me to go into the woods in South Carolina?"

"What's the problem with that?" I ask.

"Did you see *Deliverance*?"

"I did, Hike. I don't want to nitpick this, but it took place in Georgia."

"Talk about your six of one, half a dozen of the other. You ever see the bugs in those woods?"

"I don't think I have," I say.

"You know why everybody has a pickup truck down there? Because they have bugs so big that they carry off regular cars. A couple of years ago, two beetles dragged off a Winnebago with an entire family still in it. They were never heard from again."

"Hike . . ."

"And people get malaria down there like we get a cold. The doctors have given up; they can't handle it. The drugstores stock over-the-counter malaria medicine. That's why Steve Spurrier left."

Steve Spurrier was the football coach at South Carolina for years. I had no idea that Hike had any football knowledge; he's pulling out all the stops.

"Spurrier was there for eleven years," I say, "and he retired when he was seventy. I don't think malaria was a factor."

123

"Is there anyone else you can get to go?" Hike asks.

"Hike, you'll get twice your hourly rate, even when you're asleep."

"When do I leave?"

"Does that mean you're willing to go?"

Hike is always sure the world is coming to an end, but he wants to have enough money to deal with the fallout.

"You know me, Andy. I'm a team player."

"Good. You leave right away. And, Hike?"

"Yeah?"

"It's great having you on the team."

Finding Home sounds like the name of a small, intimate company that might run schmaltzy TV commercials. In real life, it is anything but that. Located in Park Ridge, it is a gleaming, modern, four-story building, with four satellite buildings, each of them quite substantial, spread out on what looks like a college campus.

It would remind me of my college days except for the fact that I went to NYU, in Greenwich Village, and there aren't enough drugs in the world to make someone confuse Park Ridge, New Jersey, with Greenwich Village.

I don't see many employees around, but maybe they're all in the buildings doing whatever it is that chemists do. I'm here to see one particular employee, Zachary Alford, CEO of Finding Home. He's been with the company for more than three years; he arrived while Jill was doing the crucial fund-raising.

When Jill elevated herself to chairman and stepped back from day-to-day involvement, Alford became CEO. I assume that if Jill ever decides she wants the title of Emperor of the Realm, then CEO Zachary Alford will become Chairman Zachary Alford.

I've gotten an instant appointment with Alford mainly because Jill asked him to see me. Laurie asked her to make the call, and she reported that Jill wasn't pleased. As I predicted, she is not taking particularly well to the new arrangement, in which we are working for Keith and not reporting details to her.

Her attitude is certainly understandable. She is desperate to know everything, in the hope that it could lead her to her missing son. Making matters worse, we are now working for the very person she believes is responsible for her personal agony.

She didn't verbalize it to Laurie, but Laurie thinks Jill sees it as a betrayal of sorts. I suspect the reason that she didn't speak out about it is to avoid antagonizing us. We are still Jill's best chance to finally get closure. She doesn't want to blow that chance.

It is a very tough spot for her to be in, and it's no walk in the park for Laurie and me either.

Alford sets the ground rules as soon as I walk into his office. "I'm willing to speak with you, Mr. Carpenter, but I do have another meeting in thirty minutes, so let's get right to it."

I'm not liking this guy already, probably for the wrong reasons. He has a frown on his face, as if I walked into his white-carpeted office with shit on my shoes. It also bugs me that he said *thirty minutes,* rather than *a half hour,* but I don't know why it does.

"Sure. No problem," I say. "I'm interested in knowing the details of Keith Wachtel's departure from the company."

He seems a bit taken aback. "The only reason we are meeting is that Ms. Hickman said that I should be forthcoming with you."

I nod. "Good advice; she's a smart lady. It's no wonder she's made it all the way to chairman. Or chairwoman. Or chairperson."

"We use *chairman.*"

"Okay. Good. Glad we got that cleared up. Now, about Keith Wachtel."

"Keith is a fine chemist. Outstanding, really."

"If you've got a meeting in twenty-eight minutes, it might be helpful if you could answer my questions. For example, had my question been, 'What kind of a chemist is Keith?' then your answer would have been directly on point. And I'm not counting, but I think I've asked twice about the circumstances leading to his departure from the company."

"So you did. We had credible evidence that Mr. Wachtel was engaging in unethical behavior. And that is putting it mildly."

"What did he do?"

"He was removing sensitive documents from the premises in violation of company policy," he says. "It was a policy that he was quite familiar with; in fact, he was instrumental in creating it in the first place."

"What was he doing with the documents?"

"We believe he was sharing them with a competitor."

"Do you have proof of that?" I ask

"If we did, he would have gone to jail for it." He hesitates and then adds, "And if he had, Ms. Hickman might still have her child."

"How did you discover the theft of the documents?"

"It was reported anonymously to our security department, who in turn followed up and confirmed it," he said. Then, "I assure you that there is no doubt about what happened."

His answer is interesting to me. If Keith is telling the truth that he did not steal documents, and Keith's truth-telling is increasing in credibility by the moment, then someone within the company already had it in for him. That same person could have set Keith up to take the fall for the kidnapping and might even have been the kidnapper himself.

"Who replaced Mr. Wachtel in the position of chief chemist?" I ask.

"Steven Emmonds," he says.

"Was he already here when Mr. Wachtel left?"

He shakes his head. "No, he was not. The circumstances that led to Mr. Wachtel's departure made it prudent to bring in a fresh team. We did not want to retain anyone who had a misguided loyalty to him."

"So you fired all those people just for knowing him?"

"We did so on the advice of counsel."

"Please tell Mr. Emmonds that I'll be wanting to talk to him."

He frowns, not pleased to be taking orders from the likes of me. "Mr. Emmonds is a busy man."

"Good for him. Please tell him I'll be wanting to talk to him."

"When?"

"I'm not sure. I'll call him directly. I just have a couple of additional questions for you. Are you aware if Jill Hickman's nanny, Teresa Mullins, ever came into these offices? Is it possible she knew someone here?"

"Not to my knowledge," he says. "But Ms. Hickman could better answer that."

"Fine; I'll ask her. Last question: Who hired you?"

"I believe it was a joint decision between the co-owners."

"Meaning Jill Hickman and Ted Parsons?"

"Yes."

I look at my watch and stand up. "We're done here. You'll make your next meeting with time to spare. I'm so relieved."

"Sam, did Linda Sanford have a cell phone?"

"Obviously," he answers, without hesitation. "Everybody has a cell phone."

"Can you get the number?"

"Why do you hurt me?" he asks.

"That means you have it?"

"Of course I have it. But she made very few calls in the last months, mostly to businesses, car service places, that kind of thing. If she had any friends, they didn't chat much on the phone."

"Did she have the phone when the kidnapping happened?"

"No, not until much later. She got it after she changed her name."

"What about e-mails? Can you access any e-mails she sent?"

"Sorry, can't help you there. I'd have to have the actual devices."

"What about tracking her movements?"

Every phone has a GPS in it, and the phone company knows where it is at all times. Sam has the ability to access their computers, which is how he got Mullins's phone information in the first place.

Of course, he's doing it illegally, a fact I am willing to overlook. We can't use the fruits of that illegal labor in court, but if he finds helpful information, I can always subpoena it legally later on.

If I ever get in front of a judge or jury in this matter, it could be helpful to place Teresa Mullins at the foundation building on the morning Cody was left there. Technically, I'd only be putting her phone at the scene, but that should be good enough.

Uh-oh . . . I'm thinking like a lawyer.

"I can definitely get the GPS data," Sam says. "They usually keep that information going back six months."

"That's more than enough. Most important is whether she was at the foundation the morning Cody was dropped off. And I hate to pile this on, but can you get me her financial information?"

"What are you looking for?"

"I want to know where her income has come from since the day of the abduction."

"You got it."

I ask him to get right on it, and then I

place a call to Hike down in South Carolina. I could ask Laurie to call him, but that might technically be considered spousal abuse.

Hike doesn't answer his cell phone, and though I want to hear what's going on, my inability to talk to him in the moment doesn't exactly crush me.

I leave a message on his voice mail, and fortunately, or unfortunately, he calls me back ten minutes later.

"You called?" he asks. "I was in with the chief."

"Of police?" I ask.

"Yeah. Billy's a good guy. We're going out for beers when he gets off."

I move the phone away from my ear and look at it, not believing the noise that's coming through. Hike is making friends?

"You're going out for beers with the chief of police?"

"Billy, yeah, and some of the other cops. Great group of guys; I like it down here."

I have never heard Hike say he liked something or someone, not ever. The closest I've ever heard him come to saying something positive about anything was when he said that the chicken wings at Charlie's "don't taste like shit."

"Hike, have you been taken hostage? Are

they forcing you to say these things?"

"Come on, Andy, you know me. I'm a fun-loving guy."

Clearly, a pod has taken over Hike's body, leaving me unsure as to how to continue the conversation. I've never actually spoken to a pod before.

I decide to proceed as if I'm talking to the actual Hike, not the Pod Hike. That way the pod people won't know I'm onto them.

"Have you been out to the cabin?" I ask.

"I went straight there from the airport; really nice drive."

"Really nice drive? What did you find?"

"A burned cabin."

"Has it been declared arson?"

"That's what the chief thinks, but they're not ready to say so for sure."

"The police chief?"

"No, Richie, the fire chief."

"Richie going out drinking with you tonight as well?" I ask.

"Good idea. I'll call him," says Pod Hike.

"So what do we know?"

"Well, they obviously know that Linda Sanford doesn't exist, or at least hasn't existed since the real Linda Sanford died. They're trying to figure out who this new victim really is, but I haven't told them."

"Good. Don't." It's a chip I want to play

when I need it.

"The body was pretty badly burned, but the coroner sees an indentation in her skull, as if she was hit over the head."

"It would be good if you could bring back a copy of the coroner's report," I say. "Do you know him also? Are you guys on the same bowling team?"

"No, his wife doesn't like him going out with the guys. You know how it is," Pod Hike says.

"Have you talked to the dead woman's neighbors? It would be helpful to know if she had a dog."

"I'm doing that tomorrow. I'll call you as soon as I know anything."

"When are you coming home?" I ask.

"I was thinking of staying the weekend. Billy's having a barbecue on Sunday. He wants to introduce me around."

"I don't know what you've done with the real Hike," I say, "but if you've hurt him, I'll track you down if it takes me forever."

Pod Hike ignores that and says, "We should think about opening an office down here."

"Open an office in South Carolina? I'm still sorry we have one in New Jersey."

"I'm just trying to think big."

"Speaking of big, have you seen any of the

Winnebago-dragging beetles?"

"Turns out that's a myth," he says. Then, "Hey, Andy . . . gotta go. Some of the guys just got here. I'll call y'all tomorrow."

Click.

Y'all?

There is one upside to my not having a clue as to what is going on. That is the fact that nothing I do feels stupid, because anything is just as logical, or illogical, as anything else.

This morning, I'm at the Alpine Medical Building in Alpine, New Jersey. It's about thirty minutes and many, many millions of dollars from Paterson; you would be hard-pressed to find a more upscale community in the state.

This is where Dylan Hickman was found, abandoned, three years ago. He was one month old at the time, and the identity of whoever left him there was, to my knowledge, never uncovered.

Laurie has done the legwork, or in this case phone-work, and discovered that the person who found Dylan was Barbara Woodson, the executive administrator of the facility, which I suppose is akin to being the office manager. The building itself seems to contain a wide array of physicians of all types who apparently decided they can more easily be found if they're in one place.

Ms. Woodson is a pretty, petite woman, one who comes off as being in total control. When I finally get into her office, she quickly fields three calls, each one ending with her giving crisp orders about how to handle a particular situation or problem.

Then she turns to me and smiles. "Sorry about that." She reaches over and flicks a switch on the phone. "Ringer off," she says.

"Thanks. Laurie told you what I wanted to talk to you about."

She nods. "The Hickman child. That was a day here unlike any other."

"Can you tell me what happened?"

"Really not that much to tell. I'm always the first one here; I get in about six thirty. I like to do things before the phone starts ringing. The first thing I noticed was that the door to the lobby was unlocked. That had never happened before."

"That worried you?"

She nods. "It did. But I didn't notice any damage or sign that the lock had been broken, so I went in anyway." She smiles. "Carefully, and prepared to run."

"Was the lock found to be broken?" I ask.

"The police said it was picked, but professionally, and the alarm was disabled. As were the lobby and outside cameras; in fact, power to the entire building had been shut off. I can only assume that it was done by the people who left Dylan," she said. "I don't believe in coincidences."

A woman after my own heart. "Doesn't sound like a distraught or overwhelmed parent," I say.

"No, it doesn't, although I have a hard time understanding anyone who could leave a child like that. Anyway, I took maybe half a dozen steps inside, and I saw the stroller . . . it was actually one of those that lies back and becomes a small bed, with a cover over it. The child was inside, apparently sleeping comfortably."

"So you immediately called the police?"

"I did. I also called for an ambulance, just in case. But they were not needed, as it turned out. The police took the child and all that came with him away. Then they questioned me, but I didn't have any more to tell them than I have to tell you."

"Was there anything else noteworthy about it?" I ask. "Anything that surprised you?"

"Actually, yes. Everything was expensive, first class all the way. I had just bought a stroller for my niece's baby, and this was much nicer than the ones I saw. I'll bet it was a thousand dollars. And the blanket covering him was cashmere. I can't even imagine what that cost."

That does seem to be unusual. It's not so much that wealthy people are more devoted to their children; it's rather that if they wanted to give a child up, they'd have resources that would let them do it in a better way than simply leaving it in a doctors' office lobby.

"Was there a note left behind?"

"No, nothing. Do you know what happened to the child?"

I realize that she is not aware that the baby was adopted by Jill and later abducted. Since she did not know the child's name, and since adoption records are sealed, it makes sense that she'd be in the dark about it.

I have no intention of telling her what happened; there's no reason to upset her. And the truth is that upset women are high up on the list of things I don't handle well, just below crazed gunmen and a notch above feral cats.

I shake my head. "All that I can say is that he was adopted into a very good home."

It's time once again to talk to Jill. Laurie has told me that she's still a bit upset with me for, in her view, taking Keith's side by representing him full-time. Laurie senses that Jill feels that we got into this to help her, and that by moving over to Keith, we are abandoning her.

From her point of view, she's not wrong.

Because I may have mentioned that I don't handle upset women well, I am bringing Laurie along to protect me. I am not ashamed of doing so; I have long ago come to terms with my own cowardice.

It turns out that my fears are unwarranted. We go to see Jill in her office, where she apparently works one day a week. She greets us with a smile and an offer of coffee or anything else we might want. Her assistant nods eagerly, demonstrating his willingness to accommodate our every whim. My whim is coffee, while Laurie is

141

whim-less.

Once we've dispensed with very little small talk, I say, "I know Laurie has told you that we're representing Keith full-time."

She nods. "She did. At first, I was upset with it." She turns to Laurie. "Sorry I over-reacted."

"Understandable. I would have reacted the same way," Laurie says.

"Thank you. The point is that I know you are trying to find out where Dylan is. How you come at it is something I trust you on."

"Thank you," I say.

She continues. "And Laurie told me that this means you will be less able to confide in me as this goes along. I understand that, but I just hope you'll tell me whatever you can. As I'm sure you know, I am desperate for any shred of information about Dylan."

I'm afraid she might start getting teary. When upset women turn into crying women, they move up past crazed gunmen on the list of things I can't handle.

"We'll share whatever we can," Laurie says, riding to the rescue. Jill thanks her, even as she's reaching for a tissue.

"How did you come to adopt Dylan?" I ask.

"I was wanting to adopt, and I had my name on a list."

"What list?"

She shrugs. "I don't really know. My lawyer took care of it. Then I got a call that a baby boy was abandoned at some doctor's office in Alpine, and I dropped everything and went to see him. He was in the hospital, although he was fine."

"So you were immediately first on the list?"

She grins with a little embarrassment. "There was a donation I made to a charity for unwanted children. It was a fairly substantial donation."

I nod my understanding. "And you've never had any idea who might have left Dylan there?"

"I've never wanted to know," she says. "I was afraid I'd be inclined to contact them, and they might then become part of our lives. The truth is I didn't want to share Dylan. I know that's selfish."

Time to change the subject. "Do you know who told your security department that Keith was stealing documents?"

She shakes her head. "No. They didn't know either. They got the information anonymously, but they confirmed it, and we took action."

"And you were in Europe at the time?"

"Yes, raising funds. I was gone for more

than two months, but I obviously kept in touch with the office here on a daily basis."

"Can you think of any enemies Keith had within the company, someone who might have wanted to report him or even create fake evidence against him?"

She pauses for a few moments, considering this. "No, I can't think of anyone."

"No one ever disliked him?" I ask. "Maybe was jealous of his job or his relationship with you?"

"I can't think of anyone, but it's obviously possible. You think someone framed Keith for the document thefts? And for the abduction? Is that where you're going with this?"

Laurie jumps in. "Jill, we want the guilty party found, whoever it may be, and we have reason to believe it is not Keith. Only by following this wherever it leads can we learn what happened to Dylan."

"Why do you think it's not Keith?" she asks.

I'm able to answer the question without violating client confidentiality because I did not learn this from the client. "Jill, Teresa Mullins is the woman who dropped Cody off at the shelter."

Jill's hand goes to her mouth, her shock evident.

I drop the other bomb. "And she died in a

144

suspicious fire shortly thereafter, just a few days ago."

"Oh, my God. No . . . this can't be happening."

"We're sure of it, Jill," Laurie says. "And that means Teresa lied in her testimony. It's why we're looking at this with fresh eyes."

Jill doesn't say anything for at least thirty seconds; it's as if she is trying to digest this new information. Finally, "So you think this was all about framing Keith?"

"We're not there yet," I say. "It could have been about Keith, or you, or Dylan."

She takes a deep breath. "So what can I do?"

"Think back to any possible enemies Keith may have had. Especially in business, but not limited to that. Also think of people that might want to do you harm."

"Okay. I will."

"And we'll need full access to everyone in your company, including security personnel."

"Of course," she says, clearly happy to be able to focus on something within her control. "You talked to Zachary, right?"

She's talking about CEO Zachary Alford, who I spoke to in his office. "I did," I say. "He didn't seem too happy about it."

"I'll try to make sure everybody speaks to

145

you with a smile," she says, forcing a smile herself.

"Including Ted Parsons?"

She frowns. "He doesn't work for me."

"He's your partner. He'll see me if you ask him to."

Jill looks as if she is going to argue the point but then sort of shrugs in defeat. "I'll call him. I really hope something comes from all this."

"Me too," I say. "By the way, Alford said that you and Ted Parsons were both instrumental in hiring him. Is that true?"

"Actually, no," she says. "I was in Europe raising money . . . I wasn't paying much attention. It was really Ted's choice, though, of course, I signed off on it. I'm glad I did; he's done an outstanding job, which is why we promoted him."

We say our good-byes, and then Jill, apparently unable to resist, once again addresses the issue that hangs over all of this.

"Please tell me what you can, when you can."

It is very possible that the answer we are looking for is connected to Finding Home. The company is a source of substantial wealth, and with that comes power. Throw in a little sex, and you have the trifecta for criminal motives. When you then add in the fact that two of this case's very key players, Jill and Keith, were connected to the company, that makes it a likely candidate to be at the center of this.

The truth is that I know very little about the company, other than what Jill and Keith have told me. I know that they do DNA testing and that a new process vaulted them into a position of prominence. But that's all.

Fortunately, I have Sam Willis at my disposal, and at my request, he's prepared a folder full of material about Finding Home, taken off the Internet. Of course, I could ask him to illegally penetrate the company's internal computer system, and he could probably do so in less time than it would take me to ask the question. But for right now, public information is sufficient.

Before I start digging into this material, I put Ricky to bed, kiss him good night, and tuck him in. It's a routine that I really enjoy, and I think on some level it's become even more important to me because of my involvement in the Dylan Hickman case. As a new parent, I don't have quite the imagination to conjure up how awful it must be to have a child taken away.

I'm that rare rich person that only accidentally stumbles onto the business pages when I'm looking for sports, so Finding Home's story is mostly new to me. But the articles Sam provided leave no doubt that the story of the company's growth played out in the public spotlight.

Most of the stories written about Finding Home were written after the fact, meaning after it became successful. That makes sense; why write about a small, unimportant company that's struggling? Who would care?

Jill Hickman comes off as fairly heroic in this portrayal, and it seems deservedly so. As a start-up entrepreneur, she was going against some large, established, and well-financed companies, and there were a number of occasions when it looked like Finding Home, the company on which she had staked her career, wouldn't make it.

She is said to have removed herself from the scientific end, which was not her specialty anyway, and plunged into the world of high finance. Her company simply would not survive unless some deep-pocketed investors were found, and Jill set out to find them. It became an all-consuming mission.

She worked both Europe and the U.S. but finally struck gold right here, just thirty minutes away in Manhattan. A private equity firm called the Parsons Group, named after Ted Parsons, its founder, first invested some funds to provide a much-needed quick influx of cash. They then followed through by purchasing half the company.

Jill retained the other half, as well as the authority to run the company. The Parsons Group was known to be a passive investor, and they were content to put their faith in Jill. However, the abduction of Dylan changed everything. Work became less important to Jill, and she pulled back considerably.

She took the title of chairman, and she and the Parsons Group elevated Zachary

Alford to CEO.

Jill's retaining her half of the company was fortuitous. With the money to compete in the research labs and the marketplace, Finding Home thrived. They've been able to expand their business well beyond just the retail side, and even government labs have farmed out much of their work to them.

The company now has so much business that they operate twenty-four hours a day. So while there didn't seem to be that many people around when I was there, it's possible the night shift is as busy or more so.

The bottom line is that everyone involved in the company made an immense amount of money. All the participants have lived happily ever after, except for Jill, who has lost her son, perhaps permanently.

Reading through this stuff is so far not getting me any closer than before to understanding what role the company might play in Keith's case.

He was removed from Finding Home for alleged ethical violations. Whether those violations were real or fabricated, the key fact is that he was removed. If the reason to harm him was related to the business, then that was already accomplished, the damage already inflicted.

What would they have to gain by going a

150

step further and framing him for the abduction of a child? How would that further a business goal?

So what was true before I started reading is equally true now.

I just don't get it.

I finish reading at ten thirty, and I no sooner close the folder than Laurie calls out from the bedroom, asking if I'm coming to bed soon. When she asks a question like that, the true answer is that I will be there in as much time as it takes me to run up the stairs. I'd get there faster if I knew how to beam myself into the bedroom.

I'm on the sixth step, taking them two at a time, when the phone rings. By the time I get to the bedroom, Laurie is handing me the phone and saying, "It's Sam."

"Tell him I'll call him back in a half hour," I say.

She smiles. "A half hour? Aren't you being overly optimistic?"

"I'm including eighteen minutes of post-coital bliss."

"Take the phone," she says.

So I do. "What's up, Sam? In as few words as possible, please."

"GPS records place Linda Sanford at the foundation when Cody was dropped off."

"Great." This comes as no surprise to me.

"Is that it?"

"No. She got an untraceable wire transfer from the Cayman Islands three years ago, two weeks after the trial ended."

"How much?"

"Seven hundred fifty thousand dollars. She spent seventy thousand of it at some kind of senior residential facility and was living off the rest until the day she died. She didn't exactly live life in the fast lane; there was more than six hundred thousand still there when she bought the farm."

In a normal circumstance, I would torture Sam for his use of that phrase by asking him how much she paid for the farm. But this is not a normal circumstance; Laurie is waiting for me in bed.

So I simply say, "Great work, Sam."

"There's more. She placed an interesting phone call about six months ago. Actually, three of them, all to the same person."

"Who is that?"

"Stanley Butler, Keith Wachtel's attorney. The calls were placed three weeks before he died."

Boom.

I need to dramatically change my approach. Until now, my goal has been to find out what really happened three years ago and to learn who was actually responsible. An additional, far worthier goal has been to find out what happened to little Dylan Hickman.

I can't focus on any of that anymore; or at least it can't be my priority. It's simply not my job.

My job is to get Keith Wachtel out of jail, to prove he is not guilty of the crime for which he has been convicted. It is not incumbent on me, or any defense attorney, to identify the actual perpetrator. What I must do is show that there is reasonable doubt that it was my client. Not an easy task, but they don't pay me the big bucks — or in this case, one single buck — for nothing.

So my focus now has to be on securing a new trial for Keith. It certainly is not where

Jill Hickman wants me to direct my attention; she only cares about where Dylan is and how she can get him back. But Jill Hickman is not my client.

I call Richard Wallace and tell him I need to meet with him again, this time more formally. I also say that he might want to have Mitch Kelly sit in on the meeting. Kelly was the attorney who prosecuted Keith at trial, and I have to assume Richard will want him to continue on the case, since he knows so much about it.

Richard must know what I want to talk about, since I've already told him that I'm representing Keith. Suggesting Mitch sit in will remove any doubt in Richard's mind. He doesn't ask me about it; he knows that if I want a meeting, then a meeting is when and where I want to make my pitch.

It's on the way to Richard's office that Hike calls.

"Let me guess," I say. "You bought a house down there, and you're going to commute to work in New Jersey."

"No, but houses are really cheap. And Billy's brother is a real estate agent."

"We'd miss your wit, Hike."

"I know. Anyway, I've got something for you."

"What is it?"

154

"A photograph of Teresa Mullins with the dog."

"Are you serious? How did you get that?"

"She took him to some kind of canine dog show that the local Rotary Club ran . . . it was like a fair, with all kinds of funny events."

"So someone took a picture of her?"

"Billy's brother — a different one, not the real estate agent — had the job of taking pictures for the Rotary magazine. He remembered she was there and went through the pictures. She showed up in two of them with the dog, but one of them is hard to make out. The other one is her, no doubt about it."

"Hike, you did a hell of a job. You are hereby made the official South Carolina representative of the Andy Carpenter law firm."

"I accept," he says.

"When are you coming home?"

"I'm in the car now. Billy's wife, Sheila, is driving me to the airport."

"Don't look back, Hike."

I'm brought right into Richard's office, and Mitch Kelly comes in soon after. Mitch is not a big fan of mine; we went against each other once at trial, and he lost. Mitch is also not a big fan of losing.

"So what's on your mind?" Richard asks, but I have no doubt that he already knows.

"I'm filing a motion for a new trial for Keith Wachtel. I wanted to give you a heads-up about it first."

Kelly makes a noise, sort of a derisive, aborted snort.

"Thanks for sharing that," I say.

"You have new evidence?" Richard asks, ignoring both Kelly's noise and my comment.

"I expect to, but my motion is based on discrediting old evidence."

"What might that be?" Kelly asks.

"Teresa Mullins lied in her testimony. Without going into details right now, I can prove it."

"Has she come forward and recanted?" Richard asks.

"She came forward in a manner of speaking. But she won't be doing any recanting. She's been murdered."

They are obviously taken by surprise by this.

"When?" Richard asks.

"Just last week. She was murdered as a result of coming forward in the manner that she did."

"That's a little cryptic," Kelly says.

I nod. "Yes, it is. Thanks for noticing." I

don't want to reveal anything else just yet.

It's Richard's turn. "So you can prove that she lied about Keith Wachtel being the kidnapper without further testimony from her?"

I shake my head. "Not exactly. But I can prove she lied about other parts of her testimony. *Falsus in uno, falsus in omnibus.*"

I love saying that phrase, because I get to speak Latin so rarely and can almost never work it into a conversation. Maybe I should look up more phrases and speak Latin to Laurie; I think it makes me sound pretty sexy.

In English, *falsus in uno, falsus in omnibus* means "false in one, false in all," meaning that the jury can distrust all of a witness's testimony if that witness is shown to have lied in any part of it.

Kelly tries to get more out of me so that he can get a head start in preparing a rebuttal, but I don't want to play any more of my cards yet. One of the reasons for that is I don't want him to have the head start, and the other reason is that when it comes to playing cards, I don't exactly have a full deck.

Finally, Richard says, "So what is it you want from us?"

"Not much," I say. "I'm here really as a

courtesy. But I would hope that you don't put up any unnecessary delays. Keith has been in jail a long time."

"He's right where he belongs," Kelly says. "And he's not going anywhere. That case was a no-brainer."

"Is that why you were given the assignment?"

Richard intervenes. "Boys, boys . . . let's behave or I'll have to give you a time-out." Then, "When are you filing the motion, Andy?"

"Hike is writing it today, and we'll file tomorrow. We're requesting an expedited hearing."

Richard smiles. "Then I guess we'll see you in court."

Hike is much better at preparing motions and filing briefs than I am. He's actually a brilliant lawyer whose career has only been held back until now by his, shall we say, difficulty with interpersonal relationships. His bleak view of everything doesn't help either; people listen to him and think the world is ending, although if the alternative is spending more time with Hike, then the end of the world doesn't seem like such a bad thing.

Of course, that's all changed since Pod Hike came into being. Based on his performance in South Carolina, he is apparently now the gregarious center of every room he's in. Hopefully, his legal skills have remained intact.

In any event, I've turned the writing of the motion to get a new trial over to Hike so I can do other stuff. My next step is to visit with Robbie Divine, the richest person

I know, and, coincidentally, one of the smartest.

Robbie is an investor. That's his job; he invests. And he must do it pretty well, because according to *Forbes,* he is a multibillionaire.

I met Robbie at a charity dinner a few years ago, and we've sort of become friends. I have close to $40 million, mostly the result of inheritance, and Robbie thinks of me as a member of the struggling lower-middle class.

I've called on him a number of times to get insight into how the other side lives when I've needed it to help on a case. He's always ready and willing, as he was when I called him this morning. He suggested I meet him in the lobby of his building on Fifty-seventh Street between Fifth and Madison, and we'd go to lunch.

I arrive at twelve thirty, and he's already downstairs waiting for me in a limousine. It's not one of those ostentatious stretch ones, more like a large sedan with a chauffeur. He opens the rear passenger door and says, "Get in."

As always, Robbie is wearing a baseball cap. Usually, it's a typical Chicago Cubs hat; he's a fanatic. This is a different Cubs hat; it says WORLD CHAMPIONS on it.

I haven't spoken to him since the Cubs won, so I congratulate him. "The first of many," he says, grinning broadly. "The first of many."

"This is the Mets' year," I say.

He laughs. "Be serious."

We head uptown, so far uptown that for a moment I think we might be heading for the George Washington Bridge back to Jersey. Instead we pull up to a small storefront pizzeria on Broadway near 101st called Sal and Tony's.

"You, my boy, are about to experience a culinary masterpiece."

We both get pizza with nothing on it except beautiful cheese, and we sit at a small table in the corner. One bite tells me that the rich really know how to live; this is a pizza for the ages. He has four pieces, and I have three; I pick up the tab, and with drinks, it costs thirty bucks.

"So what do you need?" he asks.

"Two pizzas to go."

He laughs. "What else?"

"Well, I'm investigating something in connection with a DNA company called Finding Home, and I —"

He interrupts. "I know them well."

"How?"

"A few years ago, the owner, a woman

named . . . I can't think of her name . . ."

"Jill Hickman," I prompt.

"Right. Jill Hickman. She came to me for money."

"She did?"

He nods. "She went to everyone for money; you as a poor person would have been exempt. They had some kind of new process, which as I recall sounded promising. But it wasn't right for me, so I passed."

"They got the money from the Parsons Group. Do you know them? That's the private equity company that bailed Jill Hickman out by first investing in Finding Home, and then buying half the company."

Robbie's mood changes immediately. "Don't get involved with them."

"You know Ted Parsons personally?"

"Forget about Ted Parsons; he's not a player."

"Doesn't he run the company? Isn't that his name on the door?"

He frowns. "Remember that scene in *The Godfather* when Don Corleone and Tom Hagen are driving back from the big meeting?"

I do remember it, and I tell him so. Robbie and I share a bizarre devotion to the first two *Godfather* movies, but he outdoes me. He can virtually quote every line.

He proceeds to demonstrate that talent. "After the don referred to Barzini, Tom said he thought the adversary was Tattaglia. So the don said, 'Tattaglia's a pimp. He never could've outfought Santino. But I didn't know until this day that it was Barzini all along.' "

"I'm not sure I'm following," I say, demonstrating my capacity for understatement.

"Ted Parsons is Tattaglia. He's nothing. A puppet in a suit and a dumb one at that."

"So who's Barzini?"

He pauses for a moment. "Okay, I want to be precise here. I'll tell you what's fact and also what I have heard and believe to be true. And I'll tell you which is which, so pay attention."

I nod. "Got it."

"The fact part is that Ted Parsons is an empty suit; I wouldn't hire him to do my laundry. He's a front man for other people's money; people who don't want to be seen."

"And the belief part?"

"Most of the money comes from Renny Kaiser."

"Renny? Strange name . . . what's it short for?"

"Who gives a shit?" Robbie asks.

"That makes sense," I say. "If I were named 'Who gives a shit,' I'd shorten it to

163

Renny also. What do you know about him?"

"I don't know anything; not firsthand. But I have little doubt that he has made his money, very big money, providing drugs to people."

"He's a drug dealer?" I ask.

"That is a natural assumption based on what I just said."

"So he would be using drug money to invest in legitimate companies?"

"Of course. Understand that by the time it shows up at places like Ted Parsons's company, it's been washed more times than the sweatpants you've had since college. The only difference is that the money doesn't shrink."

"Where does he live?"

"Depends on the day; he gets around. But he is in New York a lot; New York is where the money is."

"Do you have a New York address for him?" I ask.

"What do you think I am, Google?" Then, "Yeah, I think I do; I'll e-mail it to you. I was at his apartment once for a charity fund-raiser; one of those things where we rich people get together to pretend we give a shit about you poor people. He's got the top two floors of a building on Park Avenue. I think he also has a place up in Connecticut . . . I may have both addresses."

"He's doing charity fund-raisers and hanging out with legitimate people?"

"That's the nicest thing you ever said to me. Here's what you need to realize; he thinks he's a businessman. He buys and sells and manufactures. And the truth is that he's right; he *is* a businessman. His product is just illegal, and it kills people and destroys lives."

"Amazing," is all I can say.

"He's probably got kids who play Little League baseball and a wife who goes to PTA meetings. I'd bet he has season tickets to the Knicks and orders in pizza. He's a typical citizen who happens to be a scourge to society."

"Is he as rich as you?" I ask.

"Let's not get carried away. But if Renny Kaiser put his money in Finding Home, then there's something going on there, so be careful. You might want to call Luca Brasi." Robbie met Marcus once, and that's how he refers to him.

"Why?"

"Because Kaiser is a bad guy — a very bad, very dangerous, very evil guy. He might even be a Cardinals fan."

Once again, I take Laurie with me to see Jill. Laurie brings extra insight to these kinds of interviews, but this time, I'm bringing her to give me someone to hide behind. Jill is not going to be thrilled with what I'm going to talk to her about.

We meet this time at Jill's home, at my insistence. And once again, she asks us whether we have any news at all.

"Nothing close to concrete," I say, "but I wanted to talk to you about Dylan."

"What about him?"

"We're trying to cover all our bases here," I say. "I told you that last time."

She nods. "I know. What about Dylan?"

"It could be important to find out who his natural parents are. Or maybe it won't be important at all. There's no way to know until we know."

"I told you, I have no idea who they are."

I nod. "I understand that. Which is why

we need to test his DNA."

"Test his DNA?" she says, getting upset. "How is that going to help you?"

Laurie jumps in. "If either or both of his parents are in the DNA registry, it will show up. It's worth a try."

"I don't want to know who his parents are. I deliberately made no effort to find out."

"We understand that," Laurie says. "And we won't reveal it to you if you don't want us to."

"But you'll contact whoever they are, and then they will show up and be in my life," Jill says. "I don't want the people who could give up Dylan to be in my life."

"We won't contact them unless it's absolutely necessary, and even then, we will do everything to ensure that they don't seek you out."

Laurie jumps in to deliver the closing argument. "This could be important, Jill."

She thinks about it for a few moments and then seems to sag in defeat. "How will you get his DNA? Do the police have it?"

"You left his room intact," Laurie says. "I'm sure it will be in there."

Finally, Jill gets up and leads us to Dylan's room. When we get there, she says, "You go in. I only go in when I'm alone."

Laurie and I go in and start to look around. It really has been left intact, though obviously, Jill or a housekeeper has cleaned it regularly.

It doesn't take long to find three items that might well have Dylan's DNA on it, even after all this time. We take two pacifiers and a baby's hairbrush, putting them into three separate plastic bags so as not to contaminate them.

I give one of the pacifier bags to Laurie, to hold in case we need testing done from an independent lab later on. By the time we get back to the den, Jill has regained her composure and is just finishing a phone call.

"Did you get what you needed?" Jill asks.

"We did."

"I just called Steven Emmonds. He's the chief chemist at Finding Home, and I told him to conduct the tests on an expedited basis. He'll send a messenger to pick them up."

"Actually, I was planning to talk with him anyway," I say. "Can you tell him I'll bring the samples down there myself?"

"Of course. When will you be there?"

"Two hours."

I drop Laurie off at home so she can be there when Ricky gets home from school, and I head for the Finding Home offices.

Once again, the place does not seem at all crowded, especially in the satellite buildings. The receptionist tells me that Emmonds is expecting me, and I'm ushered right in.

For some reason, I expected a younger guy, maybe because I see this as cutting-edge work, but Emmonds is probably pushing sixty. He's also probably pushing two sixty, which looks pretty large on his frame. He's shorter than I am, and I'm five eleven and a quarter. Don't ever forget that quarter.

"Jill said you have some samples for me?"

I nod. "And some questions."

"She didn't mention that."

"I could call her, and she could then call you and mention it. Or I could just ask the questions and you could answer them. I think the latter approach will be faster and will involve less dialing."

"You're a lawyer?"

"I am."

"I haven't had many positive experiences with lawyers," he says.

"Join the club. Do you know Keith Wachtel?"

He shakes his head. "Just by reputation and seeing the work he produced when he was here. We never met; I came after he left."

169

"He did good work?"

"Absolutely."

"But he wasn't involved in the new process the company has developed?" I ask.

"Doesn't seem to have been. I can't be sure of that, but I haven't seen any records indicating it."

"You know why that is? You're involved with it, right? And he had your job."

He shrugs. "I really can't say. But later on, I heard they didn't trust him."

"Has there been a lot of turnover since he left?"

"For sure," he says. "Almost a completely new staff."

I can't really think of anything else to ask him; his not having even met Keith cuts down on my options.

I take out the plastic bags and hand them to him. "These are the two samples."

"What is it you want to learn?" he asks.

"Who his parents are. Since your company does government work, you have access to the national database, right?"

He nods. "Right. But there are a limited number of people in there."

"I understand. But if they are in the registry, you can get a match based on half the sample?"

"Within a range of probability," he says.

"But it will be in the billions, so you can trust whatever we come up with."

"How long will it take?"

"If we rush it, a few days, maybe as much as a week, depending how much we can get off of this."

"Rush it," I say.

"I want you to check out a guy named Renny Kaiser," I say.

"Renny?" Sam repeats. "What's that short for?"

"Who gives a shit."

"Who is he?"

"That's what I want you to tell me, Sam. All I know is he's really rich, and he's rumored to have gotten that way by selling drugs to people."

"What is it you want to know?"

"I won't know that until you tell me. For now, assume I want to know everything."

"That's what you always say," Sam points out.

"Yet you keep asking."

I also tell Sam to call Hike and ask him to subpoena everything that Sam has provided to date in the case. We need to get the information through legal means so that we can introduce it in court.

172

"Hike can be a little difficult to talk to," Sam says.

"Really? I hadn't noticed. What do you mean?"

"For example, if I cough, he tells me that I probably have tuberculosis."

"Maybe you should get it checked out; it might just be cholera. Tell Hike to get the subpoenas out quickly."

"He won't listen to me."

"Sure he will. Just say it this way: 'Y'all need to get to those dadgum subpoenas in a dadgum hurry, dadgummit.' "

I call Laurie and tell her to ask Jill whether or not she knows Renny Kaiser. Robbie's information is usually correct, but he admitted he didn't have firsthand knowledge of Kaiser's funding the Parsons Group.

Laurie has checked with some people she worked with in the DEA when she was a cop. They've confirmed Kaiser's drug dealing and say they have been unsuccessfully trying to get him for years.

According to them, he does not deal in heroin and cocaine but rather pills and drug cocktails. His clientele are upscale people that can afford to pay his prices and are willing to do so because they know the supply will always be there. And they are based in countries all over the world. It's an exclusive, highly lucrative business.

I head down to the office to meet Hike, just back from his idyllic adventure in South Carolina. I'm not sure how I will react to a personal, up-close view of an upbeat Hike; we're charting new ground here.

It starts to snow on my way to the office, and by the time I get there, the roads and sidewalks are becoming slippery. Since I wear sneakers whenever I'm not in court, it takes me a few extra minutes to navigate the walk from the parking lot to the office.

No one is in the office when I finally get there. I'm not surprised; Edna's work appearances are often weather related. If it's snowing, or sleeting, or raining, or cloudy, or partly cloudy, she has a tendency not to show up.

Hike arrives ten minutes after I do, and the first thing he says is, "I almost killed myself getting here."

"What happened?" I ask.

"My car was slipping all over the road. Four-wheel drive my ass."

"Four-wheel drive your ass?"

"They claim it's four-wheel drive, but who the hell knows? Can you tell the difference? Nobody can. If it were three-wheel drive or two-wheel drive, would you know? It's like the undercoating they sell you. Undercoating my ass."

"Undercoating your ass?"

He must consider that a rhetorical question, because he plows right through it. "The whole industry is a rip-off; those car companies don't care if we live or die."

"Yet if we live, we can buy more cars," I say. "Therein lies the conundrum."

He ignores me. "I'm going to get sick and die from this weather anyway, so I guess it doesn't matter. I've been coughing up phlegm for the last three hours."

"Thanks for sharing that. Did you by any chance stop in a phone booth and change back into the real Hike?" I ask.

"What do you mean?"

"Never mind. Anything to report that I don't already know?"

"I found at least six people that knew Mullins, or Sanford, or whatever her name was. She was a loner, but they saw her in town in places like the grocery store, and a couple of them talked to her regularly."

"Did they see Cody?"

"Three of them did, but it doesn't matter. I've got the picture."

He takes it out of an envelope and hands it to me. It certainly looks like Cody, but obviously, it could be any border collie.

"Will the person that took the picture

175

testify?"

"He will if we need him to; I just have to tell him the timing. I'll be seeing him next weekend."

"Where?" I ask.

"I'm heading back down there. Billy's daughter is getting married."

"Police chief Billy?"

He nods. "Yeah. Carla and Danny . . . sweet kids — a terrific couple. You'd really like them."

Watching him go back and forth from miserable New Jersey Hike to upbeat South Carolina Pod Hike is like watching a tennis match.

"I'm sure they're lovely," I say. "Did you finish the motion?"

He nods and hands me an eleven-page document. I read through it and make a couple of notations for changes, although they're probably not necessary. Hike has done a typically outstanding job on it. Our case sounds a lot better the way he phrases it than it does in real life.

"Good job, Hike. And thanks for having such a great attitude about South Carolina."

"It was great, Andy, I really enjoyed it. Had a lot of fun." South Carolina Pod Hike puts on his coat and changes back into New Jersey Hike. "Now if I can only get home without killing myself or getting pneumonia."

"Lunch at Charlie's?" Pete asks. "With no game on? What are we going to do, talk?"

"I'm going to talk, and you're going to listen," I say. "Then you'll talk, and I'll listen, and so on. I know you're not familiar with the process, but it's how humans interact."

"Is this about a case?"

"Yes," I say.

"So why don't you come to the precinct?"

"A, because I'm hungry and it's lunchtime. And B, because you have the home-field advantage there. Charlie's is neutral turf."

"You buying?" he asks.

"Of course."

"Meet you in fifteen minutes. I'm starving."

Pete is already waiting at our table when I arrive. When we finish ordering, he says to the waitress, "And I'm going to need a dozen bacon cheeseburgers to go, with fries."

"What the hell is that about?" I ask.

"The guys aren't happy that I'm having lunch with a defense attorney. This is like a peace offering. Best money you ever spent."

I shake my head to show my disdain, but I don't think it affects Pete too much. Head shaking is a little subtle for him.

"So talk to me," he says. "This more bullshit on the Wachtel case?"

"I filed a motion for a new trial."

He laughs a short laugh. "Good luck with that. That's what you wanted to tell me?"

"No, this is about the Stanley Butler case."

He thinks for a minute, searching his memory bank. "I don't know what you're talking about. Wait a minute, that's the lawyer who ran his car into a tree? He was Wachtel's attorney, right?"

"Correct."

"That's not a case. The guy was on drugs."

"He was murdered."

"What makes you say that?" Joking time is over; Pete is a damn good cop, and he takes comments like this very seriously.

"Teresa Mullins has been living her life under a fake name, with Cody, the border collie. Her testimony was a lie."

"I thought this was about Butler."

"I'm getting there. She was murdered a couple of weeks ago in South Carolina."

He interrupts. "Is this lawyer talk or real?"

"I can prove everything I've said, including this: Teresa Mullins called Stanley Butler three times in the weeks before he died. Whatever she told him made him optimistic about reopening the Wachtel case."

There are two problems with that last sentence. First, while I know that she called Butler, I am making the assumption that those calls resulted in his hopeful outlook. Secondly, I've technically broken a confidence in telling Pete about Butler's optimism, since my client told it to me. But I'm sure Keith wouldn't mind, and it's harmless.

"That's all you got?" Pete asks.

I nod. "That's all I got."

"I don't remember who in the department handled the car crash, but it was investigated and found to be an accident."

"Maybe someone could look at it again, with a fresh perspective."

"He was strung out," Pete says.

"Maybe he was helped along with that. Maybe it was involuntary."

"You know you didn't have to buy me lunch to get me to look into this," he says.

180

"I didn't want you to have to do it on an empty stomach."

I don't want to meet the teacher, and I don't like "meet the teacher night." Who came up with this idea anyway? Why do teachers get this honor and get to hold it at the school? I don't hold a "meet the lawyer" night in the courthouse. Anybody you know attend a "meet the gardener" luncheon out on the lawn? Or a "meet the proctologist" morning at the hospital?

I'm not the most self-aware person in the world, but even I am sensitive to the fact that I'm afraid Mrs. Aimonetti will say something bad about Ricky. But Laurie attended the last one, and since one of us has to stay home with Ricky, she thinks I should be there this time.

Mrs. Aimonetti starts our meeting with a smile and the words, "I'm sure I don't have to tell you that Ricky is a friendly, highly intelligent, and all-around wonderful child."

As meeting starters go, that's a beauty.

"You don't have to tell me," I say, "but I wish you would."

The rest of the conversation goes just as well, and by the time I leave, I'm thinking that whoever started the "meet the teacher" tradition really knew what he or she was doing.

I'm about two blocks from the school when the phone rings, and I see by caller ID that it's Laurie. I pick up the phone and say, "It went great."

The serious tone in Laurie's voice tells me that something isn't so great. "Andy, you're being followed."

"What are you talking about?"

"There's a dark blue car following you. It's a Toyota, license plate 345MJR."

I look in the mirror, but while I see a few cars, I have no idea if Laurie's comment is accurate. "How do you know that? What the hell is going on?"

"I've had Marcus following you for a while, ever since we found out that Teresa Mullins was killed. He just called me. He doesn't have your new cell number."

"You shouldn't have done that," I say.

"We can argue about that later. For now, here's what you need to do. Drive to the foundation building, but take your time getting there. Don't make crazy turns to give it

183

away that you know you're being followed, but take a longer route than usual."

"What do I do when I get there?" I ask.

"Park in the back. Most of the lights will be off, so it will be dark there. Turn your car off after you park, but do not get out until you see Marcus."

"Shouldn't I just drive to the police station?"

"You should not."

"And are we sure Marcus will be there?" I realize how stupid a question that is as soon as it leaves my mouth.

"Andy, we're talking about Marcus."

"Okay. Do we know who is following me?"

"Not yet, but we will."

I don't like this at all, even with Marcus calling the shots. Who knows how many people are in that car or what kind of weapons they have? What if they start shooting before Marcus can intervene?

He's sending me to a dark, uninhabited area. For people who follow other people for the purpose of hurting or killing them, it's a dream scenario. If they could choose where they'd want me to go, that would be where I'm going.

I take two extra turns and don't go through a light when it just turns yellow. Hopefully, that will give Marcus enough time to get ahead of me. I still can't see for sure if anyone is following me, but Marcus has a tendency to get things like this correct.

I'm driving fairly well considering my hands are shaking and squeezing the steering wheel so hard I'm surprised it hasn't broken. I finally reach the foundation building, and as I do, I think that maybe I should have called Willie to serve as reinforcement. But I probably wouldn't have even if I had thought of it; the only reason I am still alive today is because I have learned to trust Marcus in these kinds of situations.

So I park in a dark area, not too far from the back door entrance. There's a small light over the door, so I park far enough away that the light doesn't reach where I am, but not so far away as to draw suspicion about why I'm not closer.

I can't see anything, and I can't hear anything. Since I certainly can't taste, touch, or smell anything, that sort of leaves me senseless. It is one of the least comfortable, most helpless feelings I can ever remember experiencing.

I open the window halfway. This way I can hear things without increasing the danger to me. It's not like the windows are bulletproof glass; they are no protection, so lowering one doesn't exactly change the balance of power.

I have no power; it doesn't get less balanced than that.

I was hoping to see Marcus's car already here, but I don't. Maybe I'm just not seeing it in the dark, but I don't think that's it. I don't want to call Laurie, because the light from the phone could be visible, and they might hear me.

If there was a problem with the plan, I think she would have called me. I make a mental note to give Marcus my cell phone number so if I happen to survive this, the next time my life is in danger, he can call me directly.

I think I hear another car, but it's hard to tell, because the building is close enough to the street that it might just be normal traffic. I do hear some barking; the dogs inside have really sensitive hearing and must know there's something going on. I'd much rather be in the building with them.

Five minutes go by, and they seem like a month. I'm not quite sure at what point I should leave, or call Laurie, or start crying. But the pressure is getting to me.

Suddenly, my cell phone rings, and it sounds like a marching band in the silence. The caller ID says it's Laurie, hopefully about to tell me that the coast is clear and to get my ass out of here.

"You okay?" she asks.

"Yeah, what the hell is going on?"

"We've got a little problem. The guy who was following you drew a gun on Marcus, so Marcus grabbed it and hit him in the head with an elbow."

"Uh-oh."

"Right. He hit him really hard. So you should call Pete right away, and —"

"Should he bring an ambulance?"

"Sounds like the coroner would be the way to go."

"Where are they?" I ask.

"North side of the building."

I hang up, start the car, and drive toward the side of the building so I can shine the car's lights on whatever is there. I see Marcus, standing next to a large, prone body. I hate seeing dead bodies. They're so . . . lifeless.

I call Pete on his cell phone, since I know he'll be at Charlie's. "Where the hell are you?" is how he answers. "We're running up a tab here."

I tell him that someone was following me and Marcus intervened when I got to the foundation. "You need to get over here," I say.

"Bullshit," he says. "I'll get a black and white over there. I'm a hot-shit homicide captain."

"Well, there is a dead body here, if that motivates you any. The guy drew a gun and was about to shoot me when Marcus got involved." I'm lying and not remotely ashamed of it; I have no knowledge of the guy pointing his gun at me. But I want to avoid any chance of Marcus getting blamed for this.

"He killed him?"

"Let's just say he got involved really hard."

The bad guy's head is tough to look at. Imagine carving a face in a pumpkin, the eyes, nose, and mouth all perfectly formed, and then dropping it from a fifth-story window. And then running over it with a bus.

"Thanks, Marcus," I say, but he doesn't respond. He rarely responds, which is fine, since when he does, I can't understand what he's saying anyway.

"Where's the gun?" I ask, since I don't see it. If it turns out that the guy didn't have one, Marcus might have a problem.

He points to the side of the body, and I see the gun, mostly obscured by the dead guy's shadow. He was a large man; not the type I'd want to run into in a dark alley or in a dark parking lot behind a foundation building.

"I told Pete that he was going to shoot me," I say, which may or may not be an accurate statement. "Does he have a cell phone?"

Marcus just shrugs and nods toward the body.

"I'm not a big fan of touching dead bodies. Would you . . . ?"

It's hard to tell in the dark, but I think he frowns. He leans over and checks the guy's pockets and then extracts a cell phone and hands it to me.

"Do you know how to find out what phone number it is?"

This time, he definitely frowns, but he takes back the phone and presses some buttons. He hands it to me, and I see that the phone number is now showing on the face. I make a mental note of the number.

I hand the phone back to Marcus. "Would you mind returning it to its rightful owner? But wipe the prints off first."

He does so, just before three police cars pull up, lights flashing. The officers get out, take in the scene, and tell Marcus and me to put our hands against the car so they can frisk us. We do, and they find and take a small handgun from Marcus.

One of the officers points to the perp's body and asks, "Where's the club he was hit with?"

I point to Marcus and say, "It's attached

to his shoulder."

Another car pulls up, and Pete gets out. He speaks to the officers, and they set off to secure the scene. Then Pete looks at the body before coming over to us.

"He's going to be hard to interrogate," Pete says. "Any idea who he is, or was?"

"None at all," I say, and Marcus doesn't say anything.

"We'll do the questioning and take your statements down at the station. Too cold out here, and too much barking. One of the officers will take you down there."

We wait for two hours for Pete to get back to the station. I call Laurie to update her on what is going on, and then I spend some time thinking about the implications of what happened tonight.

I think it's a good assumption that the dead guy was following me because of something having to do with the Keith Wachtel case. It's my only case, and I doubt it had anything to do with "meet the teacher night."

He was either going to threaten me, hurt me, or kill me. The fact that he drew his gun seems to indicate he wasn't planning only to call me names or engage in vigorous debate. And the likelihood that he or one of his colleagues probably killed Teresa Mullins

191

would serve to support that theory.

His actions indicate that whoever employed him must think I present a danger, which comes as news to me. I think I'm floundering, but someone else must believe otherwise. That in itself is interesting.

The Teresa Mullins killing has been bugging me, though not as much as it must have bugged Teresa Mullins. The only reason to kill her, as in my case, is if she were a real danger. And the only way she would be a real danger is if she knew who the bad guys were. I don't mean the muscle, I mean the person or people at the top.

But if she did, she showed no inclination to reveal what she knew. By returning Cody, all she did was essentially give us our marching orders, to provide incentive for us to find out whatever we could. If she had more information, she could have told us.

Same thing was true with Stanley Butler. If she had told him damning information about the real abductor, Stanley would likely have gone to the police with it. Certainly, he would have done something that left some trace of what he might have learned. It seems that she simply enticed him with some information, as she did with us.

My view is that by giving us Cody, Teresa

was doing all she was going to do, so why kill her? She must have known more, or at least the killers must have believed she knew more.

When I find out what that is, I'll have found out everything.

Pete finally comes back and interrogates me himself, assigning one of his colleagues the unenviable task of questioning Marcus. Pete is no dummy.

I tell him all that happened from the time Laurie called me until the time he arrived on the scene. I advance the theory that the events were connected to the Keith Wachtel case, but I can't supply evidence to that effect, because I don't have any.

When he's finished, I say, "Do you have the guy's name yet?"

He nods. "Kyle Gillis. That mean anything to you?"

"No. Is he local?"

"He'd be local if we were in Vegas."

I'm surprised to hear that; there are enough tough guys around here without having to import any.

"What else can you tell me about him?" I ask.

"Is that my role here? To keep you informed?"

"Until I can find somebody better suited

to the job," I say.

He shakes his head. "I don't know anything yet. But you'll be the first person I tell."

It's almost one o'clock in the morning when I finally get home. Laurie is waiting up for me, and she meets me at the door with an outstanding hug. She was obviously more concerned about me than she let on.

"You okay?" she asks.

"Are you kidding? I laugh in the face of danger, babe. That's what I'm about."

"The guy's name is Kyle Gillis. Here's his cell phone number," I say.

Sam looks at the number and says, "That's a Vegas area code."

"That's where he's from."

"Where is he now?"

"On a slab in the coroner's office. He messed with me and Marcus."

"Man, how come I'm never around when stuff like that happens?"

"Sorry, Sam, I get all the luck."

"You want the full treatment on this guy's phone? Location, calls made and received, the works?"

"Absolutely. Anything yet on Renny Kaiser?"

"He's a tough one; the guy is layered up."

"What does that mean?"

"He hides behind companies that are layered, one over the other. Very hard to penetrate, but I'm working on it."

"What do you know so far?"

"He's got three dollars more than God, and he has business interests all over the world. Some of them are in countries that cruise ships don't visit . . . dangerous places."

"He's a drug dealer."

"Based on the financial dealings I can see, I'm not surprised."

"Is he a big investor in the Parsons Group?" I ask.

"He is the Parsons Group, or at least 80 percent of it."

"You have local addresses for him?"

He shakes his head. "Not yet, but I'll get there."

I smile; this is a moment of rare triumph. "You want me to give them to you?" I ask.

"You have them? How did you get them?"

"You ever hear of Google, Sam? You type stuff in, and it gives you information." Of course, I neglect to mention the fact that Robbie Divine sent me Kaiser's addresses on Park Avenue and in Greenwich.

Sam is not amused. "Yeah, give me the damn addresses."

"I'll e-mail them to you," I say. "You do know how to use e-mail, don't you?"

Sam hangs up on me, which I take as a yes, so I send him the addresses.

196

Laurie's at Jill's house, and since it's Sunday morning, Ricky doesn't have school. Laurie assigned me the job of making breakfast for the "men in her life," but it's unlikely to end well, at least by Laurie's standards.

"Here are your choices, Ricky: cold cereal with milk, or cold cereal dry."

"Frosted Flakes?" he asks hopefully.

"No, some kind of granola stuff that your mother bought. It's good for you."

"What does it taste like?"

"I don't know; I wouldn't eat it if you strapped me into the chair. Probably sawdust."

"What about the frozen pizza you got the other day?" he asks.

"I was sort of saving that for a special occasion."

"Like now?"

"Ricky, Mom would not want me to give you frozen pizza for breakfast."

"Aw, come on, Dad."

"It doesn't have any vegetables on it."

"Good," he says, "I hate vegetables."

"That's my boy," I say. "All right, pizza it is. But this has to be our secret."

"I promise."

I put the pizza in the oven, leaving it in a long time so that it's crisp, the way we both

197

like it. Then I cut it into eight pieces, of which Ricky has two and I have the other six. I'm pretty full after the fifth one, but he doesn't want any more, and I don't want to leave any trace evidence.

Laurie comes home an hour later, after I take the empty pizza box outside to the garbage where it can't be discovered. There is now nothing to be gained by her in searching the crime scene.

The first thing she asks Ricky is, "How was breakfast?"

He looks at me. "Can I tell her that?"

"Of course," I say, already not liking where this is going. "We've certainly got nothing to hide." I add a little fake chuckle at the end, to show how unworried I am about the breakfast question.

"It was good," Ricky says.

"What did you have?"

"Nothing," is Ricky's answer, which just might be insufficient to satisfy Laurie.

"You had nothing, but it was good?" Laurie asks.

"We had something, but I forget what it was," Ricky says. This is not a kid who would hold up well in cross-examination.

Laurie walks over to the refrigerator and opens the freezer door. "You had frozen pizza for breakfast?"

I need to jump in here. "First of all, it wasn't frozen when we ate it; it was warm and nourishing on a cold winter's day. Second of all," I say, pointing to Ricky, "it was all his fault."

Once we put the frozen pizza caper behind us, Laurie tells me about her conversation with Jill regarding Renny Kaiser.

"She's never met him," Laurie says, "but she's heard the rumors that it's his money behind the Parsons Group."

"She never tried to confirm it?"

Laurie shakes her head. "I don't think so. She hadn't heard of him until the transaction was long over. She said she's only dealt with Ted Parsons and that due diligence didn't show any red flags. I think she was just relieved to be able to make the deal."

"Okay," I say. I'm not terribly surprised, nor do I think badly of Jill for it. The Parsons Group is considered a reputable firm, and to have attempted to unwind a deal that saved the company over some unsubstantiated rumors would have been too much to expect of anyone.

"The fact that a big-time drug dealer might have invested money in the company doesn't exactly implicate him in a child abduction," Laurie points out.

The problem is, she's right.

I don't have a hell of a lot of time to dwell on it, because Rita Gordon calls. She's the court clerk, so this is a very important call.

"Nine o'clock tomorrow, Andy. In Judge Moran's chambers."

This means that the judge is likely to rule on our motion for a new trial. If that's the case, he's doing so faster than I thought, which I don't consider a good sign. Of course, it's just possible he wants to entertain oral arguments.

"Do you know which way this is going to go?" I ask.

Rita and I once had a forty-five-minute affair, so I like to think I have earned some friendship points with her.

"I believe I do," she says.

"Do you care to share it with me?"

"I believe I don't."

Maybe the forty-five minutes didn't go as well as I thought.

"I've studied your written briefs," Judge Moran says. "Do either of you have anything to add to them?"

The question is posed to Mitch Kelly and me as soon as we're seated in chambers.

"Yes, Your Honor," I say. "Since ours was submitted, the coroner in South Carolina has ruled that Teresa Mullins's death was in fact a homicide." I don't mention that I had that news minutes after it was determined, thanks to Hike getting a call from his police chief buddy, Billy.

Kelly shakes his head. "That's not technically accurate, since they actually haven't even determined that she is Teresa Mullins. Her identification is that of Linda Sanford."

"I have documentation of Linda Sanford's death years ago," the judge says. "Is it the prosecution's contention that she came back to life, only to be murdered?"

"Of course not, Your Honor," he says.

"But we are not ready to concede that the newly deceased is Teresa Mullins."

"We would be happy to let a jury decide that question," I say.

Judge Moran ignores that and turns to Kelly. "Your original case would have been a lot more difficult without Ms. Mullins's testimony."

"Only marginally," Kelly says. "We believe we would have prevailed anyway. But she did testify, and nothing in their brief proves that she perjured herself."

I smile. "Another question for which we would welcome a jury's decision."

"A jury made their decision three years ago," Kelly says.

"After being lied to," I point out.

"How long would it take you to prepare for trial?" Moran asks, which is as good a question as I could have hoped for under the circumstances.

"Very quickly, Your Honor. As an innocent man, Mr. Wachtel, has spent far too much time in jail already."

"I would like to restate that the county strongly believes that a retrial is not called for," Kelly says.

"Noted," Judge Moran says. "Now if you will answer my question."

"We could be ready very soon, since the

evidence is unchanged and compelling. But because it is unchanged and compelling, it should be unnecessary to re-present it."

Judge Moran nods. "I will be issuing an official notice that a new trial of Mr. Wachtel has been granted. I will set a date, based on the earliest available opening on my schedule."

"Thank you, Your Honor," I say. "My next motion will be for bail to be granted."

"Then your motion-winning streak will end at one. No bail will be granted."

I head down to the prison to tell Keith the news in person. It's rare that I bring positive news to inmates, so I'm looking forward to this one.

"You're amazing," Keith says, even though that goes without saying.

"It's only step one," I say. Slightly mixing metaphors, I add that the huge hurdle is still to come, and later on I throw in that it will be an "uphill struggle." Listening to me is like going to the gym.

"Can I testify?" he asks.

It's the earliest in the process that a client has ever asked that.

"Way too soon to think about that," I say. "And that will always be your decision, but it's rarely a good idea."

"Stanley said the same thing, and I've

always regretted not telling my side of the story."

"You don't have a side of the story, Keith. The story is the abduction, and you weren't there. You don't know any more than the jury does. All you can say is that you didn't do it, and your denial is assumed based on the fact that you didn't plead guilty. I can get your point of view across in other ways without you being cross-examined."

"Think about it, okay?"

I nod. "We both will."

I leave the prison to discover a message on my voice mail from Steve Emmonds at Finding Home.

The message is, "Give me a call or stop in. I've matched the father."

"Most people don't have their DNA on file," Emmonds says when I get to his office. "But more do than you would think. Almost all military people do, which is where we found the father."

"He's in the service?"

"I have no idea what he's doing now," Emmonds says. "But he was when his DNA was put on file."

"How long ago was that?"

He looks at some kind of notebook that's in front of him. "It'll be two years this July."

"And the mother? No match on her?"

"None. Came up empty."

"What's the father's name?" I ask.

He looks at his folder again and says, "James Ware. He's thirty-two years old and is from Pomona, New York. It's in Rockland County."

Rockland is about forty-five minutes to the north of here, in New York State but on the Jersey side of the Hudson River. To get to the New York side from there, you would take the Tappan Zee Bridge or drive down the Palisades Parkway and take the George Washington Bridge.

Emmonds gives me the only other piece of information he got from the registry, which is the address in Pomona. It's a year and a half old, so it may not still be where he is. But it's a good start.

"Are you going to share this with Jill?" he asks.

"No. She asked me not to. So you shouldn't either."

"Okay. Glad I asked."

I call Sam Willis and give him Ware's name and address and ask him to find out whatever he can about him. "Please let me know the basics as soon as you can," I say. I've been leaning on Sam a lot, but he doesn't seem to mind.

Once that's accomplished, I head home to discuss the situation with Laurie. This has to be handled tactfully, and Laurie possesses 80 percent of the tact in our family. Tara controls the other twenty. Sebastian and I are basically tact-free.

"How are you going to approach him?" Laurie asks when I tell her the DNA results.

"Here's my plan, and I think it's a good

one," I say. "I'm going to ask you what I should do, and then I'm going to do it."

She nods. "Very good plan."

"So what should I do?"

"Hard to say at this point, until we learn more about him from Sam. For instance, if he's married, I might recommend a different approach than if he's single."

"Why?"

"Because we don't want to ruin his life. We don't know whether he was a party to the decision to abandon the baby. It's even conceivable that he doesn't know about the child at all. This is not going to be a casual conversation."

"But it's one I have to have. Otherwise I'm not doing all I can to defend my client."

An hour later, Sam calls with the first piece of information. James Ware still lives on Tamarack Lane in Pomona and is a licensed plumber. He is unmarried and seems to live alone, though there is no way to be sure of that. The only thing Sam can say with certainty is no one else has a driver's license with that address on it.

When she hears this, Laurie says, "Well, at least we don't have to worry about breaking up a marriage. I think you need to just confront it head-on, tell him straight out."

"Right."

"You want me to do it with you?"

"Probably better if you don't. He'd be more forthcoming with just another guy."

"I agree," she says. "But a Rockland County plumber doesn't sound like a Central Casting sinister figure. It increases the chance that the abduction was not about Dylan at all but rather one of the adults."

I don't respond; I'm trying to anticipate what the conversation is going to be like. Laurie asks me what's wrong.

"I'm picturing how I'd react if some stranger showed up and did what I'm about to do to James Ware."

"Do you know what he did in the service?" she asks.

"No, why?"

"Well, if he was a Navy SEAL, you might want to bring Marcus."

James Ware's office is in Spring Valley, about fifteen minutes from Pomona. I didn't call ahead, because I didn't really want to reveal anything over the phone. I was just hoping that this would be a slow day for plumbing in Rockland County. The fact that there is a van in front of the store that says WARE PLUMBING AND HEATING on it tells me I may have caught a break.

I enter, and there's a man sitting behind the counter punching some keys on an old-fashioned calculator. He looks up as if surprised to have a visitor; I guess most people call plumbers rather than just show up. It's fairly difficult to drop your plumbing off at the store, like you would your shirts.

He smiles. "Hey, can I help you?"

"You can if you're James Ware."

"That's me. What can I do for you?"

"My name is Andy Carpenter; I'm an attorney."

"Oh, shit. Is this about the Anderson job? Those people are crazy. The leak had nothing to do with the work I did. I told them that. It came from an entirely different area of the pipe. I've got pictures of the whole thing."

"I don't represent the Andersons."

"Oh, then who do you represent?"

"Actually, I'm not at liberty to say. What I can tell you is that your name came up in connection with an adoption case I am working on."

He looks surprised and confused. "You mean like a child adoption?"

"Yes."

"How did my name come up?"

"DNA test results show that you are the child's father," I say.

"Excuse me?"

I know he heard what I said the first time, but I repeat it anyway.

"No chance," he says. "Total bullshit. Are you trying to shake me down?"

"One thing I can promise you is that no one is after your money. We are simply trying to get to the truth. But the test results don't lie."

"Well, in this case they do, because I've

never had a child with anybody. Absolutely no chance. Who is the mother?"

"I was hoping you could tell me that."

"Well, I can't, and this is a little too weird for me."

I nod. "Not exactly another day at the office for me either. Let's back into this, okay?" I give him the month and year that Dylan would have been conceived, which is almost four years ago, and I ask him if he had a girlfriend around that time. "Is it possible you impregnated a woman and she never told you about it?" I ask.

"No, it's not possible."

"Did you have a specific girlfriend back then?"

"I was engaged. I'm getting a little tired of these questions." Ware is getting angry, which is not good. There aren't many plumbers I can beat up. There aren't even many librarians I can beat up.

"But you didn't marry her?"

"No," he says.

"So maybe your fiancée had a child and didn't tell you?"

"Which part of 'no chance' don't you understand?"

"I'm sorry to pry like this, but it really is important."

"It ain't important to me, pal. Your test

211

results are bullshit, or you're making them up."

"Did you have relations with other women around that time?"

"I'm done talking to you."

"If you answer my questions now, you can avoid me asking them in court."

He laughs. "You gonna sue me? Go ahead and do it. I'll prove you don't know what you're talking about."

"I'm not going to sue you. I —"

He interrupts. "I don't care. Just get the hell out of here."

So I leave.

That didn't go well.

I have no idea if James Ware was telling the truth, but my guess is that he was telling at least a partial truth. I don't think he knows anything about the existence of a baby; his reaction to that news seemed genuine.

Where he's obviously less forthcoming is the question of whether he had other relationships, even one-night stands, while he was engaged. He wouldn't even answer that question. I'm not sure why he'd want to conceal the information, other than either he's embarrassed or just doesn't want to confide in a stranger, or maybe he sees a future of having to pay child support.

Most people are afraid of being dragged into court, but Ware wasn't, and his certainty that he could prove his position in a legal proceeding seemed genuine.

One thing I'm more certain of is that James Ware is not the type to be a conspirator in any sinister plot that might have led to Keith Wachtel's being in jail. He's not involved with big money, and it's unlikely he's out partying with dangerous criminals.

I simply cannot see Ware being a key player in whatever the hell it is I'm looking into. The mother of the child, whoever she is, might be a different story. But unless he has a major change of heart and attitude, we're not going to be able to learn her identity through James Ware.

The one piece of good news for the day comes in a phone call from Pete Stanton when I'm on my way home. "I just wanted to tell you that I'm starting an investigation into the death of Stanley Butler," he says. "I thought you'd want to know."

"I'm very glad to hear that. What tipped the scale?"

"According to the autopsy report, he had needle marks in his arms and drugs in his system. That information about the needle marks never came out, because there was no hearing of any kind. The coroner just came up with the cause of death, and apparently, no one questioned the details."

"So?"

"So I spoke with his wife. It turns out he was deathly afraid of needles, totally phobic. She said he was over his problems with drugs, but even when he was using, it was always pills. She said he wouldn't even get a flu shot; no needles, never."

"And that's enough to open the case?" I ask.

"That and what you told me. I'm not saying he was murdered, but I think it's time somebody checked it out."

"I don't want to overstate this," I say, "but you're doing the right thing here, and there is a chance that you might be a decent human being."

"Thanks. I live for your approval."

"Gillis called the company," Sam says. "And the company called him."

"Which company? Finding Home?" I ask.

"The very one. He called it from his cell phone three times over a six-month period, and they called him once."

"Is there any way of telling who he spoke to there?"

"No, it goes through a switchboard, so it could have been anyone in the building."

"You have the dates and times of the calls?"

"Of course."

"When did the company call him?"

He gives me the exact time of the call, and I tell him to hold on for a minute. I check my calendar, and for the first time in a while, my hunch pays off. Kyle Gillis received a phone call from Finding Home literally minutes after I left my meeting with Zachary Alford. So it appears that poor, overworked Mr. Alford, before he had to rush to his next meeting, had time to make a call to a guy who would soon be following me at night with a gun.

"You have his other calls?"

"Yeah, but I haven't gone through the list yet. The company calls just jumped out at me."

"Great job, Sam. I'm going to get Zachary Alford's cell phone number. I think it's time for Mr. Alford to get the equivalent of a cyber rectal exam. And while you're at it, that guy you checked out, James Ware . . ."

"What about him?"

"He was engaged about four years ago. I need the name of his fiancée. Any way we can get that?"

"Five minutes on Facebook."

"What do you mean?"

"When people get engaged, they tell the world. Unless they are the exceptions, either he or his girlfriend posted about it. I'll check it out."

I hang up and call Laurie. "I need Zachary Alford's cell phone number," I say.

"And you think I have it?"

"No, but Jill must. I assume all those top executives share their numbers. Can you get it from her?"

"She's going to ask me why," Laurie says,

which is a point worth considering.

"True, and I don't want her knowing we are suspicious of Alford. I don't know her relationship with him or who she talks to. She could say the wrong thing without knowing it."

"How about this?" Laurie asks. "I'll ask her for a company list with all the cell phones, and I'll tell her we don't know who we might want to reach or when. That we're just covering our bases, just in case."

"Perfect. Once you get the number, please give it to Sam."

There are all kinds of explanations for anything if one wants to find them. But sometimes if it walks and quacks like a duck, it's a duck.

Zachary Alford, the multimillionaire CEO of Finding Home, with an emphasis on the *multi,* spoke on the phone with Kyle Gillis, the hired gun whose head Marcus Clark crushed like an overripe melon.

It's true that I cannot definitively say that it was Alford who spoke to Gillis, but a call was placed from the company moments after I left. To think that it was anyone other than Alford is to violate my strict "no co-incidence" policy. And Alford was put in place by the Parsons Group, which means he was put in place by notorious bad guy

Renny Kaiser.

Zachary Alford is a duck.

It is obvious that if Alford and Gillis had a relationship, then there was money involved. Based on their relative positions, it is even more obvious that Alford was the employer and Gillis the employee.

And if I accept all that obvious stuff, and it's obvious that I should, then Alford employed Gillis to either track me, warn me, hurt me, or kill me. And he would not have done so because I am sarcastic and annoying; he would have done so because he believed I posed a threat to him or to his company.

Obviously.

So whatever I'm doing is causing him to worry big-time. I just wish I knew what I was doing.

I believe all the answers to all my questions in defending Keith Wachtel can be found at Finding Home. It's where the key players were, and it's where the money is.

The actions of the company are by themselves revealing. In a short time, they raised a large amount of capital and executed an almost complete changeover of personnel.

Keith was removed, very possibly because of fabricated evidence of corporate espionage, and then his team was dismissed because they were feared to have been tainted by him.

Then, and possibly most important, Jill essentially withdrew from the company as a result of Dylan's abduction. Could that have been the reason for the abduction in the first place? To get her out? It seems unlikely, but not impossible.

I wish I could devote full time to this new development, but I can't.

I've got a trial to prepare for.

I hate jury selection and juries . . . not necessarily in that order. I hate jury selection because I consider it a total crapshoot, and a boring one at that. I've used jury consultants in the past, but I found that they don't know any more than I do, and I don't know anything.

Conventional wisdom in this case is to avoid choosing women for the jury. The theory is that the victim, besides Dylan, is Jill. A mother has lost her child and has been left with no answers as to his fate. Any decent woman juror would be horrified by such a thing and would want to lash out and punish whoever was accused of it.

Of course, I don't know a man who wouldn't be similarly horrified. Would a father be less out to punish Keith than a woman who has never borne children?

It all depends on the person, not the gender, or economic status, or race. And as lawyers, we simply do not have the time or opportunity to understand these potential jurors as people.

Of course, our job is made infinitely more difficult by the fact that almost every potential juror lies. That may be too strong; let's say they either lie or shade the truth. The nature of the lie, or shading, depends totally on whether they want to be selected.

If serving is something they want to avoid, they say what they think we don't want to hear. If they want to serve, then they try to please us with their answers. Very often their lies are misguided, since they are not sophisticated enough to know what we are looking for.

We don't even know what we are looking for, so how could they?

So we guess, and we do our best, and then they spend the entire trial deliberately looking impassive and detached, while we continue to try to analyze their every twitch. But the truth is we don't know how well we guessed until they deliver their verdict.

Which is why I hate jury selection and juries. I would prefer that they would let me experience the trial and then decide guilt or innocence. The Andy Carpenter justice system would be fair and impartial.

Mitch Kelly has three lawyers and a

consultant with him to consider and analyze their every move. I have Hike, who is positive that every single potential juror would be a disaster for our side. I haven't seen any sign of Pod Hike since he came back from Billy's daughter's wedding.

I considered asking for a change of venue for the retrial but ultimately decided against it. I do understand that there is no doubt that most of the potential jurors will have some memory of the first trial or at least the crime.

It was a big deal around here, and I sincerely doubt that there were many people who thought Keith was wrongly convicted. Most would have the attitude that if a jury put him away after examining the facts, they were most likely right.

And they usually are.

But the awareness of the Hickman abduction was by no means limited to this area. It was a national story, and certainly widely talked about all over the northeast. Unless we reconvened in Outer Mongolia, the jury pool would be tainted by previous knowledge of the case.

And that knowledge could also work in our favor. Just the fact that there is a retrial by definition gives the impression that something was wrong the first time. All I have to do to take advantage of that fact is get across the point that the retrial is not the result of a technicality.

Jurors are people, and people hate technicalities, unless they have occasion to hide behind them.

If I had to guess, I'd say that the only person in the courtroom who is enjoying the process is Keith. It has been a welcome change in his routine and represents the first time in a very long time that anyone is taking up the fight on his behalf.

He sees action, and in his mind, action is good. I don't blame him.

It takes two days and two hours of the third day, but we finally impanel a jury. There are seven women and five men, six Caucasians, four African Americans, and two Hispanics.

It's a group of people that will carefully consider the evidence and ultimately will be swayed by the power of my logic and arguments.

Or they won't listen to a word I will say and take an hour to send Keith back to prison for the rest of his life.

I don't have the slightest idea which.

I hate that.

The reason for the retrial also represents the most difficult legal issue to handle. That is the questionable veracity of the testimony of Teresa Mullins, and more specifically, the fact that she is not here to repeat or defend it.

So the court must decide how to treat that initial testimony, and the solution will provide benefits and difficulties for both sides. The overriding concern is whether or not it would be considered hearsay, since Teresa is not going to be at the trial. Of course, it is literally hearsay, in that it will be introduced only by people who heard her say it.

To eliminate it entirely would be damaging to the prosecution, in that they relied heavily on it during the first trial. Not having it would take away some, but not all of their case.

But that will not happen, and legally, it

shouldn't. Teresa's testimony falls under two exceptions to the hearsay rule. The first is that she is legitimately unavailable; death can do that to a person. The second is that the original testimony was under oath.

So it will be heard, and while on the face of it that would appear to hurt us, there is also one significant way in which it helps. We are not saying that Teresa was wrong in her testimony, that it was an error or a misidentification. We are saying that she lied and that she did so in collusion with the actual perpetrator.

If the jury buys that, we are home free. It flies in the face of common sense to think that the person she is colluding with is the person she is sending to jail with her testimony. If they don't accept and agree with our point of view, Keith is never going to be home free again.

Judge Moran makes his ruling on the first morning of court; the testimony of Teresa Mullins will be heard by this jury. He then prepares to make two more crucial rulings on the same basic issue. The first concerns how the testimony will be read into the record.

Kelly wants a third party, even the court clerk, to read Mullins's entire testimony at the start of the trial. This will be deadly dull, and I'm opposed to it. I want both sides to be able to introduce whatever portions they or we like and have the lawyers determine who will read each part into the record.

Judge Moran agrees with me, and he then brings up the final matter, which is whether our jury can learn that there was a previous trial in which Keith was convicted.

Kelly is obviously fine with our jury knowing everything, and while I have the power to veto it, I don't. I think every single member of the jury already knows about the first trial anyway, so I'd rather confront it head-on.

Judge Moran is leery of telling them about the first trial, but in the face of both lawyers having the same position, he allows it. That effectively settles the last matter before the court. The judge calls in the jury, and we're off and running.

"Good morning, ladies and gentlemen," is Kelly's totally conventional beginning to his opening argument. Not that he isn't fast on his feet and able to improvise in the moment; he certainly is. For instance, if he were giving his statement after lunch, I'm sure he would adjust the opening to, "Good afternoon, ladies and gentlemen."

He continues. "I will make this opening statement to you, and then Mr. Carpenter will make his, and then you will hear witnesses and see and hear evidence.

"I'm a stickler for details, and I tend to overanalyze and agonize over things, so I can spend a long time preparing for a case and even for my opening statement. It drives my colleagues and my wife crazy." He grins. "Especially my wife."

The jury laughs in response. They're extra alert now, by the end of the trial, it will be all we can do to keep them from falling over asleep.

Kelly continues, "But I spent much less time than usual on this statement and even on trial preparation. That's not because I don't consider this case important. On the contrary, it's at least as important as any trial I've ever been a part of.

"The reason this took less time and effort is because I've done it before. This same defendant, Keith Wachtel, was on trial for the same crime, the abduction of little Dylan Hickman, less than three years ago. I was the lawyer for the county in that case, so I did my preparation then.

"And while Mr. Carpenter and I will disagree on most everything in this trial, there is one thing we will definitely agree on: the previous jury came back with a verdict of guilty.

"So why are we back here? Why are you called upon to do exactly what twelve of your fellow citizens were called upon to do back then? Because the defense believes that one of the witnesses against Mr. Wachtel was less than truthful, and the court believes that question to be worthy of your consideration. And that is because we do not take away a person's liberty lightly; we bend over to give them the benefit of the doubt. It's one of the many aspects of our system that contribute to its greatness.

"I also believe this issue to be worthy of consideration, and after consideration, I have concluded that it is also worthy of rejection. But my opinion does not matter . . . yours does. So you will hear all of the facts. Mr. Carpenter and I will both see to that, and then you can make up your own minds.

"But there is one other fact that you need to understand going in. The testimony in question was not the only evidence implicating Mr. Wachtel in this horrible crime, not by a long shot.

"And we will present all that additional evidence, just like we did for the jury less than three years ago. And I strongly believe that you will find it compelling, just as they did.

"You know, in all the legal maneuverings, it's easy to lose sight of the big picture, the human dimension to all of this. A baby boy, Dylan Hickman, was abducted, kidnapped. One day, he lived in a wonderful home, experiencing all the love that a precious, innocent baby deserves. And then he was gone, and to this day his fate is unknown.

"That is why you are here today. It will be your job to decide whether or not Keith Wachtel is responsible for this horrible crime. It is a true service you are providing, just as your predecessors provided the same service before you.

"I am confident that you will reach the same conclusion they did."

"You and I have something in common," is how I begin. "I was not part of that trial almost three years ago, just as you were not. Mr. Wachtel had a different lawyer, a wonderful man named Stanley Butler, who has since passed away. The circumstances of his passing are actually relevant in this case, and they will be included in what you will hear and consider.

"There is one thing that Mr. Kelly didn't mention that I want to make sure you understand. I don't know how many of you are football or baseball fans, but I want to start by describing something that happens in those sports.

"A play happens on the field, and the referee or umpire makes a call in the moment. You could say that he is delivering a verdict on what happened, based on his eyewitness view of the evidence.

"Under certain conditions, that call is

then subjected to replay, where officials look at video of the play to determine whether the call that was made was the correct one."

Three of the men and two of the women are nodding as I'm describing this. We've apparently got some sports fans on the jury, for whatever that's worth.

I continue. "The way it works is that the call on the field becomes the status quo, and for it to be overturned and reversed, there must be clear and convincing evidence on the video that it was wrong. If the video is inconclusive, then the call on the field stands. Had the opposite call been made on the field, then that would stand as well, because the video is deemed not clear and convincing. So the call on the field is given deference; you could say it is the law of that play unless proven otherwise beyond a reasonable doubt.

"That's not the way it works here. If you think of the jury's decision three years ago, it is treated almost exactly opposite to the way the referee's or umpire's decision is treated. By that, I mean that the decision of that jury is to be given no deference; you are starting from scratch. Their decision is not the status quo; there is no status quo. You must decide this case as if it has never been decided before.

"Just like any defendant that appears before any jury, Keith Wachtel is innocent until proven guilty. Because he has never been proven guilty, despite what Mr. Kelly said. The ruling of that previous jury no longer exists; it's as if it never happened.

"The other major difference between this and my sports analogy is that to overturn that sports call, there must be clear and convincing evidence that it was wrong. If it is not clear, if it is vague, then that call stands.

"Not so with the verdict almost three years ago. The only way you can agree with that jury is by finding clear and convincing evidence that they were right. If the evidence is vague, not proof beyond a reasonable doubt, then you must disagree with them. The burden is on Mr. Kelly and the prosecution to prove their case conclusively, beyond that reasonable doubt, or they lose.

"Mr. Kelly refers to our view of the testimony in question as our considering it to be 'less than truthful.' Those are his words. Let me give you my words. The witness lied. It was not a mistake, it was not a misidentification, and it was not a shading of the truth. It was a flat-out lie.

"You live in the real world. You've been lied to; you may have even told some yourselves. I've told a few beauties. You know what a lie sounds like; and you'll know these lies when you hear them.

"Mr. Kelly said that there was other conclusive evidence and that you will see it. I look forward to that, because I believe you will consider it and decide that by itself it does not come close to establishing guilt beyond a reasonable doubt.

"No, it is the testimony in question that will carry the day one way or the other. Mr. Kelly tells you it is solid-gold honest, and we tell you it is a blatant lie. It cannot be both.

"And the truth is, Ms. Mullins didn't just lie. She conspired with the real criminal to let him go free and to convict Mr. Wachtel in his stead.

"But you'll hear both sides, and you'll decide one way or the other. That's the way the system works, and I am always, and especially at this moment, thankful for that."

When I sit back down at the defense table, Keith leans over and says, "Thanks, Andy, you were great. I think the jury was really into what you were saying."

"The stuff that matters is coming up, Keith."

"Andy, what did you mean when you said that the jury would hear the circumstances of Stanley's death and that they are relevant? What does that have to do with anything?"

I realize that I never mentioned that I suspect Butler might have died because of something Teresa Mullins told him.

"I think he may have been murdered," I say.

"Because of me?"

"Because of this case. Because of something he knew. Not because of you."

"That's awful," Keith says, clearly shocked. "He was a great guy. A lawyer shouldn't die for doing his job."

I'll go along with that.

"What brought you to the scene, Detective Steitzer?"

Kelly's first witness is Detective Matt Steitzer, who was the first one on the scene of the abduction in Eastside Park.

"A 9-1-1 call was made, and my partner and I were the closest, so we were the first to respond."

"By the way, I called you Detective Steitzer, but you were not a detective back then, were you?"

"No, I was a patrolman."

"So you've since been promoted?" Kelly is demonstrating how Steitzer must be a good cop because of his ascension up the ladder.

Steitzer smiles with as much modesty as he can manage. "Twice."

"Congratulations; that's quite an accomplishment in such a short time," Kelly says.

235

I stand up. "Objection, Your Honor. Unless Mr. Kelly is going to bring in a cake and sing 'Hail to the Chief,' none of this is relevant."

"Sustained. Move on, Mr. Kelly."

"Yes, Your Honor. What did you find when you arrived?"

"There was a woman who identified herself as Teresa Mullins. She had made the 9-1-1 call. She was bleeding from a laceration on her forehead, and she told me that someone had taken the baby she was caring for."

"What was her state of mind?"

I object again. "Your Honor, unless Detective Steitzer was also promoted to vice president in charge of mind reading, he is not qualified to describe someone's state of mind."

Judge Moran sustains again; I am on what could be called a meaningless roll.

Kelly rephrases. "How would you describe her behavior?"

"She was rather hysterical. She was crying and was hard to understand. Like she was in shock."

"Did she say what her relationship was to the missing child?"

"Eventually. She described herself as the nanny."

236

"Did she mention a dog?"

"Yes, though not at first. She said that they were also walking a dog and that the abductor had taken the dog also."

"How long were you in charge of the crime scene?"

"Until Captain Stanton arrived. Then he assumed command, and we took our orders from him."

"Detective, did Ms. Mullins tell you whether she knew who perpetrated the crime?"

Steitzer nods. "She said that she was confident she could make a positive identification based on his voice and eyes and based on previous contact with the person. She said he was wearing a scarf that concealed most of his face. She also said she got most of his license plate number."

"Did she give you his name?"

He nods again. "Yes. Keith Wachtel."

"Thank you. No further questions."

I get up to cross-examine. This is just the preliminary round; this witness has not hurt us. He's just accurately describing what he saw and heard. Still, it's nice to remind the jury that the defense has a point of view.

"Detective, in the place in the park where this happened, how far is the road from the area where you found Ms. Mullins and the empty stroller?"

"Probably fifty feet."

"If I told you that I measured it and it was seventy feet, would you think that could be true?"

"Yes."

"Well, I did. I measured it, and it was seventy feet."

"If you say so."

"It would make sense to assume that the abductor pulled up parallel to the targets, wouldn't it? That way he would be the closest to them?"

"Yes."

"So Ms. Mullins, were she to look toward the car, would be seeing the driver's side, correct?"

I introduce into evidence a photograph of a Ford Fusion, the same make and model as the one that Keith owned. I point out to the court and witness that it is not Keith's car, but rather one like it. The photograph is from the side, so that the viewer is looking at the driver's side.

"The angle would basically be this, would it not?" I ask.

"Yes, I would think so."

"Please read me the license plate number on this car," I say.

"I can't. It's not in the photograph. But

Ms. Mullins could have seen it as it was pulling away. She would have seen the back of the car."

"Did you find it remarkable that a hysterical woman, in shock as you describe it, bleeding from the forehead . . . by the way, blood is affected by gravity, isn't it? It goes toward the ground?"

"Yes."

"And the eyes are just below the forehead, are they not? I'm talking specifically about Ms. Mullins's eyes and her forehead."

"Yes, but she could have wiped the blood away," he says.

"Was she still bleeding when you arrived?"

"Yes."

"Okay, back to my question. Did you find it remarkable that a hysterical woman, in shock, just pistol-whipped and wiping blood from her eyes, could read a license plate as a car is fleeing a crime scene from seventy feet away? Actually, it's more than seventy, because when it's pulling away, it's no longer at the closest point."

"I can't say."

"Why can't you say whether or not you found it remarkable? Do you need Mr. Kelly's permission? I can wait while you ask him."

Kelly springs out of his chair with an

objection, accusing me of disrespect for him and the court. Judge Moran sustains and warns me.

I turn back to Steitzer. "So you thought she was telling the truth?"

He nods. "Yes. I had no reason to doubt her."

"Then maybe you should stick around for the rest of the trial, Detective. You'll have plenty of reason to doubt her."

Kelly leaps to his feet to object, and Judge Moran strikes my last comment from the record. He's clearly pissed at me, but fortunately, he can't strike the comment from the jury's ears.

Rather than try to squeeze another witness in, Kelly and Judge Moran agree that we'll adjourn for the day a little early. Which is fine with me, because I've got a meeting to go to.

The offices of the Parsons Group are on Seventh Avenue, near Fifty-sixth Street. The neighborhood makes me feel sad; it makes me think about the Carnegie and what will never be. I don't mean Carnegie Hall; since I don't sing or play an instrument, I'm pretty much okay with never playing there. I'm even okay with not going there; you can't place a bet on classical music.

Alas, my pain is about the Carnegie Deli, which was located nearby. They've closed for good, and the fact that I will never again taste their pastrami weighs heavily on me.

I need to get better at dealing with loss.

The Parsons Group only has one corner of one floor of the building. I guess when you don't build or create anything, and all you do is invest other people's money, you don't need a lot of space to do it in.

I checked, and they have eleven employees, with Chairman Ted Parsons at the top. It's him that I'm here to see; Jill had called and cleared the way, and he agreed to give me a half hour. Zachary Alford had also only been willing to spare me a half hour; someday I hope to be worth forty-five minutes.

Parsons has a large glass desk with nothing on it, not a phone, not a piece of paper, nothing. Because it's clear, I almost didn't even realize it was there; at first I thought he was just sitting on a chair in the middle of the room.

It raises a series of interesting existential questions. If a desk is not used or seen, is it really a desk? Does it even exist? If you break it, does it make a sound?

Somehow I've got a feeling that I shouldn't use the precious granted half hour pondering these imponderables, so after thanking him for making time to see me, I get right to the point with Parsons.

"Whose money did you invest in Finding Home?"

"Our money," he says, pretending not to understand the question. "It's proven to be an excellent investment."

"Where'd you get the money? Who gave it to you in the first place?"

"As a private company, we are not required to disclose that. It's one of the advantages of investing in private companies."

I lean over and talk softly, as if pretending we're close buddies. "Just between us . . ."

He smiles a fake smile. "I don't think so. Is that what you wanted to know?"

"Among other things. Maybe we can try this a different way. I do this with my son. I'll mention a name, and you tell me if I'm getting warmer or colder."

"Mr. Carpenter . . ."

"Ready? Here's the first one. Renny Kaiser."

I can see the reaction in his face; it's a look of surprise, with a dash of fear and worry mixed in. It's all I was looking for; it doesn't matter what he says. But just for the record, he says, "This meeting is over."

"Amazing. That's what my son always says when I play the game with him."

"Have a good day," is his response.

I put on my most puzzled look. "Is it something I said? Does it have to do with the fact that you're rich and buying invisible desks with drug money?"

"I can call security."

"All by yourself?" I ask. "You can dial it and everything? I obviously underestimated you. But next time I won't — and I promise you, there will be a next time."

243

"Be careful who you threaten," he says.

"Somehow I'm not worried. Plumbers and librarians I might have a problem with; you I can handle."

I leave, actually quite satisfied with the meeting. My childish performance didn't hurt anything, since it's not like Parsons was ever going to willingly reveal anything. But his reaction left me with little doubt that Robbie Divine was right; the money behind Parsons comes from Renny Kaiser.

I've got a hunch that at some point Renny and I are going to get together.

I call Sam on the way home, and he opens with, "I was just going to call you."

"What have you got?"

"The name of James Ware's ex-fiancée. He's only been on Facebook for about a year, but she's been on forever, and almost four years ago, she started posting about their engagement and wedding plans."

"But they never got married?"

"No, the engagement ended about a year later. But it doesn't seem to have been a bad breakup; she was sad but didn't have bad things to say about him. And since then, they've become Facebook friends."

"Touching," I say. "What's her name?"

Mary Sullivan. She lives in Nanuet. "I've also got Zachary Alford's cell phone records;

I'm going through them now."

"Good. Keep me posted."

"Roger," he says.

"No, Andy," I say.

He doesn't laugh at that. It's possible that I need to come up with new material.

Kelly's next witness is Sergeant Xavier Jennings. He was in charge of the forensics unit that worked the Hickman case three years ago. He's still doing the same kind of work now and has an excellent reputation within the department.

I've questioned him before and always found him to be honest and unflappable. That last part is unfortunate; I much prefer flappable witnesses, and the more flappable the better.

Kelly spends about fifteen minutes establishing Jennings's credentials and then asks him if he was involved in investigating the Hickman abduction.

"Yes. I was in charge of the forensics."

"Did you execute a search warrant on Mr. Wachtel's house and car?"

"Yes."

"What prompted you to do that?"

"An order from my captain, Pete Stanton,"

246

he says and then grins. "He's a really good prompter."

Kelly smiles in return. "I meant, what caused a search warrant to be issued?"

"I have no firsthand knowledge of that. I wasn't involved in getting it."

"Did you find any forensic evidence that was relevant?"

"Yes. We found canine hairs. It was considered relevant because a dog was reported to have been taken in the abduction along with the child."

"Did you run any tests on the canine hair?" Kelly asks.

"We did DNA testing."

"And the results?"

"It was shown to be hair from a border collie. That is the same breed as the dog that was abducted."

Kelly pretends to be surprised. "You can tell the breed from a dog's DNA?"

"Absolutely," Jennings says. "And not just pure breeds. If the dog is a mixed breed, you can learn exactly what it is mixed with, by percentage."

"Fascinating. Did you make any effort to learn whether the dog hair from Mr. Wachtel's house matched the Hickmans' dog?"

"Yes, we collected hair from the grooming brush that Ms. Hickman used on Cody . . .

that was her dog's name. We ran the DNA on that as well."

"And the result?" Kelly asks.

"A match. There is no question that the hair in Mr. Wachtel's apartment was from the Hickmans' dog, Cody."

"Can you quantify that likelihood?"

Jennings nods. "Yes. The chance that it is not the same dog is one in slightly over eleven billion."

Kelly pauses a moment to let that sink in and then asks about the blanket fibers in the car. In Mullins's testimony, she had said that the blanket was around Evan when he was taken, so the abductor took that with him as well.

Jennings says that the blanket fiber was a cashmere that matched the type and color Jill had purchased.

Kelly turns the witness over to me.

"Do you have a dog, Sergeant?" I already know that he does; Laurie had checked it out for me.

"Yes. A yellow Lab."

"Does he ever shed?"

A smile. "Oh, yes. Pretty much all year."

"Did you ever go out and discover that you have dog hair on your clothes?" I ask.

"Never as much as was in that apartment."

248

"That doesn't answer my question; I'll ask it again, and please try to give me a yes or a no. Did you ever go out and discover that you have dog hair on your clothes?"

"Yes."

"Is it possible that some of that hair might be transferred to your car, or to wherever you're going?"

"Yes."

"What's your dog's name?"

"Bernie."

"So Bernie's hair might wind up being somewhere that he had never been himself?"

"It's possible."

"To your knowledge, were Jill Hickman and Keith Wachtel ever a couple?"

Jennings nods. "Yes, I believe so."

"Did they live together?"

"Yes."

"Along with her dog, Cody?" I ask.

"So I understand."

"Are you also aware that Mr. Wachtel had occasionally been back to that house, after they split up, to pick up some of his things?"

"I have no firsthand knowledge of that."

"I do, and there will be testimony to that effect later in the trial."

Kelly objects to my statement, and Moran strikes it.

"Sergeant Jennings, did you take any

photographs of Mr. Wachtel's apartment when you were there?"

"Certainly. That is standard procedure."

I introduce very large blown-up images, copies of three photographs that Jennings and his team took while they were in Keith's apartment. I also have twelve eight by tens of the same images, and when I submit them as evidence, I ask that they be circulated among the jury.

"Now, Sergeant Jennings, you seemed to indicate before that there was so much dog hair in the house that it would be very unlikely that it was the result of transference. Am I stating your view accurately?"

He nods. "Yes, very accurately."

"Looking at these photographs, would you say that Mr. Wachtel kept his house neat?"

"I'm not a good judge of that," he says.

"That's okay; the jury can make their own assessment. But can you point out a place in these pictures that was evidence of a lack of neatness?"

"No, but this only represents a small portion of the apartment."

"To your knowledge, are there vacuum cleaners on the market that pick up everything except dog hair?"

"Of course not."

"Did you check the vacuum cleaner bag

250

in his machine to look for dog hair?"

"No."

"That's unfortunate."

I then take him through a discussion of the blanket fiber evidence from the car and get him to admit that there are many such blankets made and that transference could conceivably be an issue there as well.

Neither he nor I believe I am right.

The difference is that I believe all this evidence was planted.

He doesn't.

During the morning recess, I see Jill Hickman in the courtroom. I'm surprised, because she told Laurie she had not attended any of the previous trial and was planning the same approach to this one.

I walk over to her, and she says, "Sorry, Andy. Mr. Kelly said I have to testify. He was going to send a subpoena if I refused."

I had seen Jill's name on Kelly's witness list, but there are always many people on those lists that don't get called. Lawyers, including myself, do that to make the other side work harder in preparation so as to stretch their resources.

"No problem at all," I say. "Just tell the truth."

"It's funny . . . no, *funny* is definitely the wrong word . . . it's disconcerting not to know how I want the trial to end. If Keith didn't do it, then he shouldn't be in prison. I just want to know what I don't know."

I nod my sympathy. "Hopefully, we'll get there."

"Are you making progress?"

"I think we are," I say, because that's really what I think, and she deserves the truth, even if it might lead to disappointment later.

As soon as the recess is over, Kelly calls her to the stand. Last time, he used other witnesses to cover the ground Jill will speak about, possibly in deference to her raw emotional state after the abduction.

Using her in this trial also probably reflects the fact that he has a weaker case now, with Teresa Mullins's testimony in dispute. Jill can do a better job than those other witnesses, and she will also evoke sympathy from the jurors.

Kelly starts by going through her business history, and it is an impressive one. It culminates, of course, with Finding Home, a very successful business she basically built from scratch.

"Mr. Wachtel worked for you?" he asks.

She nods. "He did. He was our chief chemist."

"Good at his job?"

"Yes. Very."

"Did you have a relationship outside of work?" Kelly asks.

"Yes, a serious one. We even lived together for almost a year."

"Were you planning to be married?"

"We never officially set a date, but I believe we both felt that was where it was going. But it never got there."

"Why?"

"A lot of reasons, and I'd rather not speculate here, if you don't mind," she says. "It just went from a satisfying relationship to something much less. I also couldn't trust that he was being faithful, and I've since found out that I was right. So we just gave up, and he moved out. Very adult, and quite painless."

"And did he leave the company at the same time?"

"No, that was months later."

"So you felt you could continue to work together, even after your personal relationship ended?"

"Oh, yes. I didn't consider him an enemy. Besides, I did not involve myself much in the scientific end. I know very little about it. I was off raising money so the company could survive."

"What was the cause of his eventually leaving?"

"Our security department had reason to believe he was removing highly sensitive

254

documents, possibly to share them with competitors."

"Did you believe that to be true?"

"I was traveling on business in Europe at the time. I was away for more than two months. I accepted what security told me; they were professionals, and that was their job. And Zachary Alford, who had just arrived at the company and is now our CEO, was firm in his belief that Keith had to go."

"So Mr. Wachtel was fired?"

"We positioned it as a mutual decision, but we had determined he could not stay on."

"So he accepted it?"

"I can't answer that. At one point, I was told he was preparing a lawsuit, but that never came to pass."

Kelly then takes her through the adoption of Dylan and the hiring of Teresa Mullins, allowing her to point out the outstanding reference that the agency provided for her.

The testimony of Jill about the Dylan stuff, leading up to her learning of the abduction while at the office, is a four-tissue affair, not counting those needed by the women on the jury. Kelly wraps it up by getting her to say that to this day she doesn't know what happened to her baby.

It's a defense attorney's nightmare. Unfortunately, I am the defense attorney to whom I refer. So I'm going to be quick and gentle on cross; there is very little to be gained here.

"Ms. Hickman, after you and Mr. Wachtel broke off your personal relationship, things between you remained amicable?"

"I would say reasonably so, yes. Certainly from my point of view, and I thought from his as well."

"In fact, you were able to continue your work relationship, going to the same office every day, for almost six months?"

"Yes."

"So he had never done anything violent or criminal to cause you to end the personal side?"

"No."

"You did not consider him dangerous?"

"I did not."

"Do you, as you are sitting here today, have any personal knowledge as to who may have abducted Dylan?"

"I do not."

"Thank you."

Jill leaves the stand and makes eye contact with me and then offers a slight, exhausted smile to me as she passes. This was not an easy experience for her, but she held up well.

She most definitely does not look at Keith.

Laurie and Sam are waiting for me when I get home. Laurie's presence isn't a surprise, because she lives here. Sam doesn't, but he's the one who greets me at the door. I refrain from saying, "Honey, I'm home," to him.

"I've got something for you," he says.

"I hope it's not my pipe and slippers," I say. "That would be weird."

"No, it's information." Then he turns to Laurie. "You go first."

She nods. "Okay, I checked out James Ware's ex-fiancée, Mary Sullivan. I spoke to some of her friends and a few of her coworkers. She's a waitress at a Buffalo Wild Wings."

"What excuse did you give?"

"Said it was a financial thing; a loan application. Nobody questioned it. She's been married for a year, no kids. Everybody likes her; they were falling over themselves to say positive things."

258

"What's your assessment?"

"Well, I certainly have no direct information as to whether or not she is Dylan Hickman's natural mother or whether she put him up for adoption. But I strongly doubt it."

"Why?"

"She's one of seven siblings and has sixteen nieces and nephews. They're a very close and very large family; they could hold their family circle gatherings in Madison Square Garden. It just doesn't fit with giving up a child."

"Okay," I say. I completely trust Laurie's instincts on things like this and also on things not like this.

She's not finished. "But even if she's the mother, I still don't think it gets us anywhere."

"Why is that?"

"It's the same thing you said about James Ware. These are not big-money conspirators; they don't fit the bill. If they gave up their child, they gave up their child. But there would be nothing about that child to have triggered everything that followed."

I agree with her assessment. I've thought for a while that if it was not just a random abduction, then the answer has something to do with Finding Home and Renny Kaiser. Zachary Alford sent Kyle Gillis after me that night; he didn't do that because I was mean to him in our meeting.

"You're up, Sam," I say.

"I went through Zachary Alford's phone records. The guy makes a lot of calls. Some I identified, some I didn't. There was one cell phone number he called fourteen times, and I couldn't trace it to a person. I kept coming up with a company name."

"How does that help us?" I ask.

"I told you before that he had called Gillis, and Gillis called him. So I decided to compare all their calls to each other, to see if there were any common numbers."

"Were there?"

He nods. "You'd better believe it. The cell phone number Alford called fourteen times was also on Gillis's list. But here's the kicker. Remember I told you how Renny Kaiser was layered? How he was hiding behind all kinds of corporations, most of them probably dummies?"

"I do."

"Well, the phone these guys called is listed to one of those companies."

This removes all doubt. Renny Kaiser has been talking to both Kyle Gillis and Zachary Alford. Whatever has been going on is as a result of Kaiser pulling the strings. He's got the money, and he's got the power.

"I need to talk to Renny Kaiser," I say.

"Why?"

"Because he's got the answers. Whether I'll learn anything or not is beside the point; I've got to find out how to get to him."

"Guess what? I've got his number," Sam says, smiling.

From out of the mouths of accountants . . .

Once I tell Sam that I want him to monitor Renny's phone calls from this day forward, I dial the number. My hope is that if Kaiser answers, I'll be able to hear him over the pounding noise coming from my chest. I'm scared even to get him on the phone; I can't imagine what it will be like if he agrees to a meeting.

One time, in a rare moment when we weren't insulting each other, Pete admitted to me that there were a number of times he was frightened while doing his job. He said that the key is not to show it, to pretend you're calm and confident and in control. Not only does it affect the other person, but faking confidence can actually inspire confidence in oneself.

Sometimes I'm able to pull it off, and sometimes not. This is one of those times I'm going to try.

Of course, down deep, I'm actually hoping that he won't answer at all and that I'll get a machine and be able to avoid the conversation. In that regard, it's similar to every time I ever called a girl to ask for a date in high school.

But someone does answer with only the one-word question, "Yes?"

"My name is Andy Carpenter. I'm trying to reach Renny Kaiser."

"And so you have. How did you get this number?"

"You'd be amazed at how much I know about you. I can tell you about it when we meet."

"Why would I want to meet with you?" he asks.

"So I can make you a proposition, and you can accept it."

There is a fairly long pause, to the point where I think he might have hung up without me hearing the click. Then, "Tomorrow night, nine o'clock, at my home."

"Which home is that?" I know from Robbie Divine that he has homes in Greenwich, Connecticut, and Park Avenue in Manhattan.

"Greenwich. The address is —"

I interrupt. "I know the address. Nine o'clock tomorrow."

"Come alone, or don't come at all," he says.

I hang up the phone. I find hanging up first in situations like this gives one the psychological upper hand. It's always better to be the hanger-upper rather than the hanger-uppee. I know that because when I did get those high school girls on the phone, I was invariably the uppee.

I turn to Laurie and Sam. "Nine o'clock tomorrow night at his house in Greenwich. I'm supposed to come alone."

"You're supposed to, but you're not going to," Laurie says. "I'll call Marcus."

Zachary Alford is Kelly's next witness. He testified at the first trial, so I'm sure he's just going to reprise his previous testimony.

Kelly spends some time establishing Alford's business background, up to the time he arrived at Finding Home. He also gets him to talk about the success of the company under his direction, as if that will make his subsequent testimony more credible.

"Was Keith Wachtel working at Finding Home when you arrived?" Kelly asks.

"Yes. He was the chief chemist."

"Did his position change after you got there?"

"It changed as soon as I got there. His title remained the same," Alford says, "but his responsibilities definitely were adjusted."

"In what way?"

"We were developing a new process of testing DNA, much faster and requiring less time. We brought in some new people to work on it, and Keith was not involved in that effort."

"Did he ever complain about that?"

Alford nods. "Oh, yes. Close to every day. It created a morale problem in the office."

"Did you consider terminating his employment?"

"No, he had been there a long time, and Jill . . . Ms. Hickman . . . had established a culture of loyalty to employees. We did not and do not fire people casually or precipitously."

"What caused him to finally leave?"

"Within a couple of months, our security people obtained evidence that Keith was gaining access to confidential documents that he should not have been privy to and that he was attempting to share them with our competitors."

"What did he say when you confronted him?" Kelly asks.

"He denied it, said it was nonsense, but he used much stronger words than that. I told him that under the circumstances he would have to leave the company but that we would give him a healthy severance package to put it all behind us."

"What was his response?"

"He wanted to talk to Ms. Hickman," Alford says. "He said that she wouldn't believe that he was guilty and would back him. She was in Europe at the time."

"Did you agree to that?"

Alford shakes his head. "No, she was there for an extended period raising money. Besides, I had already spoken to her. She had signed off on forcing Keith out of the company."

"Did you tell him that?"

"Yes, and he got very upset. Said that he couldn't believe she would stab him in the back like that. He threatened to sue us, and I told him that it was his choice whether to do so or not."

There isn't much that I'll be able to do with Alford on cross; he's basically relating a two-person conversation. The only way I'll be able to present a different version is if I put Keith on the stand during the defense case, but I'm loath to do that.

"Mr. Alford," I say, "just to get the chronology correct, you arrived at Finding Home when the Parsons Group had invested money in the company but had not yet bought a 50 percent share?"

"That's correct."

"And once that subsequent purchase was done, and Ms. Hickman stepped back and became chairman, you were made CEO?"

"Correct."

266

"So you were the Parsons Group's boy?"

Kelly objects, calling the question disrespectful, which I really never knew was a legal objection, but Judge Moran sustains it anyway.

"Mr. Alford, how much damage did the alleged theft of the documents by Mr. Wachtel cost your company?"

"What do you mean?"

"Which part didn't you understand?" I ask. "You said that Mr. Wachtel stole the documents to turn them over to a competitor, maybe even to sell them, so how damaging was that to you? You don't have to give me an exact monetary amount; you can ballpark it for me."

"I am not aware of any damage, monetary or otherwise. We acted so quickly to prevent that."

"I'm afraid that now I don't understand," I say. "According to you, he stole the documents; did you recover them?"

"No, they were stolen electronically. Recovery is not possible in a situation like that; there is nothing of a physical nature to recover."

"And they would have been valuable to a competitor?"

"Yes."

I pretend to look confused; I'm good at it

because it's a look I've had very often in my professional life. "But then he did nothing with them? Why would that be? Do you think he was suddenly showing loyalty to the company that had just fired him?"

"Perhaps the companies he offered them to behaved ethically."

"Did they ethically come forward and report what Keith was trying to do?"

"Not to my knowledge."

"What did the police say when you reported the theft?" I ask.

"We handled it internally," he said.

"So someone stole valuable documents from you, putting your company at substantial risk. You had proof of that theft, and prosecuting the thief might have made other companies leery of using the documents. But you handled it internally?"

"Yes."

I pause for a few moments to let that sink in, and then I ask, "When you told Mr. Wachtel that Ms. Hickman had signed off on his firing, did he make any threats against her personally?"

"No, but he was very disappointed. He felt betrayed, and he expressed his anger."

"No threats?"

"Just the lawsuit against the company."

"You didn't warn Ms. Hickman that she

might face retribution?"

"No."

"You said that your company does not fire anyone precipitously. Is that right?"

"Yes."

"The chemists on staff that worked for Mr. Wachtel, you testified that you fired them after he left?"

"Yes."

"Did you have evidence of their wrong-doing?"

"No, but we perceived them as being loyal to Mr. Wachtel."

"Lucky for them you don't fire precipitously. No further questions."

"Marcus, we're not in Paterson anymore."

We're driving through Greenwich neighborhoods that are remarkable, although I'm not even sure I'd call them neighborhoods, in the way that neighborhoods are a grouping of homes. Each piece of property here is an entity unto itself and neighborhood size in its own right. I think a while back we passed the Ponderosa.

The lawns are endless, and I have no doubt they are perfectly manicured under the thin snow covering. This is a very wealthy community; I've got a feeling you could walk around Greenwich for ten years, staring at the ground, and never see a dropped food stamp.

Marcus and I haven't chatted much on the way here; I've said a total of three sentences, which is three more than Marcus. I wonder what he thinks of this area; I have no idea where he grew up, but I

270

suspect it was a very different place. Of course, it's possible that he grew up on Krypton and flew here in a space capsule just before the planet exploded.

Before we left, Laurie, Marcus, and I discussed our strategy. I am going to act unafraid and talk to Kaiser, and Marcus is going to make sure I don't die in the process. By me talking and Marcus protecting, we're definitely playing to our strengths.

"You sure you want to do this?" Laurie asked.

"Not even close," I said.

"What is it you want to accomplish?"

"I want to shake things up. We're in need of that right now. However things fall out, we'll deal with it then."

Kaiser's property is as, or more, impressive and enormous than any we've seen on our tour of Greenwich. The Donner party wouldn't have made it from the street to the house; they'd have been chomping on each other halfway up the driveway. The setup increases my discomfort; anything that is about to happen will not exactly attract attention from the neighbors.

We pull up to the front of the house and get out. I'm sure I'm more nervous than Marcus is; I'm sure the car is more nervous than Marcus is. We go to the front door, and I almost trip over a small football lying on the slate path. It's not a good start.

I ring the doorbell and can hear chimes echoing loudly through the silence. Within moments the door opens, and a very large, rather ugly man opens it. He's got to be 280 pounds and six foot four; maybe that football was lying there because he brought it with him from the Giants' practice field.

The guy looks at me, then looks at Marcus, and then sort of grunts and steps aside for us to come in. I'm not feeling any warmth so far.

We follow him through what by any standards is a magnificent home. I'm not a good judge of stuff like this, but this place cost a fortune to decorate. And I'd bet that the people who painted the artwork on the walls have been dead for a really long time.

We go toward the back of the house, which feels like it's a half mile away. At one point, I can see through a glass wall to the backyard, which has a tennis court, swimming pool, and elaborate playground equipment. Just like Robbie Divine said, Kaiser has a regular family life, with a wife who probably goes to PTA meetings.

We're led into what might be considered a large den, although we've already passed two other rooms that I thought were dens.

272

At the entrance to the room is another guy, just as large as the first guy, but even uglier. I think to get a job working for Kaiser, you must have to be a huge person willing to run a gauntlet where a line of people smack you in the face with an ugly stick.

Sitting behind a large, ornate desk is a guy I assume is Renny Kaiser. He's dressed casually, in a pullover shirt and black jeans, which seems incongruous for these surroundings. He looks to be in his early fifties, thin, and in pretty good shape.

The two huge ugly guys follow us into the room.

"Mr. Carpenter," he says.

"Mr. Kaiser," is my witty comeback. "This is quite a pair of butlers you have here. Which one is Jeeves?"

"You were instructed to come alone."

I nod. "I disobeyed."

"So now instruct your friend to wait in the car."

"I trust this man with my life, Senator. To ask him to leave would be an insult." It's a line from *The Godfather Part II,* but based on his non-reaction, Kaiser hasn't seen the movie. This pretending-to-be-unafraid routine isn't scaring him any.

"You will remove him, or I will have him removed."

"Then you'd better have an extra truck-load full of ugly butlers hanging around. Because these two are not going to get it done."

Kaiser looks toward the butlers and makes a very slight motion with his head. They don't hesitate, moving with surprising speed toward Marcus.

Marcus does hesitate; he doesn't move a muscle until they are very close to him. Then he throws a forearm directly into the first guy's throat, sending him down and gasping to the ground. I'm not a doctor or a voice coach, but I can safely predict that his glee club days are over.

Butler number two doesn't even have time to be deterred and possibly rethink his approach. He's already too close to Marcus, who kicks up and into the guy's groin. This causes the guy's head to drop, maybe so he can get a look at what used to be his groin.

Marcus's fist, traveling up and in the opposite direction of the guy's head, smashes into it. His fist wins, and the head does an about-face and goes in the opposite direction before following the rest of the body to the floor.

Kaiser watches all of this without saying a word, really without any reaction at all.

"I should have mentioned that my friend

is the one who met your friend Kyle Gillis the other night. May he rest in peace."

"You have made a very serious mistake," Kaiser says. "A life-changing one."

"Whatever," I say, a dismissive word that Ricky uses when he wants to annoy me. "You want to hear my proposition or not?"

He smiles as insincere a smile as I have ever seen. "The floor is yours."

"Okay. You know about the trial and what I'm doing, and it at least worries you some, or you wouldn't have sent Gillis after me or agreed to this meeting."

I hear a slight gurgling noise, which I think is coming from the guy whose neck Marcus used as a heavy bag. Fortunately, Marcus has heard it as well, and he edges toward the two fallen guys, just in case.

"I know a lot about your business. I know who you are and what you do. I'm going to make you a focal point of the trial so the whole world will understand. No more hiding behind this upstanding citizen bullshit; by the time I'm done with you, you'll be voted drug dealer of the year by *Pharmacology Weekly*."

"And your proposition?" he asks. If he's worried about what I'm saying, he's hiding it really well. Maybe because we both know it's bullshit.

"I care about only two things, and the first is getting my client acquitted. I think you can make that happen; you can either point me to the real guilty party or give me some evidence that I can use to get my client off. I don't think you grabbed the kid, but I'll bet you know who did."

"And your second care?"

"I want to know what happened to Dylan. His mother deserves closure."

"Fascinating. Based on your reputation, I would have thought that you were smarter than this. Leave now."

So we do.

It would be wrong to say I accomplished nothing by meeting with Kaiser. Sure, our case is no better off, and yes, Jill Hickman is no closer to finding out what happened to her son. But I did manage to piss off a dangerous drug dealer who will likely make it the goal of his life to end mine.

Well done, Andy.

One thing I know for sure . . . not all is fun and games at Finding Home, and I think Jill should know about it. I call her and ask if she'll meet me for lunch after the morning court session, and after questioning me to make sure there's no bad news about Dylan, she agrees.

Kelly's first witness this morning is Pete Stanton. He was the lead detective on the case and can explain the actions of the police throughout.

"When you arrived on the scene, you took control?" Kelly asks.

"Yes."

"Did you speak to Teresa Mullins immediately?"

"No, there was a delay of maybe fifteen minutes. Emergency medical personnel were treating her facial injuries on the scene. Once they were finished, I interrogated her."

"Was she able to identify her assailant?"

"She said that she strongly believed it was Mr. Wachtel, based on his voice and the part of his face that was uncovered. She also had a description of the car and a partial license plate."

"What did you do with this information?"

"I confirmed that the license plate information in fact matched that on Mr. Wachtel's car and that the car was of a similar make and model to what Ms. Mullins described. Once that was done, a search warrant was prepared, signed off on, and executed."

"Where was Mr. Wachtel while all this was happening?"

"I have no personal knowledge of that. I know that he said he was hiking on Garret Mountain that day."

"So you were not able to confirm that?"

"I was not."

I have very few questions for Pete; he

didn't do us any damage, so there's nothing to repair. I reserve the right to call him in the defense case, where he will be a crucial witness. He may not be happy with that fact; helping defendants is not something he would ever relish.

Kelly next calls an ex-employee of Finding Home, Sarah Stafford, for the purpose of reporting how upset Keith was at being let go and how betrayed he felt by Jill.

Stafford was a chemist working under Keith, and she says all the things Kelly wants to hear. Kelly then turns her over to me.

"Ms. Stafford, did you ever see any evidence that Keith Wachtel was stealing documents?"

"I did not, but I wouldn't necessarily be in a position to do so."

"But you reported to him?"

She nods. "Yes."

"Ever see any sign that he was disloyal to the company?"

"No."

"Are you still employed at Finding Home?" I ask.

"No, pretty much everyone who worked for Keith was let go and replaced. It wasn't fair, but it happened."

"Why wasn't it fair?"

"Because it wasn't like Keith was our big buddy. He was a tough boss. And we weren't close; there was no reason to think we would hurt the company just because they thought he did."

"Has anyone that was terminated been rehired?"

"No, which makes it tough for people with our skills. Because of the new process, Finding Home has at least 50 percent more work, a lot of it from the government. And they've doubled their staff. So we can't go there, and nobody else has any openings, because they're not doing as much work as they used to. They gave us good severance, but that doesn't last forever."

"Thank you, Ms. Stafford. No further questions."

I meet Jill for lunch at a diner about four blocks from the courthouse. The distance will mean that we're less likely to be seen by people connected with the case. Not that we're doing anything wrong or unethical, but there's no need to start anyone talking.

Jill is waiting for me when I get there, and I tell her that the subject on the table is Finding Home.

"What about it?" she asks.

"Here's what I know. The money that Parsons used to buy half of the company was provided by Renny Kaiser. Renny Kaiser is a big-time drug dealer; they don't come any bigger. Zachary Alford has been in frequent contact with Kaiser, and one of them sent a tough guy to warn me, or much worse."

"Andy —"

"Let me finish, please. They are worried that I am close to uncovering some wrong-doing at that company. I can't see how it is connected to the abduction; it is likely something else. But there is something very wrong there, and not only do I think you should know it, but I want you to help me find out what it is."

"How much of this are you sure about?" she asks.

"One hundred percent."

She shakes her head sadly. "I never should have stepped back the way I did. It's my damn company."

"You had your reasons. But you need to step back in, find out what's going on, and fix it."

"How?"

"I don't know; that's not my area. You're the chairman. Audit the books, hold confidential interviews, issue edicts, fire people . . . do whatever chairmen do."

She seems either unconvinced, or hesitant,

or both, but finally she nods. "I'll do what I can."

"Alford is the only one who I know is part of it, but there could be others."

"Okay," she says. "Time to jump back in."

I've been a lawyer for a long time, but this is a first for me. I have never been involved in a case in which the key witness in a trial is a dead nanny.

But that is what is happening here. Kelly is about to call Teresa Mullins to the stand, as he did last time. She is, of course, unable to physically take the stand now, but her words will be center stage.

Judge Moran correctly feels the need to explain to the jury what the hell is going on. "Ladies and gentlemen of the jury, you have heard witnesses in this trial refer to Teresa Mullins, who was present at the scene of the abduction, and who testified at length during the first trial.

"Teresa Mullins is deceased and is therefore obviously unavailable to appear in court for this trial. However, her testimony from the first trial is permitted to be read and examined here and available to be judged by you.

"You may be familiar with the word *hearsay*, and you may know that it is rarely permitted to be presented to a jury. While that is usually true, there are two specifics reasons that the law allows it in this case.

"One is the legitimate unavailability of the witness, and I have already mentioned the circumstances that speak to that. The other is the fact that the original words were spoken under oath and are therefore given special consideration and deference by the court.

"It will be up to each lawyer to decide which portions of Ms. Mullins's testimony they want you to hear. Obviously, there can be no cross-examination, but the lawyers are free to present their own witnesses to support or refute what is being read."

With that, he turns things back over to Kelly, who has decided to let the court clerk read the parts of Mullins's testimony that he wants this jury to hear.

I think this is an error; it's read in a monotone that in my view diminishes the effectiveness. I know why he's doing it; if he had someone involved in the case do the reading, I could question that person in a way that would feel like a cross-examination.

And the words are powerful. She very

clearly identifies Keith as the abductor and speaks about the horror of that day and the loss of that precious child. I imagine that she originally spoke emotionally, and no doubt that had an effect on the previous jury. That emotion is obviously missing in our court clerk's rendition, although at one point the reading includes a reference to a break that Mullins took at the judge's suggestion so that she could have time to compose herself.

I watch the jury during the reading. They're either paying rapt attention or they're worried about whether they remembered to turn the oven off when they left home this morning. I don't have the slightest idea what they're thinking . . . I never do.

I don't have any questions when the reading is done. That's partially because there is no one for me to question, but more importantly it's because when I attempt to take the testimony apart, I will be presenting witnesses to do it.

I tell Judge Moran that I will be presenting and analyzing Ms. Mullins's testimony during the defense case; I say this because I want the jury to hear it. He tells the court clerk, and by extension the dead nanny, that she can step down, subject to recall.

And she'd better be ready, because Andy Carpenter is coming after her, and coming after her soon.

"The prosecution rests," says Mitch Kelly.

There's a major weakness in my case that has nothing to do with Keith Wachtel. There is no one else I can accuse of the abduction. The jury is going to want to punish someone for this crime or at least learn that there is someone else that some future jury will likely punish. I don't have to prove someone else's guilt, but I very much like to suggest a reasonable alternative to my client.

I've got no one to fill that role.

Renny Kaiser, despite my probably ill-advised threat to him, doesn't fit the bill. If I worked hard enough and was able to expose his drug activities and his connection to Finding Home, it still wouldn't get me where I want to go.

But the truth is that none of what I'm learning or not learning about Finding Home would be admissible in this courtroom. Not Renny's investment or the phone connection triangle between him, Zachary Alford, and Kyle Gillis. Not even the events with Kyle Gillis the night he followed me and ultimately met his Maker, or at least his Marcus.

The reason it wouldn't be admissible is that on the surface it has nothing to do with this case. We are here to determine whether Keith Wachtel abducted Dylan Hickman, not whether there is fraud or money laundering or any other nefarious thing going on at Finding Home.

I simply cannot tie anything at Finding Home to the abduction, and I have to face the possibility, even the probability, that it may well be due to the fact that there is no connection. No matter what Renny and his pals might be doing at Finding Home, how does stealing a baby help them do it?

If I can't answer that question, then there is no way that Judge Moran would let me pose it to the jury. And he shouldn't.

I'd like to find a way to nail Renny and the others for whatever it is they're doing, but that has nothing to do with what I'm being paid one dollar to do. So for now my focus is on Keith, and Teresa Mullins, and creating a reasonable doubt in the minds of the jury.

In that regard, what I have to hang our

collective hat on is what I consider the perjured testimony of Teresa Mullins. I have two angles from which to attack it. First, my position is that if the jury throws it out, there is not enough evidence remaining to convict Keith. Second, and at least as important, is our view that Teresa collaborated with the real criminals.

I'm going to construct the Teresa Mullins portion of our case along a time line similar to the way we uncovered it. Because of that, the first person I call to the stand is Sondra, Willie's wife.

When I had told Willie I was going to use Sondra instead of him as a witness, he seemed a little put off by it and asked why I was doing it.

I decided to tell him the truth. "Because she's more believable than you, people like her more, and she doesn't say stupid stuff."

He thought for a moment and said, "Makes a lot of sense. She's better looking than me too."

"By a lot," I said.

So Sondra is the first witness I call in the defense case. I have her talk about the foundation a bit, including the fact that I'm a partner in it. I don't want Kelly bringing that out and making it sound sinister or conspiratorial.

Then I bring her to the day Cody arrived and ask her to describe what happened.

"Willie and I just got there regular time, about eight o'clock in the morning. There was a dog tied up in front, a border collie. There was a note left with it."

I introduce the note into evidence. "Does this happen often?"

"I wouldn't say often," she says. "But sometimes people are embarrassed to be giving up their dogs, so they do it that way."

"What's the procedure when this happens?"

"Well, unless we definitely know whose dog it is, we scan it to see if it has an embedded chip. We did that in this case."

"What did the scan turn up?"

"That the dog's name was Cody and belonged to Jill Hickman."

I submit the scan report into evidence and turn the witness over to Kelly, who simply gets Sondra to say that she did not see who left the dog and has no idea who it was.

Next I call Dan Dowling, our vet, who confirms that he examined Cody and that the dog tested positive for anahlichtia, a tick-borne ailment that it very common to the state of Maine. I introduce the blood test into evidence, as well as a sworn affidavit from the company that Jill used to hire Teresa. The document lists her address as being in Nobleboro, Maine.

Kelly has little to ask Dowling but starts with, "Dr. Dowling, you say this ailment is common to Maine. Are there any other states where it's at all prevalent?"

"Yes, 20 percent of the cases in the United States are in Vermont and New Hampshire. It has made its way down from Canada."

Kelly acts surprised. "So there are cases in Canada as well?"

"Yes, many more than in the U.S."

"Does a dog have to have lived in one of those places to have gotten the disease?" Kelly asks.

"No, it could happen in one day, passing through. As long as the dog comes in contact with the tick."

"Thank you."

If the jury has been respecting Judge Moran's admonition and not reading or watching anything about the trial in the media, then they must have no idea why they're hearing about tick diseases. But since the next jury that actually listens to the judge will be the first, my guess is they know exactly where I'm going with this.

In any event, since it's Friday, they'll have the weekend to think about it.

I'm in very good shape in terms of preparation. That doesn't always happen; very often I'm working late into the night to completely familiarize myself with details of whatever case I'm working so that I can instantly respond in the courtroom.

But this trial, at least as it relates to the defense case, is fairly straightforward, so I've been able to relax a little more and not be so intense about it.

One of the great benefits of this is that I'm able to go to Ricky's basketball game today. It's a local Paterson league that plays at the Y and is run by terrific, dedicated people. I love that Ricky is able to participate in team sports at his age. Doing so myself provided me with many of my best childhood memories.

Laurie and I take him and sit through two other games before it's his turn. The kids in the two games are three and five years older than Ricky, and it's really amazing how good they are. They can dribble, get to the basket, and shoot. Defense, of course, is not a priority.

Ricky's game is a bit different. Kindly put, their skills have not yet significantly developed. Nor has their game strategy. As soon as one kid gets the ball, all five players on the other team descend on him. He's overwhelmed, so somebody takes the ball away, only to receive the same treatment from the team that originally had the ball.

The game lasts for forty minutes, with two fifteen-minute halves and a ten-minute halftime. Ricky gets the ball six times, sending Laurie into a frenzy of wild cheering. He takes one shot, which gets to about three feet short of the rim.

I have to admit I love watching this. I never thought I could enjoy a game this much without betting on it. Afterward, everybody goes for pizza, so we parents can spend concentrated time telling the kids how wonderful they are.

When we get home, I take the dogs for a walk and get back to trial preparation. I'm done at about ten, and since Laurie is already in bed, I head in that direction.

When I walk into the bedroom, I see that she is crying. My instinct is to get the hell out of here, but she's already seen me, so I'm stuck.

"What's the matter?" I ask.

"Nothing," she says through the sniffling.

"There must be something going on. Is it a good something or a bad something?" Laurie is able to cry from both happiness and sadness, an ability I fortunately never really developed.

"I was thinking about today and how much joy we get from Ricky being in our lives."

I exhale from relief. "So that's good. I was worried, because you were crying."

"I was also thinking about Dylan Hickman. I can't stop thinking about him in that picture with Teresa Mullins. He is so small and so dependent on adults. But adults let him down. Did you see how tiny his fingers were?"

I have no idea what to say in situations like this, so I say as little as possible. In this case, Laurie asked if I saw Dylan's tiny fingers, so I can get away with just saying, "Yes . . . so tiny."

She continues, "Not only is it so horrible for him and Jill, but when a child is lost . . ."

"We don't know that he's dead," I say.

She nods. "I know, but you and I both know it's probable. When a child that young

294

dies, the repercussions are not only devastating, but they are so far reaching. Just think of the lives that would have been impacted by him, the work he might have done, the people that might have loved him, the children and grandchildren that will never exist." She pauses, dabs at her eyes, and says, "Bringing a child into the world is a wonderful and very scary thing to do."

The pain in Laurie's face is tangible, and the tears are still flowing. I wish I could help her, but I can't. We both know that.

I also know one other thing. We won't be having sex tonight. I'm thinking no chance.

Sometimes thoughts just pop into my head, and sometimes they're actually meaningful. I wish I could control the timetable on when they happen, but I can't. So I basically just go with the flow.

It just happened now. I don't know whether it was the talk of bringing a child into the world, or the phrase *no chance*. But it's here, it's in my head, and it's clear as a bell.

"Can Nancy come babysit tomorrow?" I ask.

"I'm sure she could. Why?"

"Because we need to go talk to Mary Sullivan."

We catch a break in that Mary Sullivan is off from work today. Laurie called her, told her who we are, and said we must talk to her urgently about something relating to the Keith Wachtel trial. Mary was familiar with the trial, so Laurie said that helped overcome her wariness about being approached like this by strangers.

Our next-door neighbor Nancy has come in to babysit, so Laurie is able to go with me. As we get there, I'm thinking that maybe my hunch isn't so smart, maybe it's just a waste of time. But we'll know soon enough.

She asked that we meet at a diner on Route 59 in Nanuet, and she's waiting for us when we arrive. She looks to be in her early thirties, pretty without makeup.

"Thanks for talking with us," Laurie says after we go through the hellos and introductions.

"To be honest, I'm not sure I'm going to. It depends what this is about."

"It's about James Ware, your former fiancé," I say.

She is clearly surprised by this. "Jim? What does he have to do with that trial?"

"The child that was abducted was adopted. He had been abandoned by someone, probably his natural parents, a couple of months earlier. Testing shows that the father might have been James Ware."

"What kind of testing?"

"DNA," I say. "I went to talk to him about it, and he told me that it was impossible. He even dared me to sue him, saying he could prove he wasn't the father."

She's nodding as we talk, which is a good sign, so I push on. "We want to know if you know why he is so confident."

Mary starts to say something, then seems to catch herself and says, "I don't think it's my place to talk about Jim."

"It'll come out in court anyway," I say, lying through my teeth and earning a Laurie stare of disapproval. "This will be easier on him."

Mary nods. "Okay. Jim can't have kids. I think it's one of the things that drove us apart. I come from a big family, and he knows how important it is to me. The fact

297

that we'd never be able to have kids together made him feel inadequate. I told him we could adopt, but he never thought that would be enough for me."

There's really nothing left to say, so we thank her and leave. My hunch was right on target, not exactly an everyday occurrence.

Once we get in the car, it takes me about forty-five seconds to go from gloating about my correct instinct to berating myself for not realizing it sooner.

"I know Alford is bad; we've connected him to both Renny Kaiser and Kyle Gillis. Emmonds works for Alford, so how could I have counted on him to give me accurate DNA test results?"

I wasn't really asking Laurie the question; I already know the answer, and I'm beating myself up with it.

So I continue. "He probably just took a name off the registry; Ware was in there because he was military. Emmonds would have no way of knowing that Ware couldn't father children."

"This changes everything," Laurie says.

I know that she's right, but I want to hear what she has to say. "How do you mean?"

"We've been thinking that there is likely something about the Finding Home business that these people were desperate to cover up. But we didn't think it had anything to do with the abduction; we could never make that connection."

"Right."

"But this proves otherwise. Emmonds, and the people he works for, would have no reason to fake the DNA results unless they were somehow involved in the abduction. Or, at the very least, they were covering up for whoever was."

"Please answer yes to this question," I say. "Do you have the other pacifier?" We had taken two pacifiers from Dylan's room but only given one of them to Emmonds to test.

"Yes," Laurie says.

"We need to get it tested, fast."

"You want to bring it to Pete and have him get it done at the county lab?"

"No. Finding Home does a lot of their work, so the respective staffs must know each other well. If Pete goes in there and asks for it to be done, but not by Finding Home, the word might get back to them."

"You want me to call Cindy?"

Cindy Spodek is a close friend of Laurie's and mine who heads up the Boston office of the FBI. She's done a lot of favors for us in the past, and we've reciprocated a few times. Her career has prospered because of our reciprocations; she's been able to make some big arrests.

"Definitely," I say.

Laurie waits until we get home to call her, and I stay in the room to listen in. After twenty minutes of chitchat about things that are of absolutely no interest to me, I can't take it anymore. How can two people talk for that long without sports ever coming up?

"This is torture," I say. "Let me talk to her."

"Andy is unhappy with our conversation," Laurie says. "He wants to talk to you."

I take the phone and say, "Cindy, how are you? Okay, are we done with the small talk? We need a favor."

"Andy, what a treat to chat with you."

"Right. Just one question and then you can talk to Laurie some more about recipes and shoes and what the bridesmaid dresses for your niece's wedding look like. Can you run a DNA test for us?"

"Sure. The FBI exists to serve you."

"This is important. We're trying to save an innocent man and find a missing child."

"This the Dylan Hickman case?"

"Yes, we have a pacifier with his DNA on it, and we're trying to learn who the parents are."

300

"Doesn't the mother's company do DNA for a living?"

"Yes, but we want an independent test run, just to be sure."

"Okay, I'll do it for Laurie," she says.

"Why do you hurt me?"

She ignores that and says, "Have someone drop the sample off at the Newark bureau office tomorrow, and I'll set it up. It'll take about five days."

"I need it faster."

"Oh, do you now? That's too bad," she says.

"Let me rephrase. Laurie needs it faster."

"I'll see what I can do."

I hand Laurie the phone, and she ends the call with Cindy very quickly.

"She'll do it for me," I say when she gets off. "She considers me a special friend. It might take five days, which is a problem. Finding Home was able to do it in three days. On the other hand, it probably goes faster when you're faking the results."

"What do you think we're going to find out?" she asks.

"Sorry, I'm out of hunches."

Dr. Patricia Brenner was good enough to take the day off to appear in court. She flew in from Portland late last night, so neither Hike nor I have had a chance to prep her. That shouldn't be a problem; I just want her to tell the jury what she told me in Bridgton.

I take her through her career, which basically consisted of going to veterinary school at Cornell and then heading back to her hometown and opening a practice. I can immediately tell she'll be an excellent witness; she has that "kindly country doctor" look about her, the kind of person you instinctively trust.

I show her and the jury three photographs of Teresa Mullins and ask if Brenner recognizes her. "Yes, I do," she says. "She brought in her dog to be treated." She's fudging the truth a bit, since when we originally showed her the photo in Maine, she said she didn't recognize her. I don't think she's lying; rather I think her knowledge of the case is changing her recollection.

"What kind of dog?"

"A border collie."

"How many times did they come in?"

"Once."

"How can you be sure of your identification?"

"The dog had anahlichtia; it's a tick-borne disease." She then goes on to describe it, much as Dan Dowling had. "It was one of the first cases I'd ever treated; I've only had a handful since. It's difficult to diagnose, so I was pleased I was able to. That's why it was memorable."

"Did she use the name *Teresa Mullins*?"

"No. She gave her name as Linda Sanford."

"You're sure of that?"

She nods. "Positive. I brought the records with me."

Kelly aims his cross not on whether a border collie came in with that ailment but rather how Brenner can be sure that the person matched the photographs of Teresa Mullins.

She holds up quite well, and finally an exasperated Kelly says, "Don't you focus most of your attention on the patient? The dog?"

"Yes, but we're a friendly practice in a small town. I like to get to know my clients, so I schedule enough time to do so."

Kelly is very happy to get her off the stand. As for me, I liked her, and if she inspired as much respect and confidence in the jury as she did with me, we did very well.

I would let her treat Tara. I can think of no higher praise.

Next up, briefly, is Janet Gallo, who works for Verizon. Hike had subpoenaed Linda Sanford's phone records, among many others, and Gallo is here to verify them.

I get her to explain the process by which a cell phone GPS works and how the phone company can trace where a phone has been, even after the fact. The jury actually perks up when they hear this; I don't think most of them knew that Big Brother is always watching.

We introduce the records for a phone originally purchased in Brunswick, Maine, by Linda Sanford. Using maps, I get Gallo to say that the Linda Sanford phone was at the location of the Tara Foundation twenty minutes before Willie and Sondra found Cody.

I take this time to introduce records of the death of the real Linda Sanford and how a new driver's license had been issued to signal her resurrection. I let Gallo read it into the record; anyone could have done so.

Kelly's cross-examination correctly avoids challenging the science. "Ms. Gallo, is it your testimony that a person known as Linda Sanford was in that location at that time?"

"No, I am saying that her phone was there."

"So anyone could have been carrying it?"

"That's correct," she says.

"Do you have any independent knowledge that Linda Sanford and Teresa Mullins might be the same person?"

"I do not."

"So your testimony is simply that you believe a cell phone belonging to someone named Linda Sanford, regardless of who she is or who was carrying the phone, was there that day? Am I accurately describing it?" Kelly asks.

"Almost."

"Where was I wrong?"

"You said that I *believe* it to be the case. It's more than my belief. It's a fact."

Lunch today is a three-person affair . . . me, Hike, and Billy, the South Carolina police chief that became Hike's big buddy in the course of about twenty minutes.

Billy, whose full name is William Eason III, is not what I expect. In my biased Northern mind, I expected an overweight, loud sheriff who would be at his most comfortable chasing Burt Reynolds down country roads or arresting Vinny's cousin.

Instead, Billy stands six two and wouldn't push the scales past 170. He's got movie star looks, a gentle, friendly way about him, and an understated manner.

I take him through his testimony, but it proves to be unnecessary. Hike has already spoken to him about it, and he's completely on the same page as we are.

Pod Hike is at the lunch with us. Apparently, just the mere presence of a South Carolinian turns Hike into an affable, friendly, optimistic guy. He's cracking jokes, all of which sends Billy into gales of laughter.

When Billy says *Hike,* it comes out as *Haahyyk,* and at one point he says, "*Haahyyk* must keep you boys just rolling on the floor all day."

I nod. "He's a laugh a minute."

On the stand, Billy is a pro. He tells the jury that he had seen Linda Sanford in town a number of times, on occasion with the border collie. He says that there is no doubt that the woman he is talking about matches the photographs of Teresa Mullins. I also introduce the photograph taken at the Rotary event.

"Where is she today?" I ask.

"She's deceased; she died in a fire in her cabin soon after she got back to town."

"What was the cause of the fire?"

"Our fire investigators determined it was arson. We've got ourselves a murder investigation going on."

Later, after court when we are saying our good-byes, Billy points to Hike and says, "You need to send this boy down our way more often."

"I think that can be arranged," I say.

"Wish we could take him off your hands, permanent-like," he says.

I nod. "Make me an offer."

Laurie has some good news for me when I return from walking Tara and Sebastian this afternoon. "Cindy called," she says. "Apparently, they got a good, quality sample from the pacifier, so they may be able to shave a day or two off the estimate."

"She'll do anything to please me," I say.

She ignores that and repeats what she and I have been thinking since we learned that the James Ware ID from Finding Home was faked, that we can't understand what they'd have to gain by faking it.

"Maybe learning who the parents are will give us the answer," I say. "If they weren't hiding something, they wouldn't have given us wrong information."

"Wouldn't it be nice if the father was Renny Kaiser?" she asks. "That would help to tie things together rather neatly."

I'm not sure why I hadn't had that thought before. I know Kaiser has kids; what if some crazy set of circumstances led him to find out that it was a child who he'd fathered that Jill Hickman had adopted?

"That's worth checking out," I say, and I head to my checking-out place of choice: Google.

I type in *Renny Kaiser,* and I get sixty-one thousand results. I glance through a few pages of them, and none of the articles talk about him as a drug dealer or scumbag of a human being. Rather, they're about his business successes, and especially his philanthropy.

I click on *Images,* and there are hundreds of photographs of good old Renny. A half dozen or so include his family, usually when they are attending some charity event together. There are two male children in the photographs; one looks to be about twelve years old, and the other perhaps two years old.

I check the date on the photographs, and they are a year old. Which would make the younger child about three now.

Dylan Hickman's age.

Laurie is looking over my shoulder, and she says, "We can't be that lucky, can we?"

"I'm not even sure what it would mean," I say.

"The most important thing it would mean

is Dylan has been found and is healthy," she says, always looking at the big picture.

She gets the photo of Teresa and baby Dylan to see if we can determine whether he and Kaiser's son look the same, but we can't tell anything. Dylan is just too young in the baby picture; his features are not really formed yet.

"I'm looking forward to seeing that DNA report," she says, "although Kaiser may well not be in the database."

I nod. "If it shows that the father is not in the database, I will get Kaiser's DNA if I have to take the swab myself."

It doesn't pay for me to think of the implications of Renny Kaiser being the father, especially since it doesn't seem to make sense on any level.

Well, maybe on one level. Steve Emmonds and Finding Home faked the DNA tests in an effort that must have been to prevent us from learning the true parents. Renny Kaiser calls the shots at Finding Home.

If there's something that Kaiser doesn't want me to know, then I really want to know it.

Hurry up, Cindy.

David Browning is a vice president at the Passaic Bank and Trust. He's here to testify about Teresa Mullins's financial situation. We subpoenaed the information legally, and lo and behold, it matched the information that Sam had gotten illegally.

"Mr. Browning, how long did Teresa Mullins have an account with your bank?"

"Just two months."

"She opened it when she moved here?"

"Apparently. I have no independent knowledge as to when she actually moved."

"How much money did she deposit to open the account?"

"Two hundred and seventy dollars. In cash."

"Tell us about her deposit and withdrawal history, please," I say after I introduce the relevant documents into evidence.

"It was relatively uneventful for six weeks. Her balance never dipped below two hundred dollars and never went above six hundred and seventy. Then, six weeks after she opened the account, she received a wire transfer."

"For how much?"

"Seven hundred and fifty thousand dollars."

I can see some members of the jury react in surprise, which is very much what I wanted. "Where did it come from?" I ask.

"A bank in the Cayman Islands. The account information on the sender was sealed; we cannot access it."

"Did she withdraw any of that money?"

He nods. "She wrote a check to Lincoln Medical; it's a company in Maine. The check was for seventy thousand dollars, and the notation on it said, 'For Hospice Care.' "

I introduce documents that we got from Lincoln Medical showing that Martha Mullins, Teresa's mother, was a patient there, and that this payment was for her care. Ms. Mullins has since passed away.

"What did she do with the rest of the money?" I ask.

"She wired the remainder to another bank and then closed the account with us."

"Whom did she wire it to?" I ask.

"Linda Sanford."

I have no more questions for Browning,

and Kelly doesn't even try to make a dent in him. The facts are the facts, and even if the jury is half-asleep, they have to accept the fact that Teresa Mullins and Linda Sanford are one and the same person and that both of them are dead.

My next — and most important — witness is Pete Stanton. It's probably the first time he has ever been key to a defense case, and I'm sure it's weird for him. It's probably like playing for the same sports team for fifteen years and then getting traded and having to go to the visitors' locker room when you come back to play the original team.

I don't have to establish Pete's position and background, because he already did so when he testified as part of the prosecution's case. So I can get right to it.

"Welcome back, Captain Stanton. You testified earlier that you were in charge of the investigation into the abduction of Dylan Hickman. Is that correct?"

"Yes."

"And would you say that Teresa Mullins was a very important witness in that investigation?"

"Yes."

I have him read portions of her testimony aloud. I don't need it to conduct my direct

313

examination, but I want it in the record.

"So she voluntarily implicated Mr. Wachtel and identified him as the assailant, correct?"

"Yes."

"You didn't prompt her by mentioning his name first?"

"I did not."

"And it was her testimony that led you to obtain the warrant?" I want the jury to hear the answer, but more importantly, I want to get it into the record.

If we lose the case, I want to reserve the ability to appeal based on the idea that the warrant was based on a lie and the fruits of it should be inadmissible. It won't work, because as long as the police in good faith believed her at the time, then the search warrant will stand up. But I'd try it anyway.

"It was."

"Her testimony as you just read it was that the abductor took the dog as well. Is that also what she said to you at the crime scene?"

"Yes."

"She was positive it did not just run off as a stray?"

"She said she was certain of it."

I'm doing most of the talking, but at least

314

Pete's short answers have been the right ones.

"Did I come to you last month and tell you that I believed Teresa Mullins was missing?"

"You did, and you presented some evidence that it might be under suspicious circumstances."

"Did you commence an investigation?"

"An informal one. At that point, I would say I began looking into it. It seemed curious."

"Did you find Ms. Mullins?"

"We did not."

"Did you do any testing to determine whether the dog left at the foundation building was Cody, the dog that was taken during this crime?"

"Yes. It is the same dog."

"Are you familiar with the prior testimony in the defense portion of this trial?"

"I believe I am."

"I am talking about all the evidence submitted showing that Teresa Mullins abandoned Cody at the rescue foundation, that she has been in possession of him all along, that she received a huge amount of money at the time of her testimony, that she changed her identity, and that she has subsequently become a murder victim."

He nods. "I am aware of it. Much of it I confirmed independently."

"What is your professional assessment?"

"I believe Ms. Mullins lied to me and to the court, that she engineered her own disappearance, and that she was subsequently murdered."

"Thank you, Detective," I say. I should end it on the drama of that statement, but I realize that I forgot to bring something up. I mentally kick myself for it, but I need to fix it.

"One more thing, Captain Stanton. Did I tell you that I believed Teresa Mullins contacted Mr. Wachtel's former attorney, Stanley Butler, about a year ago?"

"Yes. Cell phone records confirmed that she did."

"Did Mr. Butler die soon after that?"

"Two weeks later in a car crash."

"Under suspicious circumstances?"

"It was originally ruled an accident due to the impairment of the driver. It is now being investigated as a murder."

His affirmative statement about disbelieving Teresa Mullins would have been a better way to finish his testimony, but this way Stanley Butler got his well-deserved day in court.

"Thank you, Captain," is what I say. What

we both know I mean is, "Thank you, Captain . . . the burgers and beer are on me."

I'm so focused on the case that I've almost forgotten a dangerous drug dealer wants to kill me. That is not the norm for me; usually, my personal safety is a priority. Of course, on Laurie's instructions, Marcus has been watching my back, which is rather comforting. Under Marcus's protection, I wouldn't be worried if the Kremlin wanted me dead.

On the other hand, it's not like Kaiser and I are going to line up at center ice after the trial for the traditional handshake. His desire to kill me will continue when the case is over, and Marcus cannot follow me forever.

I would love for events to transpire that would remove Kaiser as a threat. My first choice would be for him to get hit by a truck, but I don't have the guts or the truck to pull it off. My second choice would be for him to get arrested and go to prison for drug dealing, but I don't have the smarts or the evidence to pull that off. He's been successfully evading the authorities for a very long time.

Maybe I'll catch a break and the DNA test will show he's Dylan's father, and he can be arrested for kidnapping his own son. I think these kinds of thoughts are the textbook definition of grasping at straws, so my time is best served getting back to focusing on the trial.

The key part of our case is over, and it's gone well. I think Teresa Mullins has been completely discredited. She lied when she identified Keith; there's no doubt about that. But it's a jump from there to finding him not guilty; there's other evidence against him.

Having said that, I'm feeling pretty good as I head into the final phase of the case. I want to attack the remaining evidence as best I can and do some work on Keith's character.

Keith asks me if I think he should testify, and I say that I absolutely do not. He agrees, a change in attitude from the way he felt as the trial was about to begin. I assume he's pleased with the way things are going as well.

My next witness is Richard Eddington, a

forensic scientist who will testify about the presence of the dog hair in Keith's apartment. As an expert witness, he's costing me $5,000 for this appearance, which pretty much eats up the one-dollar retainer that Keith gave me.

This trial has not been a profit-making enterprise, but I can't in good conscience skimp and hurt Keith's chances of getting his life back.

Eddington talks about transference, how the amount of dog hair found is consistent with Keith having contacted the dog previously and then brought the hairs home with him on his clothes. He's my own witness, but I think he's full of it. I think the hairs were planted there.

Kelly does an effective job on cross, making the point that the hairs were found in the den and front hall, logical places for Keith to have entered the house with Cody and kept him for a brief time. There were none in the bedroom, where Keith theoretically would have changed his clothes and transferred more hair than in any other room.

My final witness is Thomas Holiday, who worked at Finding Home as the number-two chemist under Keith, back in the day. He's a supporter of Keith's and has contacted me a number of times with offers to serve as a character witness.

"Keith was a company guy all the way," Holiday says. "He was the first one in the office in the morning and the last one out. His work was really important to him, and he tried to instill it in everyone under him."

"So you never saw evidence of him doing anything unethical, like stealing confidential documents?"

"No. I thought it was bull when I heard about it, and I think it's bull now. And the worst part of it was that just when the company was about to take off, they cut him loose. And then they cut us loose."

I don't want to get into the mass layoffs after Keith left, because it could lead the jury to think that Holiday is just a disgruntled ex-employee testifying to stick it to Finding Home.

But he is not to be deterred, and he launches into a mini-rant about how they've doubled the staff at Finding Home yet won't rehire any of their former loyal employees. "I've got a friend in payroll who tells me they're working around the clock there," he says with obvious and probably justified annoyance.

Once Holiday is off the stand, Judge Moran asks me to call my next witness, forcing me to say something that I hate to say, because once it's out of my mouth, I can't get it back.

"Your Honor, the defense rests."

Kelly tells Judge Moran that he wants to call one witness in his rebuttal case, and that is a local psychotherapist named Karen Abernathy. She's testified in a number of my cases in the past, and always on the side of the prosecution.

"Ms. Abernathy, you are familiar with the circumstances of the crime in this case?"

"I am," she says. "Both from newspaper reports and from some documents you sent me."

"So you know that there has been testimony that Teresa Mullins changed her identity?"

"Yes."

"Does that surprise you?"

"Definitely not. She was involved in a terribly tragic, terribly stressful event. Even though it might seem illogical, she very likely could blame herself for not adequately protecting that poor child. She would want to escape the memory of that, and the ultimate escape is to forget who she is. Not only would she want to remove herself from the spotlight, from the attention of others, but she might literally want to erase herself entirely and start over."

"And if she somehow came into possession of the dog that was abducted . . . let's say hypothetically that the kidnappers let the dog loose, and he was able to return to a human that he was familiar with and loved . . . is it surprising that she would not report this event to authorities?"

"No, that is also consistent with the state of mind as I described it. Coming forward would remove the anonymity that she clearly coveted and reopen the wound. And this way, she could protect the dog in a way she could not protect the child.

"She was clearly in great pain. People in such pain do not always act the way we would like them to or the way we believe we would act in a similar situation."

On cross-examination, I start with, "Ms. Abernathy, you're essentially saying that the mind is a powerful thing, and the mind of Teresa Mullins caused her to behave in ways that we might find strange?"

"Exactly," she says.

"Let's examine just how strong a mind can be, shall we? For example, can the power of the mind conjure up seven hundred and fifty thousand dollars in a wire transfer from the Cayman Islands?"

"Certainly not."

"Teresa Mullins was murdered; someone set fire to her cabin. Is that a result of the power of her mind?"

"I'm not familiar with all the circumstances of that event."

"You say that she was racked with guilt. Is it possible that there could be another reason for her guilt? Perhaps that she incriminated an innocent person? Is that possible?"

"Anything is possible."

"Thank you. No further questions."

Judge Moran takes center stage, telling the jury what will be happening next in the trial. "The cases in chief have been concluded," he says, "and I would like to personally thank you for your attentiveness, concentration, and effort. I know it has been a long haul and that what you're doing is not easy.

"Tomorrow will be devoted to closing arguments; then you will have the weekend off before beginning deliberations on Monday. I will be offering what we call a charge before that happens, and that basically means we will talk about what is expected of you.

"For now, as always, do not talk to anyone about the trial, including among yourselves. And do not put yourself in a position where you might get exposure to any media coverage. Thank you again."

He adjourns court, and Keith leans over to me and says, "Man, you did a great job.

If this doesn't go well, it's sure not your fault."

"Think in terms of it going well," I say.

"I'll try. But either way, you were worth every penny."

At least he smiles when he says it.

As the bailiff is heading over to get Keith and take him back into custody, I notice that Laurie is standing in the back of the courtroom. It's unusual that she's here, especially since she hadn't told me she was coming.

She motions that she wants to talk to me, so I excuse myself to Keith and head back there. When I get there, she pulls me to the side a bit so that no one can hear what we are saying, although the courtroom has mostly emptied out.

"What's going on?" I ask. "Is something wrong?"

"Cindy just called me with the results of the DNA test. There's an ID for one of the parents."

I don't like the look on her face or the sound of her voice, so I gird myself for bad news.

"What did it say?"

"Dylan Hickman's father is Keith Wachtel."

I feel like Marcus just hit me in the

326

stomach. I instinctively look over and see Keith being led out of court by the bailiff. He's looking at Laurie and me, and when he sees me look over, he smiles and waves.

I don't wave back.

It's not often that I am completely baffled. Actually, it happens a lot, but this feels like a level beyond baffled. I feel like I've entered another dimension, and I forgot to bring my power to reason with me.

Keith Wachtel is Dylan Hickman's father. DNA tests don't lie, or at least they don't lie when it isn't Finding Home performing them.

The mother is not in the registry, which is a shame, because that is important. Keith was in the process of breaking up with Jill around that time, so theoretically it could be her.

But that makes no sense. It would mean that the mother of the child adopted him, and the father then was convicted of kidnapping him. That's not how it usually works. Usually parents that have a child that they want tend to just keep that child.

Also, Jill was never pregnant, which is

basically a prerequisite for giving birth to a baby.

Keith openly admitted to me that he had a few affairs around the same time. Could one of them be the mother without Keith knowing it? That would mean that Keith's child just happened to be adopted by Jill, his ex-fiancée and employer? That doesn't just violate the no-coincidence rule; it obliterates it.

In fact, the no-coincidence rule basically eliminates any chance that Keith does not know he is Dylan's father. It would mean that he first impregnated a woman that did not tell him about it. Then she abandoned the baby, after which he happened to be adopted by Keith's former fiancée. Then that child was kidnapped, and Keith happened to be accused of the crime.

Not possible.

If Keith did know, then it still leaves many questions unanswered. Did he somehow arrange for Jill to adopt the baby? Did he know she was interested in adopting a child, and did he then mention this one to her?

But if he wanted the child enough to kidnap it, why not keep him or adopt him in the first place? Why go through the process of convincing Jill to adopt him, without telling her the truth, if Keith wanted the baby himself?

And if this was all about Keith and his baby, then why did Renny Kaiser send Kyle Gillis after me? And why did they fake the DNA test in the first place? It couldn't have been to protect the mother, whoever she might be, because she isn't in the registry, and they of all people would know that.

And hovering above this all is the most important question: If Keith really was the abductor, then where the hell is Dylan Hickman? Could he have arranged the adoption by Jill and then start to hate her so much that he would abduct and kill him just to hurt her?

I do not want to believe that it is possible, yet the scary thing is that it seems the most likely of all the very unlikely scenarios I can come up with.

Ugh. Why the hell did I have to send in that stupid license renewal?

Which reminds me, I have a couple of legal considerations here. Fortunately, even though this is probably damaging to my client, I do not have to disclose this information to Kelly. If the reverse were true, and he came up with information that was exculpatory for Keith, he would be under an obligation to give it to me.

The question is, do I tell Keith what we've

learned? At this point, there's a downside to that and little, if any, upside. An example of the former would be that it might prompt him into a confession on the abduction. If he did that, I would then be prohibited from proclaiming his innocence in my summation.

I can't see any situation in which his legal position would benefit from my telling him. And the moral issue doesn't really come into play here. If he knows the truth, then by delaying telling him, he's not deprived of anything. If he doesn't know, then waiting until after the trial seems to be rather insignificant.

Whether or when to tell Jill is another issue entirely, and I'll discuss that with Laurie. But since it could somehow expose Keith to legal jeopardy should Jill take precipitous action, that will have to wait until the trial is over.

I have my poker face on when I get to court this morning. I don't want Keith to sense that anything unusual is going on; I'd just as soon not have to lie.

The problem is that the last time I won in poker was in the seventh grade, playing one-on-one with Rita Tamber. I had a slight advantage in that she didn't know how to play, and I sort of told her that a pair of kings beat three fours because, you know, they are kings.

So as soon as I sit down, Keith asks me if there is anything wrong, and I lie and say no. I don't think he believes me; he's savvier than Rita was back then.

Kelly gets up to give his closing argument, which he prefaces with ten seconds of shaking his head sadly, as if he's disheartened by all this and wishes he didn't have to be a part of it.

"Teresa Mullins is a troubled person. I

say *is* instead of *was* because among the many things the defense didn't prove is that she became Linda Sanford and subsequently was the one who died in that fire. So I'm going to use *is,* because for our purposes here, let's hope and assume that Teresa is alive.

"But wherever she is now, I think we can all agree that 'troubled' is the unfortunately accurate way to describe her after that horrible day when Dylan Hickman was quite literally snatched from her arms.

"It's important to know that no evidence was presented to show that Teresa had any emotional difficulties before that day, no ties to criminals, no history of doing anything but being a loving daughter and a wonderful nanny. Yet Mr. Carpenter would have you believe that she turned her back on her whole life to participate in some evil criminal conspiracy.

"But let's take some of the defense evidence, unproven and speculative as it is, and let's give it the benefit of the doubt. Let's say that Teresa Mullins became Linda Sanford and was later murdered.

"You've heard from a respected psychologist that her behavior made perfect sense for someone who had gone through the trauma that Teresa Mullins absorbed. She wanted to escape the world and escape herself. Perfectly understandable to a professional in psychology.

"And the murder of Linda Sanford, or Teresa Mullins, or whoever that was? Again, let's assume it was Teresa Mullins. In her pain, had she turned to drugs? Might that have brought her into contact with people who might kill? Who knows? We have heard nothing about her life.

"But Mr. Carpenter would have you believe that somehow it was the abductors that murdered her. Is that logical? He first tells us that they were her collaborators in the crime, that they were on the same side.

"If they wanted her dead, if they were afraid of what she might know or tell, why wait three years to kill her? She had already given up the dog; if that was a sign that she was going to turn on them, why hadn't she done so fully? All she did was give up a dog; she hardly pointed out the real bad guys to the authorities.

"If they went down to South Carolina to kill her, it means they knew where she lived. So why did they wait until then to do it? Why was she all of a sudden a threat to them? Because she gave up a dog?

"Teresa Mullins was telling the truth back then, and how do we know that? Because of the other evidence that corroborated her story. And because Keith Wachtel hated Jill Hickman.

"You've heard witnesses that said he felt betrayed by her. She threw him out of her house, and then she threw him out of her company. He wanted to hurt her in any way he could, and he did so in the worst way possible: he took her child from her.

"The police believed Teresa Mullins, the previous jury believed Teresa Mullins, and they were right to do so.

"Thank you for listening, and thank you for your service."

I get up to give the defense statement; I need to focus and do my best, but for a second I fantasize about opening with "Keith Wachtel is the real father of Dylan Hickman." That might shake things up a bit.

Instead I say, "Ladies and gentlemen, I too thank you for your service."

We lawyers really appreciate jurors before they render a verdict. Afterward, if they've voted against us, we would be fine if they all held hands and jumped off the Empire State Building.

"I told you when this trial started that Teresa Mullins lied in her testimony against Keith Wachtel. I also told you that we would prove it, and we did.

"We proved that she had the dog, and how could she have done that if she was not involved with the perpetrators of the crime? We proved that she went into hiding. She didn't just change her name; she took extraordinary steps to disappear from the planet.

"We proved that she was murdered, just days after giving up the dog. Is that a coincidence?

"And even though we don't have to prove or even show motive, we gave that to you as well. She received a fortune for her participation in this conspiracy, to help her ailing mother and to allow her to disappear forever.

"The rest is all smoke and mirrors; without Teresa Mullins's perjured testimony, Keith Wachtel would never even have been charged. For what — for having dog hair and a few strands of fiber in his house and car? For resenting the employer that fired him? You've heard testimony that Finding Home fired their entire chemistry staff. Don't you think they felt resentful? Why not charge all of them with murder?

"We don't know what happened to Dylan Hickman, and his disappearance is an unimaginable tragedy for his mother and for us as a society. Whoever took him should be punished; Mr. Kelly wants that, I want that, Mr. Wachtel wants that, and I'm sure you want that.

"But it does not help to punish the wrong person; it only increases the tragedy. It ruins a life that doesn't deserve to be ruined; that is obvious. But it does something else, something insidious. It tells the authorities that they have solved the crime, that the bad guy is locked up.

"But Keith Wachtel is not a bad guy, and he is certainly not *the* bad guy. Locking him up will only leave the real perpetrator out on the street, unworried, and free to strike again.

"Nobody gains from that. Everybody loses.

"Do the right thing, please. Thank you."

Judge Moran gives the jury their charge and sends them off. Once the jury and judge have left, Keith tells me what a great job I did.

"We need to talk," I say, making the decision in the moment.

"Okay. When?"

"Now. Right now."

I tell the bailiff that I'll need a few minutes with Keith in the anteroom. It's common practice; he'll wait outside until we're done.

As soon as we get in there, Keith asks, "What's wrong? Did something happen in there that I didn't pick up on?"

"Not in there. What happened is that we ran another test on Dylan's DNA."

"What did it show?"

"That you're the father."

He looks stunned. As an accomplished reader of facial expressions and reactions, I can quickly narrow it down to two possibilities: he's either stunned or faking being stunned.

"That's ridiculous. It's not possible."

I don't say anything, so he adds, "Did you do it through Finding Home again? Because they —"

"The FBI did it for us. They have a tendency to be accurate in matters like this."

"Let me think about this for a minute," he says. "There has to be an explanation."

I nod. "I'll wait."

"You think I knew about this?"

"I don't know; it's certainly a possibility."

"What would I have to gain from concealing that?" he asks. "And why would I kidnap my own son?"

Again, I don't say anything; I find that in situations like this I can accomplish a hell of a lot more by listening.

"Andy, I had no idea of this, and I don't know how it could be real. I'm at a loss."

I'd better be careful here, because I may be starting to believe him. "So let's put aside the question of whether you knew or not," I say. "Let's focus on who the mother might be. Could it be Jill?"

He shakes his head. "No. First of all, she wasn't pregnant, at least not to my knowledge. But why would she abandon her child and then adopt him?"

"I agree," I say. "So who else? You said you had affairs. How many?"

"Three women. But I was always careful."

"Not careful enough, apparently."

"Andy, I father a child, the woman abandons him without telling me he even exists, and then Jill winds up adopting him? Come on."

"Give me the names of the three women," I say.

"I'll try, but I'm not even sure I remember them; these were not exactly long, idyllic romances. What will you do with them?"

He's asking a good question; the truth is I have no plan for what to do. "I'm not sure."

"Are you just going to look them up and say, 'Hey, did you have a baby and give him up?' Why would they tell you, and what would you accomplish?"

"Here's what I might accomplish," I say. "It might get me one step closer to figuring out what the hell happened and where that kid is. If it doesn't, it doesn't, but at least I'll have tried."

He nods. "Okay."

"The truth is it doesn't matter for you," I say. "The trial is over; the jury is going to do what they are going to do, and you'll either walk or you won't. If you walk, then nothing I turn up can hurt you; they can't charge you again for the same crime."

"It matters plenty to me," he says, his voice a little softer.

"What does that mean?" I ask.

"When a child is lost, any child, that's terrible. But when it's your own, that's worse. I don't know that Dylan is my son, but if he is, that's worse, and it's different. It just is."

Keith just moved up a notch in my mind. He could still be lying through his teeth, but it doesn't feel like it.

I send him off with the bailiff, but I stay in the room to think. The fact is that my work as a lawyer is over, at least for the time being, but I don't think I can leave it like this.

If Keith gets convicted, I'll think there is a good chance that an innocent man is in prison and that I've failed. If he gets acquitted, I'll think that there is a good chance I allowed a guilty man to walk, which would represent a different kind of failure.

Regardless of the outcome, it will be uniquely unsatisfying and upsetting.

I leave the room sure of one thing: I need to find out the truth.

"Andy, what the hell is going on?"

It's Jill on the phone; the stress level in her voice is off the charts. The clock on the night table says it's seven fifteen, and she's woken us up.

"What are you talking about?"

"It's all over the news. They're saying that Keith is Dylan's father?"

What I'm thinking is, *How the hell did this get out?* What I say is, "I just found out myself."

"How could you do this? How could you tell the media this?"

"I didn't, Jill. I don't know who did."

"Get a retraction out there, Andy. And it's not possible that Keith could be the father. This is terrible."

"Let me get into this, Jill. Try to relax. But a retraction won't fly, because Keith really is the father."

"That's crazy . . . it can't be; that makes

342

no sense. And I can't relax, Andy. How can I relax? You need to fix this."

Laurie is up and listening to my end of the conversation, so when I finally get Jill off the phone, I update her on what happened.

"I think she's more upset about the public relations side of this than the possibility that Keith is the father," I say. "And she says it couldn't be true."

We turn the news on, and sure enough, there it is. I have no idea how this could have gotten out, and there are limited possibilities. Only Laurie and I knew on our end, so our team didn't leak it. That leaves Keith, but I can't imagine why he would do it. If the jury were to find out, it would most likely hurt, not help, his cause.

The other possibility is an FBI leak, and I call Cindy. She has seen the report and doesn't know the source either, but I can tell she is afraid it's from her end. "A lot of our chemists know a lot of the chemists at Finding Home," she says. "So it's possible."

She says that she'll check into it but allows that "we may never know." She apologizes just in case, but I don't blame her. I should have been more specific with her about the secrecy of this.

The media starts calling, and we screen

all of them. When the message tape fills up, we erase it and it starts filling up again. Today is Saturday, so I have no court responsibility, which means I can spend all day trying to figure this thing out. I've got the same plan for tomorrow, with a three-hour break to watch the Giants game. Even in these troubled times, I do have my priorities.

I sit in the den with all the materials relating to the case. I find that the best way to proceed when I'm looking for answers is to just go over everything, as often as necessary. Sometimes I can read the same document five times without seeing something that jumps out at me on the sixth reading.

But not this time. I spend three hours getting nowhere. Nothing strikes me; I have no new insights. After I read all the documents, I look at the crime scene photographs, and still nothing.

Then I get to the selfie that was in among Stanley Butler's photographs, the one of Teresa Mullins and little Dylan in his stroller. I look at it to see if I can see any of Keith in Dylan's face. Laurie and I had done the same thing when we entertained the thought that the father might be Renny Kaiser, so I bring the photo in to Laurie to ask her if she sees Keith in it.

She looks but says, "He's just too small, Andy. He's an infant."

She's right about that, but just how right is she? "How old do you think Dylan is in this picture?" I ask.

"I don't know," she says. "Maybe a few weeks? A month?"

"Does Brian have office hours today?" I ask. Brian Rubenstein is Ricky's pediatrician and also the father of Will Rubenstein, Ricky's best friend.

"I don't know. He alternates every other Saturday with Dr. Zander."

Laurie calls and learns that Brian is actually off today and at home, but going out. When I tell him I have something urgent to show him, he responds that he's heading in our direction, so he'll stop by.

Fifteen minutes later, Brian is in our house, and I show him the selfie. "How old is the child in that photograph?"

He studies it for at least a minute and says, "Maybe two weeks. Three at the most."

"Are you sure?" I ask.

"Am I sure? I'm a pediatrician, Andy," he says, smiling. "Would I ask you if you were sure something was a tort or a deposition? Actually, I wouldn't bet my life on it, but I doubt very much that I'm wrong."

I thank Brian, who leaves probably thinking that I'm nuts, and I call Pete Stanton. "Do you have Stanley Butler's computer?" I ask, assuming that they impounded it as part of their investigation.

"We do. But there was nothing on it we could use."

"I need to borrow it," I say.

"For what?"

"So I can find the bad guys and turn them over to you on a silver platter."

He resists but finally agrees, so I call Sam and ask him to pick it up from the precinct and bring it over. Two hours later, Sam and the computer are in the house.

"Look at this photograph," I say, showing him the selfie.

"What about it?"

"That's on printer paper, right? This would have been printed out?"

"Unless it was color copied."

I hadn't thought of that; if that is the case, this whole thing has been a waste of time.

"Sam, I think . . . I hope . . . that this photograph was e-mailed to Stanley Butler. If it was, then it's on that computer. Can you find it?"

"If it's in iPhoto, it'll take two minutes. If not, then longer. But if he downloaded it, I'll find it. If it's in e-mail, but he didn't download it, then we're out of luck without his e-mail password."

Laurie and I leave him alone to look, and thirty minutes later, he calls out, "I got it." We go in there, and he adds, "It wasn't in iPhoto, but it was downloaded." He points to the computer. "There it is."

Sure enough, the photograph is there, on the screen. Now I ask the question I should have asked earlier. "Is there a time stamp on it? Is there any way to tell when it was taken?"

Sam looks at me with a half frown on his face. "You really don't know anything about this stuff, do you?"

"Obviously not," I say. "Does that question mean you can't do it? Or you can?"

"Of course I can." Then he starts talking about "right-clicking" and "get info" and all kinds of other stuff, none of which I care about or understand. His final sentence is, "Do you also want to know where the photo was taken?"

"How can you tell that?"

Another frown, some more gibberish, at the end of which I understand that in addition to finding when it was taken, he can learn the latitude and longitude of the location at which it was taken. It is as accurate as a GPS.

What a world.

Within two minutes, we have the date, and five minutes after that, the street address.

There can no longer be any doubt; the selfie that Teresa Mullins took with Dylan Hickman was taken two weeks *before* he was abandoned and adopted by Jill Hickman.

I believe that Jill Hickman is both Dylan's natural and adoptive mother. That has to be a first. But it's the only solution I can come up with, so I'm sticking with it.

It is inconceivable to me that Teresa Mullins had or was caring for an infant, and then after giving it up and having it adopted by Jill, was coincidentally hired by Jill to care for it. And then throw in the fact that Keith is the father of that child and that Teresa was the witness against him, and it becomes too ridiculous to contemplate.

The only possible explanation that makes any sense at all is that Jill had the baby but for some reason didn't want that fact to be known by anyone. So she must have hired Teresa to care for it, all along planning to engineer an abandonment and adoption of her own child.

Just because I don't know why she would do that doesn't mean that she didn't.

"Nobody knew that Jill was pregnant," Laurie points out.

I nod. "I've been thinking about that. Maybe she didn't show until fairly late, and then she was able to cover it with the right kind of clothing. Then, when she couldn't do that anymore, she went off to Europe, apparently to raise money. Remember? She was gone for more than two months, and maybe the baby was born early."

"It's possible," Laurie allows, which I interpret as full-fledged agreement with my point of view. "But why hide the fact that she had the child if she was ultimately going to adopt him anyway?"

"I don't know. Maybe she didn't want Keith to be part of her life as the father. Or more likely an entirely different reason that we can't figure out."

"This would tend to explain why Finding Home lied about the DNA test; they must have known and were covering up for Jill."

I nod. "Right. And Jill had called Steve Emmonds to clear the way for his running the test. She could have told them to fake it then. This makes it much more likely that Keith was telling the truth, that he didn't know he was the father."

"But it doesn't explain other things," Laurie says. "Like why Renny Kaiser sent that guy after you. He doesn't seem to have a role in this at all."

Just then the phone rings. It's Rita Gordon, the court clerk, informing me that Judge Moran wants to meet with counsel before the start of the court day on Monday. The meeting is to be in his chambers.

"Did he say why?" I ask.

"I think if you turn on the news you might get a clue."

I tell Laurie what the call was about, and she asks the legal implications of the news of Keith's paternity getting out.

"Hard to say," is my weak response. "It should have no evidentiary impact, because that part of the trial is over. Kelly or I could petition the judge to reopen it, but I know I won't, and I doubt that he would. It's just not clear how this cuts, and it presents too many land mines."

"So what would the judge want to talk about?"

"I would think the jury, and whether or not they have seen anything about this. They're supposed to be avoiding it, but you know how that goes. A mistrial is a possibility if either Kelly or I push for it."

"Would you?"

I think about it for a moment. "I might; I'd have to talk to Keith first. I don't think

Kelly would want one, but you never know."

"So what's the next step, team leader?"

"Let's check out the address Sam gave us for where this photo was taken."

Laurie calls Nancy, who again comes over to watch Ricky, dollar signs dancing in her head. As we're about to leave, an upset Jill calls again, and Laurie unsuccessfully tries to talk her down off the ledge. She doesn't tell her about our suspicions, though we are going to have to do that sooner or later.

The address where the photo was taken turns out to be a large two-story apartment building down the street from an industrial complex in Englewood. The sign outside describes them as corporate apartments, available for long-term rentals. Obviously, companies put their out-of-town employees up here when they are going to be staying for a while, perhaps when they're relocating to the area but haven't found a place to live yet.

We seek out the manager, a guy by the name of Peter Wallman. We show him the photo of Teresa and Dylan and ask him if they'd ever stayed here.

He shrugs. "Doesn't ring a bell, but a lot of people stay here."

"Can you look up her name?" I ask. "It's either Teresa Mullins or Linda Sanford."

"She has two names?"

"It's a long story."

"Okay, when did you say she was here?"

I give him the dates, and he looks it up on his computer but comes up empty. "But that doesn't mean anything," he says. "Many of the people that stay here aren't in the computer; in fact, most of them aren't. We go by the company that booked them; that's who pays the bills."

I ask him to look up Finding Home and Jill Hickman, but that draws blanks also, so we thank him for his time and leave. I still think that Teresa stayed here with Dylan; she or Jill just concealed it well.

"I think it's time we talked to Jill," I say.

"What are we hoping to accomplish?"

"To find out what the hell really happened."

"Is this still in your role as Keith's lawyer?"

"More in my role as superhero defender of truth and justice."

She nods. "I'll hold your cape. But first I'll call Jill."

Laurie dials Jill on the car phone, so that it will be on speaker and we both can hear.

"Jill, Andy and I are coming over to talk to you."

"Enough talking," Jill says, panic in her voice. "I need this story corrected."

"What are you afraid of?"

"Afraid? I'm not afraid of anything. Keith is not the father, and I don't want anyone to think that he is."

"Keith *is* the father, Jill. We know that. And we also know that you are Dylan's natural mother. That's why we are coming over to talk."

"That's crazy!"

"Jill," Laurie says, calmly and patiently, "I'm not telling you what we think. I'm telling you what we know. You need to talk to us and tell us what is going on before it's too late."

There is a long pause, and the silence probably stretches to fifteen seconds. Believe me when I tell you it feels longer than that.

"Okay," she says, and I can almost see her sag through the phone. "Come on over. We can talk."

Unless Jill changes her mind in the next twenty-five minutes, this should be quite a meeting. On the way there, Keith calls me from the prison and is not exactly calm and composed himself. He's been made aware that the story of his fatherhood is out there in the world, and he obviously wants to know what effect this might have on the trial.

I tell him the truth, straight out, which is that I don't have the slightest idea. For some reason, he doesn't find that calming.

I still haven't had a chance to pursue any wrongdoing possibilities by Renny Kaiser and Finding Home; events have just been coming too fast and furious on the trial front. At this point, I don't see that whatever they are doing has anything to do with Keith's case, so it has to remain on the back burner. For now.

In the car, Laurie asks, "Do you think she

knows what happened to Dylan and where he is?"

"It's certainly a possibility," I say. "She lied about the birth, about the abandonment and adoption, and there is a very good chance she was a party to getting Teresa Mullins to lie about who kidnapped him. Why would she all of a sudden start telling the truth about where he is?"

"You think she engineered the kidnapping?"

"Certainly could be. Teresa worked for her; she cared for the baby well before Jill adopted him. It's hard to see Teresa lying about Keith being the abductor without Jill knowing about it. But I'm not sure about it, and hopefully we're about to find out."

We arrive at Jill's Derrom Avenue house, parking across the street because there is already another car parked in front of it. Laurie and I both get out and start to cross the street when I hear a sound. It's not that loud, sort of like a firecracker that might have gone off under a mattress.

"That's a gunshot, Andy," Laurie says, total certainty in her voice. I barely have time to register what she has said when a man comes out the front door of Jill's house and starts to head down the fairly long flight of stairs to the street.

He sees us instantly and stops running down the steps. The reason he stops is so that he can aim better. He has a gun in his hand, and it's pointing in our direction.

In the moment, I do the most courageous thing I have ever done in my life, though there is admittedly not a lot of competition for that honor. I turn my body and lunge toward Laurie, hoping to protect her from the bullet. At the same time, I don't take my eyes off the shooter, who I can see clearly, and almost in slow motion, start to pull the trigger.

My courageous action execution needs some work, as I come up short. I dive and don't quite reach Laurie; all I really wind up protecting is a manhole cover in the center of the street.

It's just as well. I hear the gunshot, and after quickly determining that no bullet has entered my body, I look and see that it is Laurie that fired the shot. She must have drawn her gun the instant she heard the gunshot from the house. I had other considerations on my mind, like trying to avoid pissing in my pants.

I get up and turn toward the shooter in time to see him reach the bottom step, headfirst. He doesn't move when he reaches the bottom, and a second later, Marcus is standing over him, making sure he isn't somehow a continuing threat.

Marcus has been protecting me, but this time he was a few seconds late. It's a good thing Laurie wasn't.

"Check him out, Marcus," Laurie says, now in full cop mode, running toward the house. Her gun is still drawn, no doubt out of concern that the downed shooter isn't alone.

Marcus goes over to the shooter and feels his neck for a pulse. He turns to me and gives the thumb-in-the-air "out" sign, like a baseball ump. I'm assuming he means "out" as in "out of the world of the living," because he then follows Laurie into the house.

So Marcus is in the house with Laurie, the shooter is sprawled dead at the bottom of the steps, and I'm on all fours on top of a manhole cover in the middle of the street, looking like a jerk. It is a role I am not unaccustomed to.

Finally, I get up and head toward the house. I'm in no hurry; I'm certainly not taking the steps two at a time. It doesn't take a genius to know what I'm going to find in there.

Mercifully, Laurie and Marcus are coming out as I reach the door. She's holding on to Cody by his collar, and it's a good sign that she has put her gun away. "Jill's dead," Laurie says. "One shot in the head. Not sure you want to go in there."

I'm sure I don't want to go in there, so instead I take out my cell phone and call Pete Stanton. I'm also sure that this street is going to be filled with cops in seconds anyway; there must be some neighbors who heard or witnessed the shootout at the Derrom Avenue corral.

"Pete, you might want to get over to Jill Hickman's house. We've got two dead bodies, one of which is hers."

"Shit," is his eloquent response. Then, "Where's the shooter?"

"He's the other body."

"I'll be right there."

At that moment three squad cars screech to a halt in the street in front of Jill's house.

"Your cavalry is already here," I say.

"Does anyone ever get killed when you're not around?" Pete asks. "You're a real good-luck charm."

Click.

Laurie knows two of the cops on the scene, so they don't treat us like we're the killers. They start to ask questions, but we don't bother to answer; instead I just point to the arriving Pete Stanton. He'll be in charge and have enough questions all by himself.

"You guys okay?" Pete asks. I don't think he'd be so solicitous if it were just me and Marcus; it's Laurie's presence that has him acting concerned and respectful.

"We're fine," I say.

Pete points to the dead shooter on the ground. He has one bullet, right where his intact heart used to be. "Who put him down?"

"That would be me," Laurie says.

"Where were you when you fired?"

She points. "About five feet from our car."

He looks in that direction, then back at the shooter. "Not bad."

"I taught her well," I say.

"Yeah. Where's Jill Hickman?"

"Inside," Laurie says. "Doorway to the kitchen."

He nods. "Okay, you guys wait here."

There are already a bunch of cops inside, so he goes in to join them, maybe to make sure they don't tromp around on any evidence. But this is not a whodunit; the guy whodunit won't be doing it anymore.

I call Willie and ask him to come get Cody, and he's here within five minutes. He asks if we need his help for anything else, but we don't.

Pete comes out about ten minutes later and asks us to take him through it, showing us exactly where we were and what happened at each moment. It doesn't take long to do that; the whole thing had taken a matter of a few seconds.

Once we're done, he tells us that we'll need to go down to the station to answer questions and make our statements. It's a drill I'm getting all too used to.

Just as we're about to leave, Pete takes my arm and pulls me to the side. "Is Wachtel really the kid's father?" he asks.

"One hundred percent positive."

"Damn. Did he snatch the kid?"

I shake my head. "One hundred percent negative."

He frowns. "Look who I'm asking."

Three hours later, we're heading home. While we were at the station, Laurie had made some calls and arranged for Nancy to take Ricky to Will Rubenstein's house. He's going to sleep over there.

When we get home, I walk Tara and Sebastian, and Laurie goes with me. I don't think we say five words to each other; we're both lost in thought. In fact, I think the only thing I say the whole time is, "Sebastian, get that out of your mouth."

After the walk, Laurie and I sit in the den with glasses of wine. "Maybe you shouldn't have sent in that license renewal," she says.

"Now you come up with that?"

"I know, and you have a right to be annoyed. But we have a child now, and we can't have all this ugly stuff in our lives."

"We shield him from it pretty well."

"Maybe, but Ricky is smart, and so are the other kids. And they hear things. I can imagine someone coming up to Ricky during recess tomorrow and saying, 'Hey, I hear your mother killed somebody yesterday.'"

"I don't want to reverse the roles here," I say, "but we're on the right side of this. We're the good guys."

"I know," she says, not sounding convinced. Then, "You tried to save my life today."

I nod. "Just protecting the little woman."

"It was wonderful. Not very effective, but wonderful."

"I need to work on my technique," I say.

She puts her glass down and says, "I think your technique is fine." Then, "Let's go to bed."

"Now you're talking."

"The comment about technique and the one about going to bed were not related," she says.

"Oh, I was hoping they were."

"Will you hold me?"

"If I have to," I say. "I am your willing servant."

She sees the look in my eye and says, "That's all you're going to do for now."

"What about for later?"

"We can worry about later, later."

I nod. "That works."

Judge Moran conducts a formal hearing in the courtroom, rather than the planned meeting in chambers. It's a sign that Jill's murder has elevated the issue in his mind, and it certainly should. The jury is not present, nor are any media or members of the public. Just the judge, clerk, bailiff, attorneys, and Keith.

I spent about fifteen minutes alone with Keith at the defense table before this hearing and updated him on what has gone on. He knew, of course, that Jill had been killed. It dominated the news so much that it pushed the Keith-fatherhood story to the side.

What Keith didn't know, but which I told him, was my strong belief that Jill was Dylan's mother. Actually, it's more than a strong belief; Jill's reaction when Laurie confronted her about it makes it a certainty.

"So why would she have gone through

that whole adoption thing? Why not just have the baby and keep him?"

"Maybe this was her way of keeping you out of it? You wouldn't press to be a co-parent if you didn't know you were the father."

He shook his head. "No way she or anyone would go to those lengths for that," he says.

"You're probably right, but she was very upset when she heard that you were the father." Even as the words leave my mouth, I'm aware that they aren't completely true. Jill was more upset about the news getting out than the content of the news.

But more importantly, I just figured out what that means. I don't say anything, because Keith is not the one to say it to and because Mitch Kelly walks over to us.

"Some weekend," Kelly says, shaking my hand.

I nod and return the shake. "Some weekend," I say.

So far this is not exactly an Algonquin roundtable conversation.

"I'm glad you're okay," he says and then walks away.

I don't have time to ponder this sudden burst of humanity from the opposition, because Judge Moran is calling the hearing to order.

"Well, gentlemen, we have some new developments to ponder. I am obviously concerned about the effects all of this might have had on the jury, should they have been exposed to it. Can I have your comments?"

Keith told me before court that he did not want a mistrial under any circumstances, that he did not want to go through this again or sit in prison one day more than necessary.

"The defense has confidence that the jurors followed your directive, Your Honor. We think that the proper course is for the jury to begin their deliberations."

Kelly has the opposite view. "Your Honor, the media coverage this weekend was not just intense, it was in the nature of an onslaught. Even if the jurors in good faith tried to avoid it, I don't see how all of them could have."

"So what would your remedy be?" Judge Moran asks.

"Much as I hate to say it, I think a mistrial is called for. Justice demands it."

I think that Kelly is more worried about the effect Jill's murder will have on the jurors than the unmasking of Keith as Dylan's father. This is the second murder in the case — Teresa Mullins was the first — and both have happened while Keith has been in jail. It certainly sends the message that there are other bad guys out there, and if they could commit murder, they could commit a child abduction.

It's also possible that he's starting to get the idea that Keith might be innocent and that he's spent a hell of a long time putting the wrong man behind bars. Maybe he considers a mistrial less of a humiliation than a loss and not as much of a stab to his conscience as another win.

I can feel Keith flinch next to me when Kelly says the word *mistrial*. I stand and say, "Your Honor, I don't think we can just take for granted that the jurors have violated a court directive. Your Honor should at least question them individually before making that determination. And if one or two have been exposed, well, that's what we have alternates for."

Judge Moran agrees, and the jurors are brought into court individually. He has told us that he will do all the questioning, which is fine with me.

I'm feeling pretty confident here. The jurors are being asked if they violated repeated orders from the judge, and the judge has no way of knowing if they are telling the truth. If these jurors are dumb or honest enough to admit to it, they are too dumb and honest to serve.

Sure enough, they all turn out to be as pure as the driven snow. None of them saw or heard anything in the media; they all spent the weekend huddled in the cone of silence.

At this point, having agreed to go through this process, the judge has no basis to do anything other than move forward. So that's what he does, sending the jurors off to deliberate.

Which is good news for us, or bad news for us.

As always in these situations, we'll know when we know.

Just before the bailiff takes Keith away, he leans in and asks me the key question.

"Andy, with all that's gone on . . . do you know where my son is?"

I tell him that I don't.

But I do.

Once I'm home, I tell Laurie what I realized when I was talking to Keith. "I told Keith how upset Jill was to find out that he was the father. But like I told you, she was more upset that the news got out. And I think I've figured out why."

"Don't keep me in suspense," Laurie says.

"I think Jill has either known Keith was the father, or more likely knew there was a chance it was him. But she was upset that it was out in the media, because she just didn't want other people to know, or more likely, some specific person."

"Renny Kaiser?"

I nod. "Renny Kaiser."

"Where are you getting this from?" she asks, not buying into what I'm saying, at least not yet.

"The dark recesses of my mind. But it makes sense; hear me out, okay? She had to know that Keith might be the father, I mean, she was sleeping with him, right?"

"Clearly," Laurie says.

"So why was she so freaked out about it getting out? The embarrassment? That couldn't be it, because the stories didn't say that she was the mother. So she would have no reason to be embarrassed; what's the difference who the natural father of an abandoned and adopted baby turned out to be?

"The only reason to be so upset about the publicity saying Keith was the father is that she told someone else a different story, and now they were going to find out the truth."

"Keep going," Laurie says. "You're on a roll."

"I think she was sleeping with Renny Kaiser at the same time, and she wanted him to think that he was the father. She was using that information to get something, probably money to save her company. And the news report blew the whole scam out of the water; Renny was going to find out the truth."

Laurie nods. "Which explains her reaction."

"Right. You talked to her just like I did. Think about how she sounded. She wasn't just upset; she was afraid. Actually, forget *afraid;* she was in a panic."

"It turns out that she had a right to be,"

she says.

"Exactly. The person that she lied to about the fatherhood felt betrayed by it, so he killed her. Which brings us back to Renny Kaiser. You weren't far off when you said he was the father. Because the truth is that he thought he was the father."

Another nod from Laurie. "And that little boy living with the Kaisers is Keith and Jill's son, Dylan Hickman."

"I'd bet anything on it," I say. "Keith said he thought Jill was having an affair while they were still together, and she was. She was sleeping with Renny Kaiser, at the same time she was trying to get him to invest enough money to save her company."

"But why go through the charade of adopting the baby and then having it abducted? Why couldn't Kaiser have just adopted the child in the first place?"

"I don't have the slightest idea," I say.

"You're off the roll."

I smile. "It was fun while it lasted."

"So what now?"

"Now we need to get that child away from Kaiser, for two reasons. One, he doesn't belong there. He belongs with his natural father, assuming I can keep him out of prison. And that brings me to number two. If we can show that Kaiser has Dylan Hickman, then Keith is by definition innocent and Kaiser is the guilty one."

"So we have to prove that Kaiser's younger son is Dylan Hickman."

"What do you suggest?" I ask. "Have Marcus break into Kaiser's house and swab the kid's mouth to get a DNA sample?"

"Can you get a search warrant to do it?"

"On what basis?"

"Probable cause," she says. "You have reason to believe that Renny Kaiser has the abducted child. Why would a search warrant to get DNA be different than one to get anything else?"

"It probably wouldn't." Laurie is right about this, in that an executed search warrant could search for any kind of forensic evidence, including fingerprints or blood or DNA or anything else. "I don't know if we could in effect enter the kid's body like that; I'd have to research it."

"I'm sure there are other traces of his DNA in the house. A hairbrush, a toothbrush," Laurie says. "They wouldn't literally have to go inside Dylan's mouth."

"It's a great idea," I say, "but I have no idea how to make it happen. All we have is guesswork. It's damn good guesswork, but no judge would buy it. There is nothing factual to tie Kaiser into this."

"So come up with something," she says. "You're a lawyer; you even sent in your renewal form."

"Thanks, pal."

"Think about it, Andy. We will not be able to live with ourselves if we don't get that baby back."

For the life of me, I can't figure a way to get a search warrant. We just don't have the evidence. I know instinctively that Jill had an affair with Renny Kaiser and told him that the child was his as a way to manipulate him to put up money. And I know that Dylan Hickman is the child that he has taken as his son.

The problem is that "Judge, go with my instincts and sign the warrant; trust me on this" is just not a recipe for success.

The other thing that's bugging me is Kaiser's reaction to everything that happened, from day one. First of all, if he really believed Dylan to be his son, and he wanted him that badly, there were other ways he could have gone about it.

Obviously, Jill wasn't exactly a devoted mother. Couldn't he have pulled this off without putting up hundreds of millions of dollars? He thought he was the father, so in any event, he would have parental rights, for at least joint custody.

The investment was ultimately a success, but he couldn't have known that going in. It wasn't a sure bet — far from it — which is why no one else was willing to put up the money.

And to track Teresa Mullins for years and kill her? And then to send Kyle Gillis after me? Finally, to top it off, to murder Jill for lying to him?

All of this to conceal the fact that he had his own son? At any point, he could have engineered another scam to rival the original abduction. The child could have been "found," and he could have subsequently gotten Jill to come forward and admit that he was the father.

At the risk of a very bad pun, his reactions have been at the least overkill.

What is Kaiser so afraid of, and what is he trying so hard to protect?

The one positive about spending my time trying to figure all of this out is that it takes my mind off the jury's deliberations. Usually at this point, I'm a basket case, unbearable to be around and religiously following my verdict superstitions.

The truth is that I'm very worried about the verdict. I think that I gave enough evidence to discredit Teresa Mullins, but the fact that she was a disembodied presence made it less dramatic and powerful.

And I didn't effectively go near the other evidence. No one, including the jury and me, believed that transference was the reason for the dog hairs and blanket fibers. I made an error in taking that position; I should have stuck to my guns and said they were planted. To hide behind transference sent a message to the jury that I didn't believe they were planted, because the two explanations are mutually exclusive.

Laurie interrupts my pondering to come in and ask if I've come up with any idea for getting the search warrant.

"No, they could agree with everything we think and still not go along with it. A judge has to show that he signed off on it based on real evidence. Just my saying it has no credibility."

"I wonder if after all this, Jill would have told us the whole truth. It felt like she was about to."

The idea comes to me all of a sudden, and it's a strange feeling, because I simultaneously think it's a good idea and a bad idea. I like it and I hate it, so I might as well voice it.

"What if she did tell us? What if in that

phone conversation before she died she told us where Dylan really is?"

"She didn't."

"What if she did?"

"Andy, she didn't. I was on the call. I don't understand."

"Okay . . . let me ask the question another way. What if I lie?"

"You mean tell the police and a judge that Jill said something to you that she didn't say?"

"That's what I mean."

"Andy, you can't do that."

"I'm not saying I've decided to do it, or even that I want to, but let's think this through," I say. "If I lie about this, and we're right about Dylan Hickman, then we take a child away from the person that abducted him, and we put away a big-time drug dealer. If I don't lie, we probably never get the child back, and the drug dealer doesn't get caught."

"You're an officer of the court."

"So you would think less of me if I told a lie about something I believed to be true than if I didn't do everything I could to get the child back and put a drug dealer away?"

Just as Laurie is about to answer, the phone rings, and I pick it up. "Andy, you need to get down here."

It's Rita Gordon, the court clerk. "Is there a verdict?" I ask.

"I don't know, but the jury is coming in."

There is not going to be a verdict. Not now, and maybe never. As soon as we get to the courthouse, Rita tells me that it is her understanding that the jury wants to talk to the judge but that it is not an evidentiary question.

In my experience that means only one thing: they are hung.

I go to the defense table, where Hike is waiting for me.

"This is not going to be good," he says. I haven't heard from Pod Hike in a while.

Keith is brought in, and I can see the anxiety etched into his face. "Is there a verdict?"

I shake my head. "No, they want to talk to the judge. My guess is they are going to tell him they are hung."

"What will happen next?"

"Depends on the judge," I say. "He can send them back or declare a mistrial."

As I say that, the judge that it depends on comes into the courtroom, and we all rise as instructed to greet him. He briefly informs us that the jury has a message they want to convey, after which he calls them in.

Once they're settled, he calls on the foreman, who says, "Your Honor, at this point, we are unable to reach a verdict."

If he thought that Judge Moran was going to say, "Fine, you're free to go," he is sadly mistaken. Instead, the judge lectures them on the effort they must continue to put in to find common ground.

He says that he knows it's not easy, but that they are here to do a job, and they should do everything in their power to make sure they get it done.

He says it not in a critical, but rather almost inspirational way, as if exhorting them to "convict one for the Gipper." I half expect them to start pounding each other on the shoulder pads as they head back to the jury room to restart their deliberations.

Once Keith leaves and the courtroom starts to empty out, I find Laurie near the back of the room. "We never got a chance to finish our conversation," I say.

"Andy, I understand your frustration. But even if you're right, Dylan has been with them for three years and I'm sure is being treated well. And Kaiser has been eluding the law for a lot longer than that."

"So what are you saying?"

"That I think we should exhaust every avenue before you think about crossing that line, and maybe revisit the idea later."

I think about that for a few moments; it seems a reasonable approach. "I can live with that," I say, although I think Laurie is putting more emphasis on the "not crossing the line," while I'm focused more on the "revisiting the idea later."

But for now, the key is coming up with some avenues to exhaust.

I have to apply some pressure; the question is where it would be most effective. What I need is for someone who knows the truth about Dylan Hickman to come forward. That would be all that I'd require to have the police generate a search warrant, and then there would be no stopping the steam-roller.

I'm sure Finding Home is full of such people, and the one I decide to pressure is Steven Emmonds. I choose him for a couple of reasons.

One is that he's a scientist, not a top-level business or money guy, and I imagine he's had less experience dealing with these kinds of stressful situations. Two is that I know he's in on it, because he's the one who lied to me about the test results, no doubt because Jill told him to.

It's a little after seven in the evening when I decide that either Emmonds is the weakest link or at least the link I want to test. I'm not sure if he'd still be in the office, but I call the Finding Home number.

I get a message saying that I've reached them after business hours and that I should call after nine o'clock in the morning.

I walk into the kitchen, where Laurie and Ricky are going over some of his homework. "What happened?" she asks.

"There's no switchboard operator; they're closed."

She looks at her watch. "It's after seven."

"They have a full staff on at night," I say. "Everybody says that they're a twenty-four-hour operation."

"So?"

"So why can you only call the day shift? Actually, you don't need to answer that, because I think I know why. I have to go down there."

"To Finding Home?"

"Yes."

"You are going to talk to Emmonds?"

"No, I have no idea if he's there."

"I can't go with you," she says, since we obviously can't leave Ricky alone. "What are you going to do?"

"I'm going to try to get a look at what is happening there, basically to confirm what I already know, so I can report it in."

"I'll call Marcus."

Marcus arrives five minutes later; I don't know how he always appears so fast; maybe he's living in our basement. I tell him that we'll go over the plan on the way to Finding Home; this way, I'll have something to fill the awkward silence in the car.

We park two blocks from the Finding Home campus. Fortunately, the streets around it are very dark; I don't know why, but in many suburban upscale neighborhoods, residents feel more comfortable in the dark. They're not as concerned about safety as they are about ambiance.

By contrast, in urban centers like Paterson, most people would approve the placement of klieg lights on every corner. I am among those people.

Marcus and I walk carefully and quietly onto the Finding Home campus. As I expected, the main building has only a few lights on, while two of the satellite buildings are completely lit up.

"I want to get close up. We don't need to get in, but I want to see what's happening in there," I say, and Marcus just nods.

As we walk closer, the large door on the side of the building, near the loading dock, opens. Three large vans come out and start toward us. We get out of the way before their headlights reach us, and we hide in the shrubbery along the side of the path.

As far as I can see, there is no identification on the vans at all. The name *Finding Home* is not emblazoned on what I assume are Finding Home trucks.

Even though I believe the existence of the trucks is enough to make me sure I'm right, we move closer to the building. I look in the windows, but although I can see a lot of people milling about and working in what seem to be labs, I can't tell what they're doing.

"Inside?" Marcus asks.

It's a tempting prospect. Unless there's a chemist in there with a bazooka, Marcus could get us in with little problem. But it would alert Renny Kaiser to what I'm doing, and he might disband the operation.

More importantly, we'd be entering illegally, and nothing I could say about it would be admissible either in court or on a search warrant. So the upside to going in is not enough to offset the downside.

It's disappointing that I can't see more from out here, but ultimately, it doesn't matter. I know what they're doing, and if I have to, I'll swear to it.

We walk back the way we came, and just as we reach the public street, my cell phone rings. It sounds deafening and scares the hell out of me, and the scariest part of it is that I was too dumb to have shut it off before. It could have rung while we were snooping around near the building.

The caller is Sam, and I'm whispering, even though now I don't have to. "What's is it, Sam?"

"I've been monitoring Renny Kaiser's phone like you asked, and he made a call you might be interested in."

"What is it?"

"He called an aviation company that he's used before."

"So?"

"So I hacked into their computers. Renny Kaiser and his family are flying from Westchester County Airport to Dubai tomorrow night. Their only stop to refuel is in Croatia."

Dubai. It's very hot, it's very wealthy, and it does not have an extradition treaty with the United States. Neither does Croatia.

I cannot let them get on that plane.

I now know what Renny Kaiser got out of his investment in Finding Home. I assume he wanted Dylan, whom he probably believed to be his son. But at its core, the investment was a brilliant business maneuver, and not because Finding Home became a profitable company. That was just gravy.

By all accounts, Renny Kaiser deals in prescription drugs and exotic drug cocktails. Prescription drugs are not that easy to come by. They are generally gotten through thefts of drugstores, private homes, or warehouses, corrupt doctors writing bogus prescriptions, or prescriptions written on stolen or fake forms.

But Kaiser found a way to eliminate all of that tedious stuff. He is manufacturing the drugs himself, and he's set up the perfect operation in which to do it.

In Finding Home, he has a large facility and has been able to staff it full of chemists and other workers to create the drugs without arousing suspicion. Because of the very nature of Finding Home's business, they are assumed to belong there. The company is even doing government work, so by definition, it is a trusted entity.

Kaiser has been mass-producing these drugs right under the noses of everyone; those large vans were not carrying DNA results. And they didn't fire all those chemists because they might be loyal to Keith Wachtel; they fired them because they didn't want them around to see what was really happening.

I call Laurie at home, brief her on what I've learned and what I suspect, and ask her for Steve Emmonds's cell phone number. She gets it off the company directory that she had gotten from Jill and gives it to me.

Emmonds answers on the third ring, and I tell him it's Andy Carpenter calling. "It's past ten o'clock," is his first response.

"Take advantage of it while you can," I say. "In the cell block, it's lights out at eight."

"What are you talking about?"

"I know all about the illegal drug manufacturing going on at Finding Home, I know that you lied about the DNA test, I know who Dylan Hickman's real parents are, I

388

know where he is, and I know you're going to jail."

He's either thinking in silence, or he's hung up.

"You need to be on the right side of this, Emmonds. It's going down fast."

Finally, he says, "What do you want?"

"I want to hear it from you, and then I want you to make a deal for yourself. You are in an excellent position to do that. If you say no, I move on to the next person, and you become one of the big losers."

"I'm in Chicago," he says. "Visiting family."

"Pretty soon they'll be visiting you. You can talk through the bulletproof glass."

"Okay. I'll meet you at noon tomorrow. But just you, no police."

"I can't wait that long," I say, neglecting to add that I literally have a flight to catch.

"I can't get there before then," he says. "I told you, I'm in Chicago. But I'll give you what you need."

The timing is close, but it can work. I'll make it work. "Where?" I ask.

"There's a park about six blocks from Finding Home. At the north end is a building that they used to use as storage for park equipment. I'll meet you there."

"Stevie-boy, if you're not there, or not

there on time, or not alone, the next meeting you have will be with a judge."

My self-preservation instinct compels me to bring Marcus with me to meet Emmonds. I might need him if something goes wrong, and worst comes to worst, maybe I can convince Marcus to torture Emmonds into confessing. I'm only half kidding, because above all I need to keep Kaiser and his family, including Dylan Hickman, off that plane tonight.

We find the park easily enough, but there is no way to drive all the way to the north end. We leave the car in the parking area and start walking toward where Emmonds is supposed to be waiting.

When we see the building in the distance, Marcus tells me to wait behind. He doesn't say so in so many words; instead he grunts and pushes me up against a tree. He's either making sure that it's safe to go farther or he's just sick of me.

Fifteen minutes later, I see Marcus, and

he's waving for me to come toward him. "He's dead," Marcus says, which qualifies as a soliloquy coming from him, and a scary one at that.

We break into a run and get to the greenhouse, and sure enough, there is a very dead Emmonds lying on the building floor. I don't see any blood, but his neck and head are at an angle that probably would not sustain life.

I want to ask Marcus if he killed him, but I'm afraid to. I'm pretty confident he didn't, because he'd have no reason to. He knows we came here to talk to Emmonds, not to bury him.

Instead I ask Marcus if he saw the killer, and he says, "Nunh," which pretty much says it all.

Protocol mandates that I call 9-1-1 and report this and then wait around for the police to arrive, at which point they would take hours to question me in detail. Park Ridge is out of Pete Stanton's jurisdiction, so it would take even longer with local cops who don't know me.

I don't have time for that. Marcus and I run to the car, and once we're in it, I call Pete and tell him I have to see him right away.

"What now?"

"Pete, I want you to trust me on this. It's urgent."

"Are you with another dead body?"

"In a manner of speaking."

He tells me to come right down to the station, and I hang up. My next call is to the Park Ridge police to report a dead body in the greenhouse at the north end of the park.

"Are you there now, sir?" the operator asks.

"No."

"You need to return to that area, sir, unless you feel in personal danger."

"If you need me, contact Captain Pete Stanton of the Paterson Police Department," I say and then hang up.

I get to Pete's office in less than a half hour. I ask Marcus to wait in the lobby; he's not really involved in what I'm about to say, and I'm not sure I want him to hear me say it.

Pete comes out to meet me and says, "The Park Ridge police say you're a suspect in a murder."

"What did you tell them?"

"That I'll be happy to make the arrest. What the hell is going on?"

We go back to his office, and I start by describing how we found Emmonds's body.

"What were you doing there?"

"He told me he was going to give me even more detail about what was going on at Finding Home, and then he'd let me bring him to the police to turn himself in."

"So you had spoken to him before?"

"Yes, and that's why I didn't wait around there and instead came here. You need to get a search warrant right away; you can take down the entire operation."

"Which entire operation might that be?" he asks.

I proceed to tell him about the drug-manufacturing operation at Finding Home, Renny Kaiser's involvement at the head of it, and Kaiser's planned evening departure tonight.

"Emmonds told you all this?"

It's the moment of truth or non-truth. I had agreed with Laurie that we might revisit the idea of my lying later. Well, this is as later as it gets, so here goes. "He did; in a phone call last night," I say.

"How do I know you're telling me the truth?"

"You don't know," I say. "And if you choose to, you can sit on your ass and do nothing and then find out I was right. And Renny Kaiser can sit in Dubai with an abducted child and laugh in your face."

"Give me some proof," he says, apparently

uncowed.

"Okay. Emmonds gave me the aviation company that Kaiser reserved the plane with. He's leaving with his family tonight at six. Check it out."

"What's the name of the company?"

I tell him, and Pete calls someone with the instructions to check it out, without revealing anything. Fifteen minutes later, he gets a phone call, listens briefly, and then hangs up. "It checks out," he says.

"I accept your apology," I say. "Now get the damn search warrant."

The phone rings again, and Pete picks it up. "Yeah, he's here," he says. "Okay, I'll tell him."

He puts down the phone and says, "There's a verdict."

I don't want to be in court right now. I want to be with Pete to make sure he gets the damn search warrant. And then I want to be at Finding Home when it's executed.

My fear is that if Kaiser had thought Emmonds had turned on him, and that's why he had him killed, then he might have pulled the plug on the whole operation. He could even have cleaned out the building where the drugs were being manufactured; by now it could be a day care center, or an ice-skating rink.

If the search doesn't happen, or if it doesn't turn up what I know was there, then all is lost. I also will be in very deep shit, but I can't worry about that now. All I can do is go to court, hear the verdict, and hope Pete doesn't screw it up.

I am worried about the verdict; I think we'll probably lose. All that does is put added pressure on what is happening outside the courthouse. If Kaiser is arrested and Dylan Hickman is proven to have been in his house all along, then even if Keith is convicted, he will soon be out of jail.

But if Kaiser gets away, then Keith will have lost his last chance at freedom.

Keith is brought to the defense table, and Judge Moran and the jury follow shortly. The tension is etched in Keith's face, and just before we are told to rise, he says, "What do you think?"

"Thinking is not my specialty," I say. "I'm better at listening."

"Hike thinks we're going to lose," he says.

"You will probably never say a more meaningless sentence for the rest of your life," I say.

Judge Moran asks the bailiff to bring him the verdict form, and he reads it without changing his expression. The bailiff then takes it to the court clerk, who reads it in the same expressionless monotone that she used to read Teresa Mullins's testimony.

"As it relates to count one, we, the jury, in the case of the *State of New Jersey v. Keith Wachtel,* find the defendant, Keith Wachtel, not guilty of the crime of kidnapping."

Keith sags slightly and then turns and hugs me. I'm not a big fan of hugs in any circumstances, unless Laurie is involved.

But this time I like it even less, because it eats up precious seconds.

"You did an amazing job," he says. "I can never thank you enough."

"Keith, I'm beyond happy that we won and that you're free. But I gotta go."

As I'm running to the car, I call Pete on his cell phone but get no answer. I don't know where to go or what to do, but by the time I get to the car, I've made my decision. I'm going to Finding Home.

The thirty-minute drive feels like it takes a little more than a week. When I finally get there and pull onto the campus, I see a beautiful sight: flashing red lights. There are Paterson police cars, Park Ridge police cars, and a couple of DEA vans. I'm sure somewhere in that mass of law enforcement are some FBI agents as well.

I don't see Pete or his car, so I don't even bother to stop and get out. They won't let me near the place anyway, and that's okay. Based on the activity level, I'm pretty confident that things are working out on this end.

It's the other end I'm worried about. It's almost five o'clock, and Westchester County Airport is a good drive from here. I'm hoping that is where Pete is headed, and I further hope that he called ahead to get some cops or agents there.

I hit a lot of traffic, and I'm pretty much going insane as I watch the clock move toward six o'clock. For all I know, Kaiser moved up the flight because things in his world were deteriorating; maybe he's on his third in-flight cocktail already.

I get to the airport just in time to see two police cars pulling out. I recognize the passengers in the back seats from their Google images. In one of the cars is Kaiser's wife and older child, and in the other is Dylan Hickman.

In the back seat with Dylan is a woman, hopefully a therapist of some sort brought here for this purpose. Dylan is crying; he's just been wrenched from the only family he's ever known, and while I am happy about it, it breaks my heart. I'm glad I got here a few minutes late so I didn't have to watch that scene unfold.

I go into the airport and am stopped by police, who have set up something of a perimeter. I see Pete, and more importantly, he sees me, and he instructs the cop to let me in. Pete is standing with other officers and six other guys who must be FBI agents, because they're all dressed in the same suit.

Two of them are putting Renny into the back seat of one of their vehicles. He's dressed casually in a sport shirt, sneakers, and jeans, not even wearing a coat. I wonder if he was already on the plane before they got to him.

He sees me approaching, and I give him a little smile and wave. I don't want to overdo the victory lap; even though he's not going to be in a position to kill me for many years, I'm sure he knows people who would happily step in to fill the breach.

He doesn't wave back.

Pete comes over to me and says, "This worked out pretty well."

"You're welcome," I say.

"If Emmonds already told you everything and was turning himself in, why the hell would he want to meet you in a secluded area of a park?"

"That is indeed a vexing question," I say. "But it is destined to be an eternal one, because alas, we're never going to get to ask him."

"I don't believe he told you anything. You told me what you thought was the case, and Emmonds had nothing to do with it. I think you lied to me."

"Pete, you're a hero. You made an arrest the feds have been dying to make for years, and you saved a little boy. You'll probably be on the goddamn *Today* show. You'll be

400

so famous and so admired that you might someday even be able to get a woman to go out with you. So my sincere advice to you is, let it go."

"I don't think I can do that."

"Do you think you can pay for your own beer and hamburgers for the rest of your life?"

He thinks about it for a few seconds and says, "On the other hand, all's well that ends well."

We always have a small party at Charlie's to celebrate a winning case. This one is a bit different from most of the others, though, in that the victorious defendant hasn't shown up. He said he'd try to stop in for a few minutes later, as soon as a neighbor showed up to watch Dylan.

Laurie, Willie, Sondra, Sam, Marcus, Edna, Pete, and Vince are here. I don't even know if Pete and Vince knew there was a party; I think they just came here to eat, drink, and watch sports like any other night. So for them it's no different; they never pick up a check anyway.

This time, I extract a price from Pete; I make him tell me the status of the case against Renny Kaiser. It's going very, very well.

Hike isn't here; he went down to South Carolina to go fishing with his buddies. I've come to terms with the pods having taken over Hike's mind and body; they've actually done a really good job with it.

The talk gets around to the case, as it always does, and Laurie asks me why Jill had the baby in the first place.

"I don't think she ever wanted him," I say. "She used Dylan to draw Renny in by telling him the baby was his; for all I know, she faked DNA results to make him believe it. Both Renny and his wife wanted the baby very badly; she can't have kids, and their older child is adopted.

"They believed Dylan was Renny's natural son, which is why they were so anxious to have him. Renny must have an understanding wife."

"How do you know all this?" she asks.

"Pete told me. Zachary Alford is trying to make a deal; he's been singing to the police like they were his board of directors."

"But why did Jill go through the whole abandonment and adoption routine?"

"It probably took a while to get Renny to commit; and at first he just put in enough money to keep the company afloat. They each had something the other wanted, so they were playing a game of chicken.

"But it turned out that he finally realized he could get much more out of his investment than Dylan, that the company was a potential gold mine as a way to produce his illegal drugs. That's when he stepped up and bought half the company.

"This scheme also represented a way for everybody to get what they wanted, while getting rid of Keith permanently."

"Why was that so important?" Sam asks.

"Because of the lawsuit Keith was preparing. The last thing they wanted was to have Finding Home in the kind of spotlight that a court action would bring, with the resulting depositions and financial scrutiny. That's why they gave all the people they fired such generous exit packages; they wanted a clean break."

"She gave away her own child," Laurie says, shaking her head in amazement.

"People do that every day," I say. "That's why there are adoptions."

"But she kept Dylan's room intact."

I nod. "It was part of the act, part of the show. She had plenty of other rooms in that house."

Willie's turn. "How did Teresa wind up with Cody?"

"I'm just guessing here, but I doubt that the plan was for the abductor to take him. Once he did, Jill would have wanted to make sure he was okay; the irony is she loved that dog. So Teresa, who was going to disappear anyway, was a logical choice."

"She seemed so anxious to get Dylan back, to find out if we had learned anything about him," Laurie says. She just can't wrap her head about a mother using her son as a bargaining chip.

I nod. "Alford told Pete that she knew where he was all along. I think what she really wanted was information on how our investigation was going so she could pass it on to Kaiser and Alford."

Keith shows up but again apologizes that he can't stay long.

"How's it going with Dylan?" Laurie asks.

"It's a struggle; he misses his family, and there's nothing I can do. But the therapist says he's doing very well and that it will get better each day."

"Are you going to look for work?" Laurie asks.

"No, I think I'm going to devote all my time to being a father, at least for now, thanks to you and Andy."

Laurie and I have lent Keith a substantial amount of money so that he can live and take care of Dylan without any stress.

We are preparing a civil lawsuit against Finding Home, Renny Kaiser, and Jill Hickman's estate. There is no doubt that Keith will be a rich man when it's settled, and he will pay us back. He's also said that he wants to pay what would have been my bill for representing him.

Minus the one dollar that he's already put up.

"And how's Cody?" Willie asks.

"Doing great, but I'm spoiling him with biscuits." Then he smiles broadly. "Hey, that dog got me out of prison."

It's not until Laurie and I are on the way home that she asks me the question I've been expecting for three days.

"Did Emmonds really give you the information you used to get the warrant, or did you make it up?"

"Should I tell you what you want to hear or the truth?"

"What I want to hear," she says.

"He told me everything. I would never lie about it; I'm an officer of the court. Our system depends on complete honesty and integrity from everyone involved."

"Okay. Now try the truth."

I take a deep breath. "I lied through my teeth; Emmonds never had a chance to tell me a thing. I'm sorry . . . actually, I'm not sorry. I could not let that little boy get on that plane."

Laurie doesn't say anything, which is either a good or bad sign.

"Have I dropped down a notch in your eyes because I did that?" I ask.

She nods. "Yes." Then comes a smile. "But you started from a really high place."

I exhale for the first time since the conversation started. "So we're good?"

She takes my hand; it only leaves me with one to drive, which is more than enough. "We're good," she says. "Did I ever tell you I find lawyers really sexy?"

"Really?" I ask. "Did I ever tell you I sent that form in?"

ABOUT THE AUTHOR

David Rosenfelt is the Edgar-nominated and Shamus Award-winning author of seven standalones and thirteen previous Andy Carpenter novels, most recently *Outfoxed*. After years living in California, he and his wife recently moved to Maine with the twenty-five golden retrievers that they've rescued. Rosenfelt's hilarious account of this cross-country move, *Dogtripping,* is published by St. Martin's Press.

The employees of Thorndike Press hope you have enjoyed this Large Print book. All our Thorndike, Wheeler, and Kennebec Large Print titles are designed for easy reading, and all our books are made to last. Other Thorndike Press Large Print books are available at your library, through selected bookstores, or directly from us.

For information about titles, please call:
  (800) 223-1244

or visit our website at:
  gale.com/thorndike

To share your comments, please write:
  Publisher
  Thorndike Press
  10 Water St., Suite 310
  Waterville, ME 04901